MEAN

SEASON

For Mary —

Enjoy!

MEAN SEASON

Heather Cochran

**RED
DRESS
INK**
™

First edition September 2004

MEAN SEASON

A Red Dress Ink novel

ISBN 0-373-25069-X

© 2004 by Heather Cochran.

Author photo by Laurie Steiner-Halperin

www.RedDressInk.com

Printed in U.S.A.

To Zoë

ACKNOWLEDGMENTS

Heartfelt thanks to all four of my parents for their varied support through this process. To some early and awesome readers, Brangien Davis, Aly Meranze, Dan Daley, Erica Payne, Gabrielle Dudnyk and Gwen Riley. Huge thanks also to Katherine Fausset of Watkins-Loomis and to my editor, Farrin Jacobs. And to David Allen, whose opinion matters.

ACKNOWLEDGMENT

Chapter 1

Day One

Joshua Reed was delivered to our house on Prospect Street in a police car. Lars and Judy followed in their rental, then Momma and I in her station wagon. Momma was humming, like she found it all so amusing. My oldest brother, Tommy, had got into trouble with the law a few times back when he was in high school, and each call from the police station had sparked words between Momma (who wanted to see him punished) and Dad (who thought a good scare was punishment enough). But when it came to Joshua, Momma didn't seem to care whether he learned anything from his punishment. She said that Joshua not being her son made it seem like a movie, something she might keep her distance from and maybe even enjoy a little.

The policemen who drove Joshua Reed to our house stayed for a couple minutes to make sure that his ankle sensor was working, and also to review the boundaries of our property. In the backyard, Joshua would be allowed to wander to the edge of the lawn, where the trees started, and on the unfenced side of the house, he could go as far as the stand of creepy dead oaks. In front, he could wander to the mailbox at the edge of our driveway.

Once the police drove off (after one of them had asked Joshua for an autograph, for his daughter he made sure to say), the five of us who were left stood a moment in our living room, me and Momma and Judy and Lars and Joshua Reed, newly incarcerated movie star. It was the first time that Judy and Lars and Joshua had actually been inside our house. I caught them looking around, and my cheeks burned. I was suddenly aware of the peeling ceiling paint and the frayed edge of the living room rug and how the fabric on the big couch was worn through, so that Momma had long ago thrown one of her quilts over top of it, like a slipcover that didn't fit neat around the curves or corners. We'd cleaned— well, I'd cleaned—the house all that previous week. And it looked clean, but it was still nothing like the houses you see in TV shows. And I knew it was nothing like where Joshua Reed usually called home. A year back, there'd been an article about his house in a home decor magazine, so I'd seen pictures. The magazine had called his place an "artist's cottage," though it was maybe twice as big as the largest house along all of Prospect Street, maybe in all of Pinecob.

No one looked too comfortable, just standing there. I wasn't sure what to do besides offer to show Joshua his room, and I noticed him glare at Judy and Lars before he followed me up the stairs.

"I'll call you soon, J.P.," Judy said.

He didn't answer her.

I had put my best sheets on his bed and cleared out some space in the dresser and closet. Vince's stuff was still all through the room, on the walls and the shelves. After he disappeared, Momma mostly stopped going in there, so it had stayed the same for the past decade. It was only maybe a season before that she'd started to leave Vince's door open during the day, and I noticed that sometimes, when I got home from work, the shades in his room would be up, letting in a little light.

Vince had always been Momma's favorite. Maybe I shouldn't say that—it's the sort of thing kids aren't supposed to pick up on, which pretty much ensures that they will. I picked up on it, even when I was little. So when Vince took off, well, I'm sure I won't get the words right to describe how hard it was on Momma. I can barely describe how hard it was on me. Vince had been my favorite, too.

If you knew Vince, you'd understand. He was the sort of person you'd notice as soon as he entered a room, and the sort of person your eyes would search for, as soon as you entered. He was the guy you always saved a seat for, because sitting beside Vince was like sitting in the sun on a cold day. He could make even church fly by, pointing out who was about to fall asleep, imagining who was daydreaming what, and when it came time to sing, belting out hymns in perfect pitch.

He made up silly games to pass the time, like the one where he'd give you two choices.

"Avocado or banana?" he'd ask, and if you chose differently from him, he'd make you say why. "Orange or green?" he'd ask. "Brother or sister?" he'd always end with. That was the only one we were allowed to disagree on.

Vince was a hair shorter and quite a bit skinnier than both of my other brothers, Beau Ray and Tommy. Still, he'd made varsity football his freshman year of high school, on account of being so fast. No one could catch him, and if someone did manage to get a handful of jersey, they had a hell of a time trying to keep him pinned. That's what I'd tell myself, whenever I got to thinking about him, that he was one of those people you couldn't hold down. Maybe he wasn't made for a town the size of Pinecob. Of course, me being his younger sister surely had something to do with that opinion.

Even with the shades open, it was still Vince's room. It was still full of his trophies and his football uniform and cleats; and those things, I'd left there. I didn't know how much shelf space Joshua would need. I didn't know if he was going to have boxes of clothing sent from California, or whether he planned to spend the whole of his time with us in sweatpants. I showed him the closet, and the bathroom he would be using.

"I'm going to lie down now," Joshua said, without looking at me.

As soon as I came back downstairs, Momma left to pick up Beau Ray from the adult care center.

I asked Lars and Judy whether they'd be staying for dinner—I figured they would, to make sure that Joshua was settling in okay—but Lars shook his head.

"Love to, Leanne, but we've got a flight back to Los Angeles tonight."

I nodded. I had seen so much of them in the past weeks, it felt strange to remember that they lived all the way across the country.

"Leanne," Judy said. "I want to tell you something. Lars and I both do."

Her tone made me nervous. "Something bad?" I asked.

"Nothing bad," Lars said, shaking his head.

"You must know how much we appreciate all you've done for J.P.," Judy began. "I'm not talking about the fan club. If it weren't for you, he'd almost certainly be in jail right now."

I nodded. "I guess," I said.

"But I want to say, well, I hope you're not thinking," Judy went on, "that the next ninety days are going to be some sort of slumber party."

"Judy," I said. I was embarrassed she would think such a thing. "I'm twenty-five. I'm not nine."

"Oh, I know, dear, I know. It's just that you've only really known J.P. for a week. Maybe it seems like you know him better, because of your work with the fan club. But you don't. Not really. He's a stranger. And Lars and I, well, we'd prefer that you keep that in mind."

"That he's a stranger?"

"You know, don't be too accommodating," Judy said. "Keep your distance."

"But he's stuck here," I said. "For the summer. You're saying I shouldn't be nice to him?"

"I'm saying you don't have to be. He hasn't earned it," Judy said. "He got himself into this mess," she said. "You call me for any reason at all. Okay? You have all my numbers."

I nodded.

"I'll be back in the next month or so, as things with the production start to heat up." She looked at me. "Trust me, someday this will make sense," she said.

Chapter 2

The Joshua Reed Fan Club

I was fifteen when I first fell in love with Joshua Reed. Okay, so maybe love is a strong word, but it was all I knew at that age. Joshua had just joined the staff of General Hospital—not a real hospital, but the one on the soap *General Hospital*. He played Colin Ashcroft, a cardiology resident. He ran on-screen in order to save Miranda's life with mouth-to-mouth, and I sat there, stock-still, staring at him. I called Sandy Wilson, my best friend since third grade, to ask if she'd seen what I'd just seen, but she wasn't home yet from her job at her family's service station. I watched him, wishing that I was Miranda or at least that I'd be given the chance to swoon in his general vicinity. Not that such swooning was likely—I lived outside of Charles Town and *General Hospital* was filmed in Los Angeles, about as far as you can get from West Virginia and still be in the States.

I knew that Joshua Reed wasn't really a doctor. I knew he

was an actor. For one, I'm sharper than that, and for two, he was way dreamier and younger than any doctor I'd ever seen in the town clinic where we went for shots and checkups. Even the night of Beau Ray's accident, when we went to a real hospital, and even in the weeks that followed, I don't remember seeing anyone who looked like Joshua Reed. Most of the doctors I knew were older and tired-out-looking, or young and scared-looking. I figured the young ones were scared that their patients were going to die on them. There were always a few drunks and some really gray-looking people in the waiting room at the clinic, so maybe those skittish doctors had reason to be scared. I felt so bad for them that I used to pinch my cheeks before a checkup, to look particularly healthy. When I was twelve, I pinched myself a little too hard and scared one of them into thinking I had scarlet fever. That put an end to such nonsense.

Colin Ashcroft was never scared, but there weren't any drunks at General Hospital, or old guys up from center state where all the mines are, the ones who were constantly coughing and spitting. And even if there had been, technically speaking, his character wouldn't have seen them, because he specialized in cardiology. Colin Ashcroft, as written, was a prodigy, in line to become the head of the cardiology unit, and I hoped he would someday, because it meant that Joshua Reed would keep showing up on my television screen.

Joshua Reed had also been on *The Young and the Restless* for a short time, playing Copper Malabar, a drifter who seduced a number of the leading ladies before leaving town. That was his breakout role, but I never watched *The Young and the Restless* (although back when I was fifteen, I fit the description well enough). Later, of course, I'd learn all his roles, from Copper to Colin to Nate to Stormy, and so on. But that's because it became my job to know them.

The fan thing was new to me. I'd never been a devoted

fan of anyone before, except maybe my brother Beau Ray's friend Max Campbell, whom I had one doozy of a crush on, pretty much from the word go, which is to say, when I was eight and he was twelve. Sandy always liked Eleanor Roosevelt. And my sister, Susan, had a thing for Bo Duke, the blond one on *Dukes of Hazzard*, but I was always keener for dark-haired guys. Maybe that's why I got hooked by Joshua, that day he ran on-screen to save Miranda. Even in green scrubs, he looked like I imagined a prince would— with short dark hair, deep green eyes and the end of a long day, shadow of a beard. He didn't wear glasses. He didn't smoke. He didn't drink. He didn't swear. And he was a doctor. He saved lives. I mean, it's all fine and well to bag groceries at the Winn-Dixie (like Max, my longstanding crush), or build houses (like my oldest brother Tommy, who could lift me by his forearms alone), or even sell life insurance (like Dad did, before he died). That's what normal people do, and it's fine, but Joshua Reed seemed like so much more.

So there I was, fifteen, then sixteen, then seventeen, grinding through high school in Pinecob, West Virginia, starry-eyed over the actor Joshua Reed. I wasn't obsessed. I did all the normal things a high-school girl does. I did my homework. I did my makeup. I went on dates. I got to first, then second base with Butch MacAfee, then broke up with him. I got to third with Howard Malkin, then broke up with him.

I didn't break up with Howard because I was holding out for the likes of Joshua Reed. I've always been pretty realistic. You learn to be when you're the youngest of five, and every day after school, you have to make sure your older brother hasn't died during the day from a seizure or a clot or something. But I remember that it was around then, around the breakup with Howard, a low time even though I'd called it quits, that Momma found her autographed picture of Pat Boone.

She was being surprisingly nice to me about Howard, saying things like "that Loreen can't hold a candle to you." I didn't expect the sympathy. For a few years after my dad died, Momma held back a lot of her mothering, as if she'd forgotten that I was still mostly a child, one that might need a parental sort of guidance now and again. I don't mean to say that I suffered from it. Not more than anyone else. Besides, I had Sandy, and I was always welcome at the Wilsons' house for dinner.

And every so often, Momma would muster her energy, and there'd be all sorts of activity as she hurried to catch up on the months she hadn't been paying attention. One such time coincided with my breakup with Howard Malkin. Momma was down in the basement, knee-deep in boxes of her and Dad's old papers, when she looked up and told me that Howard Malkin was a pissant who would never amount to much. A minute later, she found the Pat Boone picture, and rattled off the story behind it: how she'd had a crush on Mr. Boone back when he was first starting out, how she had written to him and been sent a signed photograph in return.

Early on, I had found a picture of Joshua—a really good one in *Soap Opera Digest* where he was in a tank top—and I stuck it inside my locker door at school. I always kept an eye out for him in *Soap Opera Digest* and *Daytime Drama Weekly* and even *People* magazine, but in those first years, he didn't get much coverage. He was certainly handsome enough, but that was back when the whole country was obsessed with the Jasper and Helen storyline and whether or not Jasper would come back before Helen married Bart. All that buzz drowned out Joshua for a time. When my mother held up her picture of Mr. Boone, I realized that if all it took was asking nice in a letter, then, sure, I'd like a signed photograph, too. The cutout in my locker was getting a little ratty by then.

So I wrote to *General Hospital*. I sent my letter to Joshua Reed's publicist, not to Joshua himself. Momma told me it would get forwarded to the publicist anyhow, so I'd get faster results that way. Besides, I didn't want Joshua Reed to think that I was the sort of girl who wrote to stars and expected a response. Publicists, they're supposed to write back. That's their job. At least, that's what I thought it was. I wrote about how I was a big fan, ever since the day Colin Ashcroft first saved Miranda. I wrote about how I'd watched the show consistently, how I had Joshua's picture in my locker and how I would like to know more about him—where he was from, what he liked, what he *was* like.

That's what started it all. It was the second semester of my senior year in high school when I sent the letter. A couple weeks later, a woman called me at home. She said that she did publicity for all of *General Hospital,* which was a huge job and growing (especially with the Jasper and Helen affair). She said that one of her duties was to organize the official fan clubs for every *General Hospital* cast member who had one. Of course Joshua Reed had a fan club, but it had been slow to get off the ground—not because he wasn't popular, but because the woman who then ran it had gotten pregnant and wasn't getting the newsletter out like she was supposed to. Judy—that was the publicist's name—said that my letter hit her desk right when she was trying to decide what to do. She asked whether I had any interest in heading up the club, at least as a trial—then before I could answer, she asked how old I was. I said seventeen, almost eighteen at that point, and I could hear her start to backpedal. I could tell she thought I was too young, so real quick I explained how I was a mature seventeen, maybe not in the bra and hips way, but in the way I took care of Beau Ray a lot and did most of the grocery shopping and made sure Momma got presents out for Susan's kids' birthdays.

"It doesn't pay anything," Judy said. "You've got to really want to do it. I'm looking for someone who really wants to do it. I don't have time to train and retrain and retrain," she said.

I swore up and down that I wanted to do it, even before I knew for sure that I did. I was old enough to recognize that such an opportunity didn't often show up in Pinecob.

She told me what I would have to do. I would have to keep the membership list current, forward membership dues and send out a welcome kit. I would have to organize and send out the newsletter four times a year. I would be expected to answer some of the basic fan mail and forward on to her anything that I couldn't figure out or anything at all threatening. And, Judy said, she would expect me to keep her informed if I heard any rumors about Joshua, good or bad. Did I want to try it, she asked me.

Would I get to meet him, I asked her. Judy said maybe, someday, and surely that could be arranged if I ever found myself in Los Angeles. Judy said that she didn't know how often J.P. (she called him J.P.) got to West Virginia. But if such a trip ever got planned, she would let me know. Judy seemed really nice—really busy, like one of those New York people you see in the movies talking on two phones at once, but really nice. I was seventeen, almost eighteen, and Joshua Reed was twenty-four. I said yes. I mean, what girl wouldn't have?

I learned right away that you have to be organized. Judy sent me all the information I needed to get started, which included the membership list and copies of his biography and a whole stack of autographed 8x10 photographs. There were only two hundred and seventy-three paying members back then, with a lot in Texas (where Joshua was originally from) and Iowa and Washington state. From West Virginia there were just two—me and Sandy.

Dues were ten dollars a year, and for that, members got (and I had to assemble) a package that included Joshua's biography and list of credits, an autographed picture, the quarterly newsletter and a membership card—Judy gave me a whole box of blank ones, and it was my job to type in the member's name. All of that was mailed out in an envelope that had a picture of Joshua (dressed in scrubs, as Colin Ashcroft) printed across the front.

At first, all my supplies fit into a milk crate that Tommy had years back stolen from behind the Winn-Dixie, but once Joshua started getting movie work, I moved into a filing cabinet. I filled it with the clippings that Judy would send to me and the clippings that I came across, and all the normal fan mail. And I kept old photographs whenever a stack of new ones would arrive, in case I needed them some day.

Being president of the fan club made me stand out a bit in Pinecob. It's not like I was an actress or anything, but people knew that I had connections to *General Hospital,* and that I could get them 8x10 glossies of just about any soap star, even those on other shows. Once you're president of a fan club, you learn how those things work. But the fact was— and I knew it—I was still Leanne Gitlin, living at home with Momma and Beau Ray, working at the county clerk's office over in Charles Town, going out on the weekends with Sandy or whatever guys would occasionally ask, and buying groceries at the Winn-Dixie each Sunday.

Momma was inconsistent when it came to my hobby. On the one hand, she was glad to see me focused on something that wouldn't get me pregnant. Momma had some professional hopes for me, and I think she realized that my fan club responsibilities provided organizational practice, the sort that you might someday be able to coax into an actual occupation. Much as Momma loved Susan's kids, Susan had been just sixteen when Kevin came along, eighteen with Kathy, and twenty-one with Kenny. Taking care of three kids when your husband is on the road all day takes skill, but not the sort you can easily turn into a job that pays well.

My oldest brother Tommy had his trade but never seemed to save a dime, and he'd taken to sometimes living out of his truck while he worked different construction jobs up and down the Shenandoah Valley. Vince—well, no one knew where he was, and it was one of those things that even my friends had learned not to mention when Momma was anywhere near. And no one ever talked about Beau Ray getting a job even though he'd had one before his fall. For a while, I'd tried to get Beau Ray to help me with my fan club duties—but even putting things into an envelope was hard for him to focus on, and he'd grow frustrated within five minutes.

But I knew that Momma also worried that the fan club would mess me up somehow, since it was different from what everyone else was doing, and different to her meant abnormal. Somehow she was fine with letting me take care of Beau Ray, and she didn't mind expecting me to do most of the housecleaning from the time I was fourteen on—but the fan club thing threw her. She worried (I overheard her say so) that I would start to think I was someone I wasn't, or want to be something I couldn't be, or decide to move to Los Angeles to be a star and end up in porno movies. Of all us kids, I'm the one who never offered her any reason to worry, and maybe that felt strange, so she made up the hows and whys. I probably stayed in the county clerk job for as long as I did because she harped on me a lot less after I took it. I guess it seemed to her along the road to somewhere called normal.

But I wasn't going to end up in pornos. Being president of Joshua Reed's fan club gave me something to look forward to, was all. I *liked* that it was different. Still, life on Prospect Street got easier once I learned to manage most of my fan club chores from the basement in a couple hours on Saturday afternoons. That's when Beau Ray went to his "Move Your Body, Move Your Mind" class at the Y and Mom went to her ages-old quilting bee, so I had a little quiet time. To tell the truth, by two years in, the fan club had become almost as routine as everything else.

Of course, it's old news by now that Joshua Reed's career really took off after he played Nate, the hero in *Villains Can't Be Choosers*. It's easy to see why. The costume people dressed him all in white and he grew his hair out, and he looked like Jesus come to life. Only sexy.

The fan club membership had been growing since I took the job, but it really jumped—it tripled in size—after that movie came out, and again when *Villains* hit video. Judy had to send a whole new batch of membership cards and glossies. By then, she wasn't working for all the *General Hospital* staff—she only had a few clients, Joshua being one of them. By then, Joshua had made it into *People* a few times. I cut out the pictures and photocopied them for the newsletter.

I know people wondered about it—what my real deal with Joshua was. Mostly, I let them guess, although it was obvious to me that I wasn't flying off to Los Angeles for weekends, and no limos were ever parked along Prospect Street. Fact is, I knew a lot about Joshua, and I could answer almost all of the questions that club members would send in. (For example, Judy called him J.P. because his real name was Joshua Polichuk. He started going by Joshua Reed when he moved to L.A.) But I never talked to him on the phone or anything. Once, when I was talking to Judy, she said that Joshua said to say hi, but I didn't hear him say it, so I don't know whether he was even in the room with her. He did write—a couple of times. Not really letters, but he would scrawl a note at the end of something Judy was sending off. He had messy, uneven handwriting, but his signature was polished. Probably from signing all those photographs. The first time, he wrote: *Leanne, Judy tells me you're my biggest fan. You're the best! xoxo, Joshua Reed.*

The second time, he wrote: *Leanne, you're the best for keeping all this together!*

The third time, it was: *Leanne, Be sure to tell all your friends about* Villains, *and also about* Celebrity Jeopardy! That was right before *Villains Can't Be Choosers* came out, and Judy was keeping him busy with all sorts of special events and appearances, mostly in California, but also in New York.

Sure, it would have been nice if he'd written more or even called on the phone once or twice. That way I might have known him in a personal way, different from the facts and stories that were out there for everyone. But it's impossible to know where a thread starts when you're looking back on things. Maybe if I *had* known Joshua better, I would have quit the fan club long before I did, and Judy probably figured that. Still, it was fun seeing my name in his handwriting, and he spelled it right, too. A lot of people spell it Leeanne, or Leann, or some other way. But Joshua always spelled it right.

I didn't stick with the fan club because I thought that we were meant for each other, Joshua and me. I'm not going to say that a seventeen-year-old girl doesn't imagine things, and I'll admit that I imagined plenty in my early days with the club. But that was before Beau Ray suffered the first of his bad seizures and before Momma went through the months she'd come to call her "unraveleds." I referred to those months as her mean seasons, since it seemed like she was pissed at everything and everyone in the world. Of course, folks in such a state never realize how ornery and off-putting they're being, so when you find yourself in the midst of someone's mean season, the best you can hope for is to stay out of their line of fire. Back in Momma's worst times, I'd call Tommy or Susan for help, but neither ever offered to head home for even a week to make dinner and check which bills were least overdue. (That was around the same time that the idea of me going off to a full-time college stopped being talked about like it was a good thing, something that might really happen.)

But whenever I thought maybe I ought to give up the club and focus on getting my own life in order, I'd feel a heaviness, almost like family, like I'd be letting Judy down. Judy, who always said "thank you" to me. Judy, who asked "would you please." Judy, who sent cards on my birthday and told me when she would be unavailable (like during her honeymoon) and called whenever she was going to send a new set of photos or an updated credits sheet or a rewritten biography—so I'd know it was coming. Part of me wanted to be like her. Even more of me wanted to *be* her, out there in California, seeing Joshua close up and making dinner for myself, just myself.

At the beginning of my seventh year with the club, membership reached 10,000. That's paying fans, and dues by then were fifteen dollars a year. A year earlier, when it hit 5,000, Judy bought me a computer. I think she was exaggerating, but she said that she couldn't have done any of it without me—that my help and organization and the way I always sent her the rumors that people wrote in about had helped Joshua's career immensely. That's why he's only doing movies now. And good ones, big ones.

But like I said, it had long grown routine by the time Judy called one Saturday.

"Leanne?" she said. "Judy Masterson here." She always told me her last name, although I didn't know any other Judys so she didn't have to. "I've got some wonderful news."

"What's that?" I asked. Joshua had been dating this Belgian supermodel named Elise, and I thought maybe Judy was going to tell me that they were getting married. But she didn't even mention Elise.

"J.P. just signed to do a Civil War epic called *Musket Fire*. Think *Taming of the Shrew* meets *Gone with the Wind*. He's not the lead—well, he's the romantic lead, but not the historic lead, you know. We're going to be filming back east, in Virginia, for about three months. Starting next month. Isn't that exciting?"

"I guess I should include that in the Summer newsletter."

I must have been tired when I said that. I wasn't thinking that it's only forty minutes from Pinecob to the Virginia border—and that once you hit Virginia where the mountains ease up, the roads run a lot quicker.

"That would be great, but mostly, I called to say that I wanted to arrange dinner with you and me and Joshua. You've been working on the fan club for so long, and I swear, J.P.'s club runs so much more smoothly than any of my other clients'—I thought it would be nice…"

"Oh—of course," I said. "That would be great. I wasn't thinking. When?"

Judy said that she and Joshua would be arriving three weeks from that Sunday, but that the movie studio had already sent casting and location people to set things up. A lot of the filming would be taking place around Winchester and Front Royal, which were only an hour and a half or so from Pinecob. Judy asked whether I wanted to be an extra in the film. She said that Sandy and I could probably both be extras. It might require getting out of work for a few days, she said, but no one was a bigger movie buff than Mr. Bellevue, my boss in the county clerk's office, so I knew he'd let me do it.

I couldn't believe it: Joshua Reed, coming to Pinecob—well, not exactly to Pinecob. He and Judy were going to stay across the Potomac in Virginia for a few days, in part because there are nicer places to stay around there than in Charles Town (and there's no place to stay in Pinecob if you're not at someone's house), and in part because Joshua's character (the fiery lieutenant Josiah Whitcomb) was from that area of Virginia, and Joshua wanted to get a sense of Josiah's history.

I told everyone, of course. How could I not? I told Beau Ray when he got back from "Move Your Body" class. I told Momma when she got back from her bee. I called Sandy and she screamed when I said how we could be extras, and she wondered whether she should try to get extra tan at the beach when she went. I even went to the Winn-Dixie a day earlier than usual, and when I saw Max, I told him.

Max didn't seem that excited, but he's a guy and Joshua Reed is one of those rare people who's better-looking than Max is. Least, I always thought Max was that good-looking. I spent way too many hours of junior high and high school embarrassing myself by hanging around when he and Beau Ray played football, just so I could see Max wipe the sweat off his brow or lean into his knees to catch his breath. He was Beau Ray's best friend up until the fall, and I think he tried to be afterward, before it became clear how different everything was.

After the fall, you couldn't talk to Beau Ray in the same way—you had to keep to simpler, shorter conversations, and even then, he might not follow. Max would turn to me, since I was often around, to ask if I thought Beau Ray had understood something, or to try to figure out where my brother was taking a thought.

They were talking about airplanes once, I remember. This was a few years after the accident. The three of us were sitting in the backyard when Beau Ray had suddenly looked up and pointed.

"What's that?" Max had asked, as Beau Ray traced his finger across something in the sky.

I looked up. "That airplane? Is that what you're looking at?"

Beau Ray nodded.

"Where do you think they're going?" I asked him.

"Hawaii," Beau Ray said. He had watched a travel program a few days before with a piece on the various Hawaiian islands and the tourists who were flocking to them.

"I don't think that's headed in the right direction for Hawaii," Max had said, squinting upward. "I think it looks to be headed east of here. Maybe D. C. or even Europe or something."

"Hawaii," Beau Ray said, sounding certain.

Max looked at the plane again, before it disappeared beyond the trees. He gave a little shiver, the kind you'd miss if you weren't watching closely.

"You okay?" I asked him.

"I'm not much on planes," he said.

"You ever been on one?" I asked him. I hadn't.

"I don't think flying's for me. I like sticking nearer to the ground."

"Max is taking the bus," Beau Ray said.

"The bus?" Max asked. "What bus?" He looked at me, lost.

"To Hawaii," Beau Ray said. "Everyone is going to Hawaii."

"I don't get it." Max still looked confused, but I smiled.

"That's one long bus ride," I said to him. "Be sure to pack a lunch."

Some folks might have viewed Max Campbell's fear of flying as a weakness, but not me. I liked him just as much for his fear, and counted myself lucky to have been sitting nearby when he'd admitted it. I liked knowing that he wasn't about to go flying off somewhere, that I could count on him being around. Sure, maybe someday he'd disappear down the road in a car, like Vince had, but at least it would take him longer to pull away from Pinecob. Hop on a plane, and you could end up anywhere.

Not that Max was going anywhere. By the time of Judy's phone call, it seemed like he was almost always at the Winn-Dixie (he was an associate manager by then), and I would stop to talk with him whenever I went in. Max had been married for a little while, to a girl named Charlene who had once won the title of Miss Junior West Virginia in a beauty pageant. She'd blown in from the Northern Panhandle, and then blew out again, only a year after their wedding. It shook him something wicked. Judy's phone call about Joshua Reed came maybe a year after Charlene had up and left, when everyone was still whispering about the torch Max carried, not dating and holding out hope she'd one day come back.

As I said, Max didn't seem too excited about my news, but Martha, the weekend manager was beyond ecstatic. She told everyone. I was surprised she didn't announce it over the loudspeaker. By the end of the weekend, it seemed that everyone in Pinecob knew that I was going to have dinner with Joshua Reed—and maybe even be in the movie!

Chapter 3

Dinner in Virginia

"What do you look like, Leanne?" Judy asked me. "It seems so funny to have to ask that, but I'm sure that the mental picture I've got is wrong. You live in L.A. long enough, and your sense of what people look like and what people *are* like gets all screwy."

So I told her how I'm pretty tall for a girl and on the skinnier side of average and about my hair being halfway between red and brown, and that it was sort of feathering past my shoulders those days. I said I was white, since I realized that she might not know, except that Leanne Gitlin always sounded like a white girl's name to me.

"But if I'm meeting you at the restaurant, won't I recognize Joshua?"

"Oh, of course. I just wanted to try to get a picture of you in my mind. Why did I have you as a bottle blonde, I wonder? I've got to run. I've asked that the driver be at your house at six forty-five. We'll see you at the restaurant."

And then I was there.

Before then, I was in the car that came to pick me up, which was a lot nicer than any car I'd ever ridden in, even the one my ex, Lionel, bought new from the dealership. And before the car came, I was getting ready, and trying to figure out what to wear. Sandy had left for the beach the day before, so she couldn't help me, but we'd pretty much decided on a sundress that I thought looked like one on the cover of the *Vogue* I saw in the salon where I got my hair cut. Except that my dress had red flowers on a white background, not yellow, and mine was cotton and faded a little and I think the one in the magazine was silk and was surely brand-new.

I looked in the mirror as I waited for my nail polish to dry. I'm pretty enough—people always say I've got good bones—but I'd never been pretty in the way of my sister, Susan. Even after she had three kids, strangers would still tell Susan how beautiful she was—like she might not have known, like they were the first to notice. People had never done that to me, although guys did cross bars to talk. Or at least, they crossed to talk to me and Sandy, but Sandy usually rolled her eyes and turned away, so I was the one who ended up in discussions about rebuilt car engines or Judas Priest vs. Motley Crüe. I'd nod and smile, and by the end of their talking, they'd look at me and say, "you know, you're real pretty." But by then, I was always unsure if it was because I'd been listening to them yammer on, or because they were tired of talking and wanted to make out, or because maybe, just maybe, I was pretty in the first place. Girls like Susan and Sandy and Max's ex-wife Charlene didn't have that to contend with.

I stared into the bathroom mirror. I dug through my makeup bag and wondered whether blue or green eyeshadow would look better against brown eyes. I put on a kiss of lipstick, then wiped it off.

I wore a lot more makeup in my teens than I was wearing at twenty-five. At thirteen or fifteen, makeup felt like magic. Wave the mascara wand, and suddenly I'd look older, more like the senior girls with their long, polished nails and cigarettes. Add lipstick, and I could imagine being the sort of girl that boys in my class whispered about, with her curvy way of walking by that would make even a football star press against the wall to let her pass. Add blush, and I might even start to resemble Brennie Critchett, who was prom queen back when I was a sophomore.

Of course, when I got older, I realized that there were a lot of things mascara couldn't change or fix. Maybe if I'd been the prom queen, I'd have felt differently.

I blinked at my reflection in the mirror of the narrow upstairs bathroom. At the same age, Joshua Reed had a publicist and a fan club and a fan club president. Of course, not everyone can have such a life, or there'd be no one to run the registers at the Winn-Dixie. But I worried a little about the discrepancy between the girl in the mirror and the folks she'd meet in a few hours time.

I put the lipstick back on, and chose green eyeshadow. I thought the night might call for a little magic. It was Joshua Reed, after all. I wondered what Judy would be wearing. I wondered if I would get to call Joshua "J.P."

And then I was there. The car ride took less time than I'd expected. Even though I was twenty-five, I'd only been to Harper's Ferry maybe five times, and then, not to the Virginia side. I'd never even heard of the resort where Judy and Joshua were staying, where we were having dinner. It seemed so far from Pinecob that I expected to be sitting on that leather car seat for hours.

I walked in and gave the host my name and he took me to a table where a woman was sitting.

She stood up and said, "Oh Leanne, Leanne, Leanne. It's a real pleasure."

Judy was shorter than I was, but she was in heels, so it was hard to tell by just how much. She had short hair, too, in a sort of blond, businesswoman cut. She was younger than I expected, older than me but somewhere in her mid-thirties. And she seemed as nice in person as on the phone. Just as nice and just as busy. Right as I walked up, her cell phone rang. She glanced at it, then turned it off without answering, which I took as a compliment.

"It's nice to meet you," I said. "Finally."

"J.P. and Lars will be down soon enough, I'm guessing," Judy said. I must have looked confused because she said, "Lars is my husband," and then I remembered the name. "He decided to come with me, last minute. You know he's J.P.'s agent, right? That's how we met."

"I don't think you ever told me that," I said.

"It's not much of a story. Lars makes it his business to know everyone. So when he signed Joshua, he had to meet with me. The rest is history," Judy said. "Listen, Leanne, before the boys show up and people start drinking, I want to thank you for your time and effort, all these years. You really keep the fan club rolling. I want to tell you that. J.P. certainly won't," she added.

"What? Why?" I asked.

"Oh, I didn't mean it that way," Judy said. "There are no complaints from his corner. Actually, there are many complaints, but none about you. He's…he's getting famous," she began, but cut off. "There you two are!"

That's when I turned and saw Joshua Reed in person for the first time. Judy stood, so I stood, too. I felt my heart start pounding a little.

"Joshua, I want you to meet Leanne," Judy said. "Hi honey," she whispered to a second man who had walked up and put his arm around her waist.

Joshua Reed leaned forward and kissed me on the cheek. "Leanne. Favorite fan. It is a pleasure," he said.

I nodded. I managed to say that it was nice to meet him, too. At least, I think I managed to say that. I was just taking it all in. There he was, Joshua Reed, Colin Ashcroft, Nate Cummings, soon to be Josiah Whitcomb. Joshua Reed.

He was shorter than the Joshua Reed in my mind. I mean, after seven years, I knew what his details were, and the official statistics put him at 6'1", but Tommy is 6'2", and I swear that Joshua was more than an inch down. But I didn't focus on that. The rest of the statistics were accurate. The dark brown hair, the dark green eyes. He was growing his hair for the role, Judy had told me, and I could tell. It was curling a bit around the bottoms of his ears. He was beautiful. I'd never seen someone that beautiful up close and in person. I tried not to stare.

Judy introduced me to Lars, her husband, the agent, and he shook my hand hard and enthusiastic and then the four of us sat.

"So Leanne, Judy says that you've lived in West Virginia your whole life. Any plans to move?" Lars asked me this, right after our drinks came.

He looked like I always imagined New England professors to look—with little glasses and a beard. And he was one of those people who looked straight at you when you talked, like everything you said was fascinating. I wondered if that made him a good agent.

I told him that I didn't have any plans as yet, that there were nice things about living in Pinecob.

"The town is called Pinecob?" Joshua asked. "What's that all about?"

"J.P.," Judy said. "Please."

"I'm just asking," he said.

"I don't know where the name comes from," I told him. "Pine trees, maybe. It's just a small town. I imagine there are lots of small towns with funny names out there."

"Of course there are," Judy said, and Lars nodded.

"Has your family been around here for long? You know, I'm from Virginia," Lars said. "Northern. Close to D.C."

I nodded, to both parts.

"My father's family is from Elkins, down south a bit. That's where Susan, my sister, lives. My mother's family is from close to Charleston, the capital—not Charles Town," I explained. "Charles Town is just the county seat. But that's probably more than you wanted to know."

"Not at all," Lars said, though I thought I saw Joshua roll his eyes. "What business is your father in?" Lars asked.

I heard Judy take a quick breath. She knew more about me than either of the men, and I imagine she was worried that I was going to feel uncomfortable, telling practical strangers about my life. But I didn't mind. I couldn't remember anyone asking before. That's the thing about a small town— everyone already knows your story. It's kind of nice to say it out loud every once in a while.

"My dad died when I was fourteen," I explained. "But he was in the insurance business. Life insurance."

"I'm sorry," Lars said.

"You must have cleaned up after that."

I looked over at Joshua, but I couldn't read his expression. I couldn't tell whether or not he was being nice.

"Why? Oh, because he would have a big policy? Yeah, you'd think that, but they say it's like doctors smoking. He didn't leave much of anything."

"But that's awful," Judy said. "I didn't realize."

"Wait—your dad was a life insurance salesman and he didn't have life insurance? Rude!" Joshua sounded annoyed.

"He had some," I explained. "But it only covered the funeral costs. Anyhow, we're okay. He had good health insurance, so most of my brother Beau Ray's care is covered from here on out."

"Beau Ray?" Joshua asked.

"Brother," Judy said.

"Yeah, I got that," Joshua said. He poured himself more wine. "What's wrong with brother Beau Ray?"

"He had a fall. Years back. He was playing touch football, no helmet, and he fell and hit up against a rock. For a while, the doctors said he was probably going to die, but he made it, only he's disabled."

"Disabled how?"

"J.P.," Judy hissed.

"I'm just asking," he said. He sounded defensive.

"No, it's okay. It's not a secret. My dad always said that families shouldn't have secrets—except around the holidays, you know, with presents and all," I said.

I told them—we talked about it pretty much through dinner and on into coffee. Judy and Lars kept asking for details. Joshua Reed didn't say much, but he did offer to refill my wineglass once, after refilling his own. I told them about Beau Ray and how he was more like a six-year-old than a twenty-nine-year-old, and how that wasn't likely to change for the better. I told them about Tommy doing construction up and down the Shenandoah. I told them about Susan and her three kids and her husband, Tim, who drove a truck down in Elkins. I told them about Momma and her job as a receptionist in a dentist's office and her weekends making quilts and how she hadn't been out with anyone since Dad died. I mentioned Vince and how he left the house that night when I was fourteen, and that except for a couple of phone calls early on, no one had heard from him, no one knew where he was and no one much talked about it anymore.

"Jesus," Joshua said. "That's fucked up."

"You never thought about going to college? You're clearly bright enough," Judy asked, waving Joshua away.

I couldn't imagine ever waving him away, and here she was acting like it was no big deal. Judy was looking hard at me, so I knew I had to answer. I explained that I had figured on college, but when the time came, Momma couldn't take care of Beau Ray on her own, and he was my brother, after all. I told her how, for a few years running, I'd been taking prelaw courses over in Shepherdstown—during the summer when things were slower at the dentist's office. Judy and Lars nodded.

"It'll happen eventually," I said. "There are worse places to be than Pinecob."

"I hope we'll get a chance to visit while we're here, don't you, Judy?" Lars asked.

"Of course," Judy agreed.

"Jesus!" Joshua said, and all three of us looked over at him. I thought maybe he'd burned himself on something. His voice was that sharp. "You think she really believes you?"

"Josh—" Lars began, but Joshua kept going.

"No offense Leanne, but if I get a day off, I plan to find a city, or at least a good-sized suburb. There are a few too many gun racks around here for my taste."

"J.P.!" Judy said.

"Josh, that's completely uncalled for," Lars said.

"It's okay," I said. I could tell that Lars was angry.

"It's not okay," Lars snapped. He turned to Joshua. "None of your behavior tonight has been okay! None of your behavior on this entire trip has been okay! I want you to apologize to Leanne."

Joshua turned and stared at me. I didn't know what to do. I felt like I was some sort of Goody Two-shoes I hadn't meant to be. Turns out, I didn't have to do anything. Joshua Reed turned back to Lars and ignored me altogether.

"I'm not your kid," he said. "You want me to apologize because I don't want to go to Pinecob? Please! Like you guys would actually be caught dead there. Why the fuck am I even here? Leanne runs the fan club. Great. Wonderful. I'm sure she does a bang-up job. But that's your bag, Judy. Don't drag me into it. I could be home in L.A., watching a Lakers game with my girlfriend. I did you a favor. I came to dinner." Joshua stood up and stepped away from the table. He steadied himself on the back of his chair. "But I didn't agree to be hauled around and shown off in random bum-fuck towns."

"You're such a prick," Lars said. "I've been with you for an evening, and I'm sick of you already."

"Yeah, right," Joshua said. "You say that and then you get your ten percent and you shut up awfully quick about how sick you are of me."

"Fuck you," Lars said. He stood, too, and stared at Joshua. "I don't care how big you think you're getting. It's not worth it. You're not worth it."

"Oh, no," Joshua Reed said. His voice was sarcastic.

"Joshua, please. Lars," Judy said, but neither man paid any attention. They reminded me of cats in a standoff, staring at each other until one backs away.

"Fuck you," Lars said again. "You want me to see to it that you don't work here again?"

"In Harper's Ferry? Go right ahead," Joshua said.

"You know that's not where I mean," Lars said.

"You can't do that anymore. You don't decide," Joshua said. "Just try." And then he stalked off.

"You're an asshole!" Lars called out after him.

There were only a few tables where people were still eating, but from where I sat, it looked like everyone in the room turned to stare at Lars. I shrank a little in my chair.

"He is," Lars said. "Sorry."

Judy took hold of Lars's arm and pulled him back to his seat.

"Leanne, I'm so sorry," Judy said. She dabbed her eyes with a napkin. "I'm sorry you had to see…hear that."

"It's okay," I told them, though I wasn't sure how I felt about it. Sure, no one likes to be insulted, or have the thing or the people they care for held up as goofy or uncool. But it was hard to take it personally. Joshua Reed didn't know me, or my family, or Pinecob. He was just mad, and I knew that, whatever the reason, it had been there before he met me.

"It's not okay," Lars said again. "It can't always be okay. It's not okay to insult you, to make Judy cry. I'm really fed up with this kid."

"He's not a kid," Judy said. "That's the problem."

"He doesn't act like any adult I know," Lars said. "So much potential and I have tried—really—to get him to use it, and not waste goodwill on these outbreaks. I'm serious. I can get a lot of agents not to touch him, but someone out there is going to offer him representation."

Judy nodded.

"Listen, Leanne. It's late," Lars said. "You can take the car back home now, if you want. But why don't you let us put you up here tonight? You can have a nice night away. We can have breakfast in the morning—I know Judy wanted to talk to you about the movie, didn't you, hon?"

Judy nodded again.

"We can put this incident behind us," Lars said.

"Oh, do stay," Judy said. "They've got a great breakfast buffet."

Like I needed convincing. I'd never stayed in a hotel that nice, and the thought of sleeping in a big bed and getting to use trial-size shampoos, that sounded fun. So I said okay, and Lars jumped up to take care of things.

"Joshua is going through a difficult period," Judy said, quietly, once Lars was out of earshot.

I nodded like I knew what she was talking about. All I knew was that he was getting more and more famous, and getting to star in a bunch of different movies, and getting to date models like Elise. I wasn't a guy and I didn't live in Los Angeles, but it didn't sound all that difficult.

"He's…he's adjusting to a new level of celebrity, and that's hard," she said.

"How long has it been difficult?" I asked.

Judy thought a moment, then shook her head. "Pretty much since I've known him, I guess." She smiled but looked sad at the same time.

"That can't be fun. For you, I mean," I said.

"It's not. A lot of the time. But he's an excellent actor. He really is. He's more talented than any of my other clients. And when I see him work," Judy said, "it's almost worth it. For Lars, it's different. He doesn't really like actors, so he's got a lot less patience."

"Was he serious about dropping Joshua?" I asked.

Judy seemed to think about it. "He might have been. Something to sleep on, anyhow."

Lars returned then, with a room key for me. He gave me a brief tour on the way to the lobby. There was a bar that stayed open late, to the left of the restaurant. There was a smaller dining room, where the breakfast buffet would be served.

"What time do you usually wake up?" Lars asked. "For breakfast."

"I'm usually up around six," I told him.

"Yow," Lars said.

Judy laughed. "You're quite the morning person, but that's a little early for us," she said. "Especially since that's three in the morning California time. How about around eight we meet down here?"

We were standing in the lobby. My room was down the hallway, theirs was upstairs.

"Eight's fine, too," I told them.

My room was small, but so neat, and the blankets were turned down and there was a chocolate coin on the pillow. I checked the bathroom, and there was a little bottle of shampoo and another of conditioner and also lotion and two kinds of soap, and a shower cap and a sewing kit. I put everything in my purse right away, then put the shampoo back, since I would need it for the shower in the morning.

I called home so that Momma knew where I was. And then I called Sandy at the beach.

"You'll never guess where I am," I told her.

"In Joshua Reed's bedroom?" she guessed, whispering.

"No. But I am in the same hotel, and I'm staying here. In my own room. For the night."

"So?" Sandy asked.

I told her all of it, and she was a lot more pissed than I was.

"What a butthole," she said, when I finished.

"Yeah, I guess," I said.

"I'm sorry, Leanne," Sandy said.

"No, I'm really okay about it," I told her.

"It still shouldn't have happened. That was a butthole thing to do."

I agreed.

After I got off the phone, I was still wide awake and figured I might as well poke around the resort, in case a maid had left her cart out, and I could get more shampoos to bring home for Beau Ray. I didn't find a cart, but I wandered through the various lobbies and waiting rooms until I found myself by the door of the bar. The bartender looked up from wiping the counter and waved me inside.

"Hey, have a seat," he said. "You were eating with that movie guy earlier, weren't you?"

"Joshua Reed," I said, nodding. "Yeah. I hope the yelling didn't disturb you."

He just shrugged, as if one man calling another man an asshole across a nice restaurant was something that happened every weekend.

"What's he like?" the bartender asked, and then he looked past me and said, "speak of the devil, I guess I'll find out."

I turned on my stool and saw Joshua Reed swagger into the bar. He looked over at me, frowned, and then walked up and took the stool next to mine. I got the impression that he had kept drinking between dinner and just then. He ordered a martini and turned to me.

"Leanne Gitlin," he said.

I turned to him, trying my hardest to look like I didn't care, or like I'd sat next to lots of movie stars in lots of bars before that particular night.

"I hope you're not angry with me." He smiled. I'd seen that same smile on Colin Ashcroft.

"Why should I be angry?" I said.

"Exactly," he said. "You get it."

"Sure, I get it," I told him, even though I had no idea what he was talking about.

"You don't know what it's like," he went on. "All these people putting demands on me, expecting me to do this, do that. I just want to live my own life. You understand that, don't you?"

"Sure," I said again. I was afraid that I was starting to sound stupid even though I did know a fair bit about demands and expectations.

He took a sip of his drink and turned and looked straight at me. "Why the fuck do you do it?" he asked, and even though I'd heard him swear at dinner, it still made me flinch. It was hard to get used to him as someone who swore so casually. He never swore in the interviews I'd read.

"What do you mean? Do what?" I asked.

"Because you seem smart enough. I figured you for the usual ditzy fan, but you seem smart, so why do it? The fan club bullshit."

"Oh. *That*." I was glad to figure out what he was talking about. "I don't know," I said. "It's different. It's something dif-

ferent." I'm not sure he heard me, because he started in again
while I was still talking.

"You fans sort of freak me out," he said. "It's like some
weird fantasy. I don't understand you people."

"I guess I do it more for Judy than I do it for you," I
told him.

Joshua looked over like he wasn't sure whether or not to
believe me.

"Really? Yeah, I can see that now. She gets a lot of people to do things for her. She's good at her job."

"She's a good person," I said. I wanted him to understand
the difference. "Other people matter to her." I hoped that was
true. It struck me that I didn't know Judy as well as Joshua
did.

"You think?" Joshua Reed asked. "Believe me, I've seen
her act like they do. But I'm not so sure, in the long run.
Hell, I know *I* matter, but I pay her bills."

I didn't want to follow his conversation to somewhere
ugly, so I switched subjects and asked him whether he
thought that Lars was serious about dropping him as a client.

"I don't know," Joshua said, shrugging. "I guess. We'll see.
I can always get another agent. I'm a prize bull at the county
fair." He stood up, unsteady. "I've got to get out of here," he
said. "The drinks are on me," he said, though he hadn't ordered me one. He dropped money onto the bar. "See you
around, Leanne Gitlin." And then Joshua Reed wandered off.

I looked back at the bartender, who I figured had been
listening to us the whole time anyway.

"Does that answer your question?" I asked him.

I slept until almost seven. After my shower, I pocketed the
rest of the shampoo, and then put my clothes back on. I was
downstairs at eight, but no one was around so I picked up a
Virginia travel magazine and sat in the lobby. I read an arti-

cle on horses until 8:10. I read an article on Thomas Jefferson until 8:15. And I read up on Richmond restaurants until Judy rushed in at 8:20.

"Leanne, oh, I'm so sorry!" she said. "This morning has been unbelievable," she said. "I've got to get some coffee, but, my God! I just got off the phone with the studio. Because of some sort of farming statute, they can't start filming for another two months."

"Is that a problem?" I asked her.

"That's not even the start of it."

Judy said she wasn't hungry and only drank coffee, but I figured I ought to take advantage of the breakfast buffet, because I'd never been to one so nice. So I was eating an omelette that the chef made special while Judy told me the story.

Apparently, after Joshua wandered out of the bar the night before, he had found the keys to one of the rented limousines and had taken himself for a ride.

"But he'd been drinking," I said.

Judy sighed. "It's not the first time," she said, then pulled back a little and looked at me. "I'm sure it was a mistake," she said, more slowly. "I'm sure he didn't realize how much he'd had." Judy said that Joshua had crossed the Potomac into West Virginia, though she didn't figure that he had actually meant to go for a late-night visit to Pinecob. "He was probably looking for a bar or a girl or something. God only knows," Judy said.

A weaving limousine stands out on West Virginia roads, and the police tried to pull him over. "And if that's not bad enough," Judy said, "I guess the lights or siren startled him. The limo ended up through a fence in a field. He hit a cow. He hit a goddamn cow!" Judy said.

I didn't know the right reaction to news like that, so I just nodded.

"Apparently, it's fine. The cow is fine," Judy went on. "I've already been on the phone, calling around to find a way to mend the fence. A perfect metaphor for my day."

"At least the cow's okay," I said. "He must not have been going very fast."

Judy shook her head. "This is my personal nightmare," she said. "This is the exact sort of thing I dread. Now I've got to either try to keep a lid on this, or put some sort of good spin on it, and at the very least, try to get him out of this mess. Lars has gone over to the station where they kept him overnight. He'll probably be able to get him out, but Jesus!" Judy laughed. "What a fuck-up," she muttered. "I'm really sorry you've had to see all of this. I can't tell you..."

I shrugged. I offered her a bite of omelette but she shook her head.

"What I want is a cigarette," she said, "but I quit, and Lars would kill me."

"All I'm saying is that there must be *something* we can do. It's West Virginia for Chrissakes. It's not like it's a serious state." Joshua was trailing behind Lars as the two walked into the breakfast room.

He wore the same clothes as the night before, though his shirt was untucked and wrinkled, and a grass stain smeared one knee of his pants. He hadn't shaved, and he looked as though he hadn't slept, but even so, Joshua Reed was striking. Actually, I thought he looked just like the character Stormy Bridges, the street-smart runaway he'd played a few years back.

Lars stopped in front of our table. "Okay," he said, turning around, "first off, how about you not driving drunk anymore? How's that for an idea?"

"Well, duh, but that doesn't help our particular problem," Joshua pointed out.

"*Your* particular problem," Lars snapped. "Because, legally, West Virginia *is* a serious state. Hi, sweetheart," he said to

Judy. He kissed her on the cheek. "Morning, Leanne. I trust Judy has brought you up to date on our most recent disaster."

I nodded.

"Leanne Gitlin," Joshua Reed said, looking down at me. "If it isn't my number one fan." He spoke with an exaggerated drawl, so that "fan" sounded like "fie-un."

"J.P.," Judy snapped.

"I'm practicing my Josiah accent," Joshua said.

"You'll be lucky if we can keep you in the picture," Lars hissed. "There are lots of pretty boys willing to play Josiah, and a call to the director says one of them's going to get that chance."

Joshua's face froze into an expression I couldn't read. For the first time, he looked something less than cocky, maybe even a little scared. He glanced back at me and nodded a more polite good morning.

"Dude, so what do you want me to do?" he asked Lars, almost quietly.

"Go to your room. Take a shower. Get dressed. Then come back down here, and we'll discuss this. You reek."

Joshua nodded and walked off. Lars shook his head and took a seat at our table.

"So what does it look like?" Judy asked.

Lars shook his head again. "Oh, it looks great. Just great," Lars said, and Judy winced. "He took a breathalyzer like he shouldn't have—he should have waited, of course—and it came through as intoxicated, and with state reciprocity in effect, we obviously can't plead first offense."

Judy nodded. This was the first I'd heard of any legal trouble Joshua'd gotten into. I looked at the two of them and wondered how much else they had kept quiet.

"So now it's pretty much a matter of mandatory sentences and precedents. Thank God he didn't hurt that cow. I know people all through Virginia, but not here. Why couldn't he have stayed in Virginia? Fuck, we'd be better off if he'd driven into the Potomac."

"Lars!" Judy said.

"I know. I don't mean it. Leanne, you know I don't mean it."

"How far did he get?" I asked. "I mean, in West Virginia. What county?"

"Jefferson, apparently," Lars said. "I don't even know where that is. The driver took me."

"That's Charles Town," I said. "That's my county."

Lars looked at me. Judy looked at me.

"You know, I work at the county clerk's office. Same building as the courthouse," I told them.

"She works at the courthouse!" Judy said, suddenly excited.

"Not exactly. But in the same building. All the same, I probably know the judge on the case," I continued. "There aren't too many."

"Oh my God, she knows…I mean, you know the judge?" Judy asked.

"I might. I probably do. At least I could find out who it is. You want me to call and find out?"

Lars handed me his cell phone without another word. I took it and stared at it. No one I knew had a cell phone, and I wasn't sure how they worked. Judy took the phone from my hand and asked me for the number, plugging it in as I told her. She pressed a button and handed back the phone. I heard the ringing tone.

Mr. Bellevue, my boss, answered.

"Hey, Mr. Bellevue, it's Leanne," I said.

"We want to keep this out of the papers," Lars whispered to me.

I nodded. "Something's come up," I said to Mr. Bellevue, and told him the story.

I knew that Mr. Bellevue would help if he could, on account of being such a big movie fan. Also I was pretty certain that he was gay, although I'd never asked, and Joshua Reed had a substantial following in that community. Mr. Bellevue listened and sighed a little, and seemed happy to hear that the cow was okay, and then he put me on hold to go find out which judge had been assigned to Joshua's arraignment.

"Your fella's a lucky boy," Mr. Bellevue said when he got back on the phone. "It's Weintraub."

"He was Charlie's, right? That is good news," I said. I asked Mr. Bellevue to please keep all this to himself, but I wasn't too worried. I knew that he respected privacy, at least the serious kind. And I promised to give him details when I got there in the afternoon. I handed the phone back to Judy to hang up.

"So?" Lars and Judy were looking at me.

"Yeah, when you paid and asked for the first available court date, that's good—you got Judge Weintraub. People say he's pretty progressive and also a nice guy. But what's cool is that, Sandy, my best friend since third grade? Her brother Charlie got pulled over about a year ago, second offense, drunk driving. Is it Joshua's second offense?"

Lars and Judy exchanged glances. Lars nodded.

"Because second is usually jail but third always is," I told them, although I got the impression that they already knew something about drunk driving sentences. "Anyway, Charlie lost his license of course, for a long time, but instead of jail he got house arrest, at home, for I think it was ninety days. Weintraub's really into families helping each other through hard times. It drove Sandy crazy to have him there. Charlie, not the judge. I mean, they let him go to work, but then he had to come right home. So you might be able to argue some sort of precedent. You know, if you were willing to plead guilty. That's the thing, Charlie pled guilty. Pled? Pleaded? You get what I mean."

"But what are we going to do about the movie? I know

you're pissed, sweetheart, but I really want him to be in this movie," Judy said to Lars. "It'll be good for all of us. We can't have him sitting at home in California."

"He couldn't do that," I told her. "Whatever punishment he gets will have to be in West Virginia. Probably Jefferson County. I remember that from my class on jurisdiction," I said.

Lars smiled at me. "You'll make a good lawyer," he said. He turned to Judy. "Leanne's right. Whatever happens, it's bound to happen in Jefferson County."

"What are you suggesting?" Judy said. "That we stick him in a hotel for three months?"

"I doubt that would count as house arrest," Lars said. "It's not a house. And I don't think there's such thing as bed-and-breakfast arrest." Lars was almost laughing, but Judy looked serious.

"So who do we know in Jefferson County?" Judy asked. "We must know someone. Can we rent an apartment?"

Lars was looking across the table at me.

"You know me," I said. "And of course, I know a lot of people."

Judy turned to me, smiling and exasperated. "I don't suppose there are any house arrest bungalows available in Pinecob, are there?" Now she was laughing. "Or guesthouses?"

I shook my head. I had a thought, bit my lip, then opened my mouth. I figured it was likely a stupid idea, that it wouldn't work so there was no harm in saying it. Knowing what I know now, maybe I wouldn't have said it. Knowing what I know now, maybe I would have kept quiet and looked at my shoes instead. But I did say it. And everything that would have otherwise stayed the same started changing. Like experiments with food coloring we did in home economics, making icing in green and blue and red shades. Put a drop of red into water, and the water will never again run clear. You can keep adding more and make it deeper red, or add blue and make purple. You still have choices like that. But to get back to clear water, you have to pour out what you've done and start over. And that doesn't work in life, with its days and geography. You can't just start over. You can never just start over.

"The thing is, Judge Weintraub is really into families. That's why he likes house arrest," I explained. I remember hearing Sandy complaining about this. "I know he's not related, but Joshua might be able to stay in Vince's room," I said. "There's probably a legal guardianship thing to work out, and you'd have to convince my mother."

Judy turned to Lars and raised her eyebrows. Lars turned to me and raised his.

"We could argue a long-term relationship, given the fan club," Lars said.

"Can you imagine?" Judy asked. "Let's think this through a minute. For starters, J.P. would hate that." Judy didn't add to her list. She stopped talking and looked over at me, too.

Joshua Reed appeared then, hair still wet from the shower but clean shaven and clean clothed. Even damp, he really was beautiful. Judy and Lars looked at him, then turned to me.

"You are really fucking lucky," Lars said.

"Yeah?" Joshua smiled. He seemed surprised. "Hey, that's great."

"Leanne here knows your judge," Lars said.

Chapter 4

Start Slow

What's crazy is how it all worked out. The court system in the United States—or at least in West Virginia—really does work on precedent. I'd heard that, but this was the first time I'd seen it in action. I'd always liked that about law. The logic of it. Knowing, at least in some small part, what you might expect.

A lot went on, I'll bet much more than I ever saw, and things fell into place. Lars and Judy hunkered down and sweet-talked the hell out of people. Lars spent a lot of time on his cell phone, and at least as much time cursing about how it hardly worked in Charles Town and Harper's Ferry. Judy spent a lot of time on the phone, too. She called it "putting out fires" and I guess she did a good job of it. The fence got fixed, and the farmer paid for his inconvenience, and *People* didn't get wind of Joshua Reed being arrested—though there was a notice in the *Charles Town Register* about a J. Polichuk. There was no mention of the cow.

Lars got Joshua's arraignment pushed up to just a week after his arrest, and in the meantime, found a lawyer from Charleston who had previously clerked for Judge Weintraub. Judy kept me in the loop with phone calls, but Lars was over at the courthouse nearly every day, so on my lunch hour, I'd cross over from the other wing and catch up with how things were going. Joshua mostly stayed back in Harper's Ferry—Judy had told me that Lars agreed to keep him as a client so long as all Joshua did that week was read and think, and that he showed up whenever and wherever Lars asked, acting polite and looking sober and sorry. Judy said she'd convinced Lars that Joshua was a good long-term investment.

There was one long meeting between the lawyer and Lars and Joshua and Momma and Judge Weintraub and the county prosecutor. It must have gone well because Lars looked relieved when they all poured out of the judge's chambers. Judge Weintraub waved at me. I didn't know the judge well, though I'd heard a few stories about him on account of working in the same building—how he'd worked at the state capitol a while, until his wife died and he moved north to Charles Town. Judge Weintraub's leanings toward family made more sense once I found out that he'd been married, though he'd been a widower some years by the time of Joshua's plea meeting. After the meeting, while everyone was still shuffling around, the judge asked my mother to come back into in his chambers for a moment. I assumed it had something to do with the temporary legal guardianship she had to take on. Momma had a short stack of forms to sign.

I never found out what Judy said to my mother to get her to agree to allow Joshua Reed to sit out his sentence under our roof. Momma didn't seem too excited about the idea when I first mentioned it, what with him being a drunk driver and all. She put down her quilting and stared hard at me.

"You know what you're asking? You really want for me to do this?" Momma asked.

"It was just an idea," I told her. "I just thought, maybe."

"You been with that fan club how long now?"

I reminded her that it had been seven years.

"I suppose you think this guy's worth some trouble," she said. "I'm not convinced of it, but maybe you know better."

The next morning, Momma told me that she'd take a call from Judy, and whatever Judy said convinced her to go along. I always figured it had something to do with money.

So it was a week after the arrest that Joshua sat in the courtroom at the arraignment, frowning as Judge Weintraub asked for the plea and the Charleston lawyer said, "guilty." And after that, it was over. At least, most of the legal part.

As Judy predicted, Joshua wasn't too excited about spending ninety days in Pinecob, even if he'd be allowed to commute to the movie set once production started. But I got the impression that whatever Lars and Judy had on him, it was enough to make him simmer down and sit tight. Lars kept pointing out how lucky Joshua was, though I didn't get the impression that he saw himself as lucky to live with me and Momma and Beau Ray, even when the other choice was the Jefferson County jail.

"Fuck that," Joshua Reed said that morning in the Harper's Ferry hotel, after he'd come back to the table by the breakfast buffet and Lars mentioned the house arrest idea. "You can't be serious." He looked at Lars, then Judy, then back to Lars. "There's got to be another way. Can't we—I mean, I—just pay a really big fine? Or, I don't know, talk to high-school kids?"

Lars and Judy had shrugged. As it turned out, Judge Weintraub didn't think that fining rich people was an effective deterrent (although he did slap Joshua with a $5,000 fine and the cost of the repaired fence and the cow's vet visit). Judge William Weintraub believed in families and he believed in house arrest for ninety days for Joshua's sort of a DUI. The terms of Joshua's sentence were this: He would have to wear an ankle sensor so that the county police would know where he was at all times. He wasn't allowed to leave the house without police supervision, except to go to required alcohol counseling classes, which in Pinecob meant AA twice a week over at Potomac Springs Senior High. And he lost his license for a year.

"Fuck me," Joshua had said, leaving the courthouse after all the plea bargaining was done. "This is going to give me a rash."

I think he meant the ankle sensor.

"Three months in fucking Pinecob. It's a fucking bad dream."

By the time Momma got back from the Y with Beau Ray—that first afternoon with Joshua Reed in the house— Lars and Judy were on their way to the airport, and Joshua was tucked behind the closed door to Vince's old bedroom. I asked Beau Ray to keep extra quiet that afternoon. I thought Joshua might be sleeping, although I didn't know. I could have walked in easy enough. There was no lock on the door to Vince's room. Except for the bathrooms, there were no locks on any of the inside doors in our house. Dad hadn't believed in them, and after he died—well, it would have felt disloyal to make an addition like that. The Gitlin family rule was that closed doors were as good as locked, so you were supposed to assume that the person who'd done the closing didn't want to be barged in on. You were supposed to knock before walking in. Although, logically, I knew that he had to eat, part of me wondered if we would ever see Joshua Reed again.

"Leanne," Momma said, "you come over here and help your brother put to right his playing cards."

I'd been in the living room, comparing our own setup against the picture of Joshua's "artist's cottage" from the home decor magazine Judy's assistant had sent me. The quilt that Momma had laid over the long couch hadn't been cleaned in a while, so I'd hauled it out to soak in the laundry tub and replaced it with one I thought was prettier, made mostly of blue shirting. But even that didn't look like something you might see in a magazine.

Don't get me wrong, our house was fine and it's not like we didn't have room enough. Momma and Dad had moved in back when Tommy was a toddler and Susan, just a baby. So I'd been conceived there, and before me, Vince and before Vince, Beau Ray. Growing up, Dad was always the one with big plans—tearing out a wall to expand a room, adding another bedroom out back. But most of those plans never materialized. And after Dad died, Momma wouldn't talk of renovations. As the seasons passed, that meant that the kitchen floors sagged a bit along one edge, and the basement tended to smell a little swampy. Ours just wasn't a home decor house.

Beau Ray had rushed off to his room upon returning from "Move Your Body, Move Your Mind." Even though I knew that extended periods of quiet were usually followed by the discovery of some sort of chaos—like the time he'd dunked all of his clothes in the bathtub or cut his hair in jagged layers or tried to repair an old model plane but only succeeded in pasting it to his arm with superglue—I hadn't felt like checking in on him. Transitions home from the Y tended to be difficult, but that day had also been Raoul's last before moving back to Mexico to be with his family. Raoul was a physical therapist's assistant, and Beau Ray had worked with him for the previous two years. There had been a going-away party the week before, but there's nothing like the very last day you're going to see someone to make the loss hit home.

"Leanne, didn't you hear me? I'm talking right at you," Momma said. She sounded mad. "Beau Ray's done mixed up all his playing cards, plus the ones from the game chest. I don't know, just fix it!"

"Yes, Momma," I told her, and I put the artist's cottage picture inside the pages of the fancy Bible that Susan had given us the year before.

Beau Ray's room was a mess of playing cards.

"Beau Ray," I said to get his attention. I could see how Momma had probably taken one look and called for me. There were cards strewn across his bed, across the rug, across the dresser, everywhere. If there'd been anyone else to ask, I'd have kept passing the buck.

Beau Ray was squatting in the doorway of his closet, pretending to play solitaire. Sometimes, even though years had passed, I'd have these split-second moments when I'd forget all that had happened, that Beau Ray wasn't exactly Beau Ray anymore, that there was a new person in our midst.

"What's with all the cards?" I asked him.

He looked up at me, confused, and it all came back.

"Playing solidtare," he said.

"Solitaire," I told him. "But what about all these?"

"Playing twenty-eight pickup," he said.

From the door, I could see that he'd mixed at least four different decks, four different designs including one from my room that had roses on the backs and gold around the edges. I don't put too much stock in playing cards, but Vince had given me the rose deck when I was twelve, so they were not something I wanted to see torn up or stepped on.

"Looks like two hundred and eight pickup," I said, doing the math.

"Two hundred eight pickup," Beau Ray said. He threw his solitaire pile into the air. On the outside, it looked celebratory, the cards fluttering around him like petals and whirligigs. But he didn't look happy.

"Momma says we've got to clean this up. Help me get the cards into a big pile, okay?"

Beau Ray nodded but didn't move. I started gathering the cards into one pile and finally he shrugged, then helped a little. I told him that I wanted him to ask before he took the deck of rose cards, and even though I was trying not to sound mad about it, Beau Ray started to rock back and forth as he did when he sought to comfort himself.

"Beau Ray, it's okay," I said. "I'm not yelling at you. It's just that they belong in my room—like this is your room and your cards live here, right?"

He nodded, but I knew that we'd be having the same conversation again about something else, some other thing he found and would take or break or both. I'd learned not to become too attached to things since Beau Ray's fall. Nothing lasted.

Beau Ray was a good guy—at least, he meant to be. That he'd always been mellow, even back when he was functioning at normal levels, was a saving grace. I'd heard stories of people, brain-injured like him, full of adult-sized rage but without the ability to put it anywhere. So my brother marked Raoul's departure by throwing four packs of playing cards in the air. That wasn't so bad.

Maybe an hour later, I was in my room replacing the rose-backed cards in my desk drawer when Joshua opened Vince's door. He stood in the doorway, stock-still for a moment, staring across the hall into my room. He looked both sleepy and mad, like a toddler roused too early from a nap. His dark hair curled out in different directions. Then he shuffled across the hall and stood at my bedroom door, frowning out my window toward the yard below and the street beyond. He looked down at his left ankle, where the gray plastic sensor with a locked band hung. He shook his left foot, and I could hear the plastic rattle and thud against his skin.

"So it's not a bad dream," he said. "Fuck."

"You awake?" I asked him and then cringed to myself. It was a stupid question, given that he was standing before me, his eyes open. "You want to see the rest of the house now?"

Joshua shrugged. "I guess. Whatever. Why the fuck not?"

He hated us, I thought, if he could be goaded to feel anything at all. At least, he acted like he hated us, and as Judy had pointed out, Joshua Reed was a fine actor.

"Great. I'll give you the grand tour," I told him.

I thought about what Judy had told me to do—or rather, how she'd told me to act. But still I heard myself being nice to him before I knew if I wanted to be, before I'd even thought about what I wanted. No one ever noticed, I don't think—that I tended to be nice as pie even when I didn't mean it. But it was a quirk that bugged me, and I realized that if I were going to be aloof to Joshua, I'd have to become a better actress. I'd have to practice.

He'd already seen most of the upstairs, what there was to it. He'd seen his room, and mine, and the hall bathroom. Besides that, there was Momma's bedroom and Susan's old bedroom, which had years back been converted into the sewing room where Momma did all her machine piecing. I pointed out both rooms on the way downstairs, but Joshua didn't seem to care. There was a lot of shrugging.

Downstairs, Beau Ray sat on the couch watching *This Old House* on television. He had quieted down and for that, Momma had given him a slice of cake. Momma sat beside him, stacking fabric squares. She nodded up at us.

"Joshua, this is my brother Beau Ray. Beau Ray, say hello," I said.

Beau Ray didn't look up.

"Beau Ray, it's polite to say hello," I said.

"Hello," he said but still didn't look up.

A streak of chocolate icing colored his face, across his mouth and cheek. I usually wouldn't have cared about something like that, but I remember being a little embarrassed just then.

"Joshua's going to be our house guest for the summer," Momma said. "Isn't that nice?"

Joshua looked a little uncomfortable. Beau Ray finally tore his eyes from the television set and glanced up at Joshua.

"Hey, man," Joshua said.

Beau Ray's eyes went wide. "That's!" Beau Ray said. He pointed at Joshua Reed, then turned to me with an incredulous smile, mouth open, icing everywhere. "That's!" he said again.

I had to smile back. Anyone would have.

"Yes. It is," I said. "Remember how I was telling you? And you didn't believe me."

Beau Ray scrambled to his feet, his eyes locked on Joshua the whole time. Chocolate crumbs fell to the floor and got mashed into the carpet as Beau Ray rushed over and enveloped Joshua in a huge hug. Joshua looked at me like he could use some guidance.

"It's!" Beau Ray said, hugging him close.

"Now, now, dear," Momma told my brother. "Of course you're excited but let the man alone!"

But Beau Ray was a lot beefier than Joshua, and he was holding on tight.

"It's!" Beau Ray said again, laughing a little. His laughter shook Joshua up and down.

"It's cool, man," Joshua said, but I thought he looked sort of scared. His arms flapped a little—as much as they could pinned beneath the hug.

"Beau Ray, please let go of him. You've got the whole summer to hug him," I said. I must have sounded serious because Beau Ray released Joshua, then came to my side. He poked me in the shoulder, like I hadn't seen Joshua yet or if I had, didn't realize the magnitude of amazement he warranted.

"Cool man," Beau Ray said to me, poking me hard.

"Ouch. I know," I said.

Joshua was catching his breath. He'd taken a couple steps away from Beau Ray and was wiping chocolate icing from his cheek.

"I'll get you a towel for that," Momma said. "You got some on your shirt, too. I'll get the soap."

"Really, don't bother," Joshua said, but she was already halfway to the kitchen.

"Beau Ray," I said. "Have you cleaned your room? Because I want to show Joshua your room, but I want to make sure it's clean first."

"It's clean," Beau Ray said, still staring, as if Joshua might disappear if he looked away.

"Really?" I asked.

Beau Ray cast his eyes to the floor. The playing cards had been only the top layer of disorganization. I'd taught Beau Ray to throw all his things into the closet and shut the door if he couldn't actually get them put away in time for company to see. I figured that's what still needed doing.

"I'm gonna go clean my room," Beau Ray said. "Cool man." He smiled at Joshua and hustled off. Joshua stared after him.

"He was just excited to meet you. He'll calm down," I told him. "He's the one I was telling you is disabled."

"I see it didn't stunt his size," Joshua said.

"He used to play a lot of football," I said.

"When did, you know, his head happen? You said it was a fall?" Joshua asked.

"I was thirteen," I said, trying to remember. "It was January, so he was seventeen. So twelve years ago. He's turning thirty this summer. You'll be here."

Downstairs, in addition to the living room with the TV and the two couches and Dad's old reading chair, there was Beau Ray's room and his bathroom, the dining room and the kitchen. Another set of stairs, near the door of the kitchen, led farther down, to the washing machine and the swampy basement with the Ping-Pong table that no one ever used, the computer Judy bought me, and my fan club filing cabinet. Joshua didn't say anything as I showed him around. He sniffed a bit and frowned a lot, but he didn't say a word.

Outside was the big backyard and smaller front yard, and between the front yard and the door, a covered porch with a clothesline and a rickety table. On one end sat half a motorcycle Tommy had abandoned a few summers back, and at the other, an old tire that Momma had fashioned into a marigold planter. We ended up out there after I ran out of things to show him inside. Joshua sank into our one porch chair, so I sat on the two-step stoop, looking out at the driveway, beyond which Joshua couldn't go. For a while, he held his head in his hands, like he had the worst headache. I asked him if there was anything he needed.

"A drink," he said.

"You mean a liquor drink or a soda or something because Lars told me he didn't want—" I started saying, but he cut me off.

"No," he said. "Nothing."

"I usually go to the Winn-Dixie on Sundays," I explained. "But if there's anything special you want, let me know. I could make an extra trip."

"What the fuck is a Winn-Dixie?" Joshua snapped.

I felt my cheeks go hot. Sandy was right, I thought just then. Joshua Reed *was* a butthole. Joshua was a butthole and this was day one of ninety. The summer stretched out farther into the future than any of us could see, like the bend in Prospect Street when you turned left. There was never any way to know what might be coming at you there, so it was best to take it slow. That's what Dad had always said.

I didn't answer him, and eventually Joshua Reed looked up at me. I still didn't answer and he frowned, then looked a little ashamed, then broke out one of his smiles.

"Sorry," he said. "Winn-Dixie?"

I took a breath and thought, okay, I'll forgive him, the way you forgive a kid who is done with time-out, even though you know that he's bound to start roughhousing again. I took a breath and thought, start slow.

"For groceries. It's a supermarket," I told him. "I guess they don't have them in Los Angeles?"

He shook his head. "There's nothing I need. Wait. I'll let you know. I can't even think right now," he said.

I looked at my nails. I was still sporting the polish I'd put on the night I first met Joshua Reed. It had begun to flake and crack, and I picked at it as I looked out into our driveway. A car rolled by. I didn't recognize who it was, but I waved like I always did and whoever it was waved back. Joshua turned to me.

"What?" I asked.

"Nothing," he said, though I knew that his look carried something with it.

"You want lemonade?" I asked.

He kept staring into the street. I stood up.

"I could use a beer," I said.

Lars had asked me not to serve Joshua alcohol so long as he was under house arrest, but that didn't mean I couldn't indulge, even if it was mostly for show. As I opened the screen door, Joshua buried his head in his hands again.

"Fuck me," he muttered. And then louder, like he was really angry, he yelled it. "Fuck me!"

"Hey," I said to him, walking back near. "About the swearing. You can't be doing that. You can't be swearing like that around the house."

He turned to me. "What?" But I could tell he had heard me, because he sounded fed up. I suddenly got all nervous.

"It's just…you can't…you shouldn't…not around the house."

Joshua looked like he didn't know where to begin. "People swear in prison," he finally said.

"On account of Beau Ray," I explained. I told him how Beau Ray had this bad habit—more annoying than bad, I guess—of mimicking. Especially with swear words. "We've all trained ourselves not to," I told him.

"I'll see what I can do."

"Thanks," I said, and went to get my beer. From behind the screen door, I heard Joshua again.

"Jesus fucking Christ," he muttered.

The house was quiet that night, but I didn't sleep well. Joshua's door was closed, and Momma had closed hers, too. As I padded down the hall, ready to crawl into bed, I wondered what Momma was really thinking. She'd been fairly closemouthed on the subject of Joshua up to then. All I knew was that she saw his house arrest as an extension of my fan club duties, as if Joshua were a hobby of mine I had to keep neat and in the right place, like the plastic horses I'd collected when I was little. She'd already told me that I'd be the one driving him to AA. I would also be the one to buy groceries and whatever else he might demand. That night, Momma had gone to bed before dinner, saying that she was tuckered and had a big day ahead. I wondered if it hadn't been the arraignment and being civil to Judy and Lars and worrying over Beau Ray. Or maybe it was just having someone in Vince's room after all that time.

I had always slept with my door open. When I was younger, it was so I could look into Vince's room and see his feet sticking up under the covers and know that he would hear anything awful or scary and could rush to my side in seconds. Not that anything awful or scary ever happened— not that he could prevent at least. And after Vince left, I'd kept my door open so that I would be able to see if he came back in the night. And years after that, it was habit. But that night, that first night with Joshua, I'd closed my door, and with all the doors upstairs closed, it felt like a different house. Like my family wasn't my own anymore. I wondered if we'd made a mistake.

Often when I couldn't sleep, I called Sandy late at night. But that night, she was with her family at the beach—would be for the next week, too—and I was afraid I'd wake everyone. Sometimes when I couldn't sleep, I'd sit on the porch and listen to the crickets. But closing my door seemed so final, and I didn't want to take a chance on running into Joshua while I was in nightclothes. So I stared at the ceiling and wondered how long ninety days would last. Start slow, I told myself.

I've been an early riser since forever—or at least since my teens. Usually I'm up around six. I don't know where it comes from, since no one else in my family gets up so early. Beau Ray had long been one of those guys who'd sleep until noon in a bright room. And Momma was more of an eight o'clock riser—earlyish, but not early. But me, I've never even had to set an alarm. I could always tell myself "get up at five forty-five" or "get up at six-fifteen" and my body would obey (although daylight saving time would have me off-kilter for a couple days). So even though I didn't sleep well, I still woke up by six-thirty that first morning after Joshua moved in.

I got up, got dressed and took Momma's station wagon to SpeedLube for an oil change, and then I drove into Charles Town and it was still but seven forty-five. I had a key that got me into the county clerk's office, no matter what the time, and I went to my desk and organized my things like I'd meant to do the day before, except the arraignment had gone longer than I'd figured. For the next eighty-nine days, I was only going to be working half-time, since it turned out that we would be getting paid for taking care of Joshua.

I hadn't been thinking anything about money, I'd swear on Susan's fancy Bible, when I offered up Vince's room. Heck, I hadn't even known it the day Momma signed the guardianship papers, though I think Momma might have. Momma had told me that Judy and Lars were fixing to pay her $200 a day for the use of Vince's room and meals and laundry and not killing him (that last part being a joke). Judy said that it was like paying for a hotel, which they would have been doing had there been such thing as hotel arrest. Judy even asked Judge Weintraub whether he thought that was fair, and he said he didn't see anything wrong with it.

Two hundred dollars a day was a lot more than I was making at the county clerk's office. It was probably more than what Momma and I together brought home. And Momma said that if we were getting paid like that to take care of Joshua, we sure as hell better take care of Joshua, which meant she wanted me to be around more.

This is the way Momma would talk: "Leanne, I'm wanting you to stick around the house more this summer." It sounds polite and all, but if I'd ever said no, all of that niceness would be gone and she'd start in with how ungrateful I was and didn't I see how hard it had been for her, and I'd end up doing what she wanted anyway. I knew it, and she knew I knew it. But it still irked me because I also knew that it was awful convenient that Beau Ray would be watched over at the same time. And that screwed me, since summer was when Momma usually did more watching so I could take my extension courses. It's like she had forgotten that I was the one she'd pushed to think about college, well, me and Vince. I remember wondering whether Vince had found his way to college, wherever he was, as I straightened my desk in case Mr. Bellevue assigned someone else to sit there on Mondays, Thursdays and Friday afternoons.

I saw that Mr. Bellevue had left a note for me.

Leanne, it read, *I'm terribly excited for you!!! Enjoy this experience—but of course you'll have to tell me everything! I'm sure it will be unique and memorable!!*

By his use of exclamation points, I had to assume that Mr. Bellevue meant memorable in a good way. But President Kennedy's assassination was memorable, too. And the space shuttle coming down in flames. And my dad dying, even that was memorable on a smaller scale.

Of course, I hoped the summer would be memorable in a good way. For heaven's sake, Joshua Reed was going to be living in my house! He was there even as I folded up the note. He was there even as I walked out of the county clerk's office. I wondered if he'd sleep late. I wondered what he'd want to do on his first full day under our roof. I had no doubt that after a good night's sleep, he'd have relaxed some and feel more himself. Maybe I'd suggest that we rent a few movies. Maybe he'd let me listen to him practice his *Musket Fire* lines.

With the first, awkward night behind us, I felt hopeful. Ninety days was ample time to get to know someone. Sandy and I hadn't needed a month to become fast friends when we'd met in the third grade. At the end of ninety days, Joshua and I might well be inseparable. We might have private jokes. We might realize that we both hate runny eggs and love Mounds bars. Maybe he'd introduce me to some of his friends—on the phone or if ever a few of them decided to fly in and surprise him for a weekend.

I knew that Joshua and I already had things in common. Like the fact that we'd both excelled in English in high school. And that we were both allergic to cats. And like me, he'd grown up in a small town, even farther from a big city than we were in Pinecob. Although he'd sure made it clear that he preferred city living.

In the parking lot, my keys fit in the car lock the same as usual. The steering wheel felt in my hands like it always did, as I spun it away from the municipal building. The road beneath the tires was smooth where I expected smooth, and the stoplight by the post office shone red, then green, as always. But back at my house, Joshua Reed was sleeping between the same sheets I sometimes slept between. How crazy was that? It felt like remembering a dream, the sense of everything just a step beyond belief. My house, but not my house. The feel of life, but not quite. Joshua Reed, movie star, was sleeping between my sheets.

I knew that a lot of women would have killed—or at least scratched and bit—for the chance to take my place. Back when I was sixteen or seventeen, I might have done the same. But at twenty-five, I wasn't holding on to the crazy fantasies I'd harbored in my teens. And besides, I knew that Joshua was dating Elise, the Belgian supermodel with aqua eyes.

I looked into the rearview mirror. My eyes were as brown as ever. And anyway, I've always been one to respect an existing relationship. I don't know what the feminine equivalent of chivalry is, but maybe you'd call it that. Sandy, on the other hand, would probably call it me not having the gumption to hold my hand out for what I wanted. But I knew what it felt like, someone moving in on your boyfriend when you're not around. The same thing had happened to me with Howard Malkin. I wasn't going to be like that.

It was around eight-thirty in the morning when I got back home, and Momma was making blueberry cottage cheese pancakes, which sounds weird, but they're the best pancakes ever. She almost never made them, so it must have been Joshua who brought out the act. She told me to get Beau Ray up and to offer Joshua more coffee.

"Judy said we shouldn't be catering to him," I told her.

"Judy's not here," Momma said. "And Judy don't make the rules in this house, so git."

I'd bought a *Charles Town Register* on my way home, and I dropped it on the dining room table as I passed. Joshua looked up at me.

"Hey sleepyhead," I said, at the door of Beau Ray's room. I was glad to see that Beau Ray, at least, had slept with his door wide open. His closet door was open, too, and a huge pile of clothes and books and sporting equipment spilled out onto his floor. "Momma's making pancakes," I said. "You don't want to miss pancakes."

Beau Ray turned over. "Pancakes?" he asked and started to sit up.

"Blueberry. Come soon," I said.

Beau Ray followed me into the dining room. He took a seat across from Joshua and smiled at him. Joshua looked up from the paper.

"Morning, Beau Ray," he said.

"Morning, cool man Joshua Reed," Beau Ray said. "Fuck me."

"Beau Ray!" I snapped.

Joshua seemed surprised, then amused.

"Beau Ray, you know we don't say that," I said.

"Fuck me! Fuck me!" Beau Ray said. Joshua started laughing.

"It's not funny," I told him, but Beau Ray looked so pleased with himself and with Joshua that I found myself fighting a grin.

"Shh," Joshua said to Beau Ray. "We don't want your mother to hear."

"Shh," Beau Ray said back, nodding and winking.

Momma brought a plate of pancakes to the table. "Who's ready for the first round?" she asked. "Morning, angel," she said to Beau Ray. She kissed him on the head.

Beau Ray was already poking at the pancakes with a fork. "Yum. Pancakes," Beau Ray said. "Fuck me!"

Joshua and I went silent.

Momma turned to me. "Leanne," she said, frowning.

I shrugged and turned to Joshua, who started to laugh.

Momma looked pissed. "It's not funny," she said to him. "I don't know how you live your life out there in California, but here, in this house, we don't use bad language."

"Fuck me," Beau Ray said. "Cool man don't use bads." He giggled.

"See what I mean?" I told Joshua, who was still laughing.

"It's not funny," Momma said again, even angrier.

"I know," Joshua said. But he wasn't doing a very good job of looking sorry. He cleared his throat. "I'm sorry. I didn't realize. It won't happen again."

"Joshua Reed say sorry," Beau Ray said.

"I am sorry," Joshua said to my mother.

He had found his focus and was wearing his apologetic look. I guess Joshua Reed always played guys who messed up, because I swear I'd seen that same look in every one of his movies. His eyes were wide open and sad, and his chin was tilted down, so that he was looking up at Momma through his lashes. After he spoke, his lips stayed slightly open, and the effect was a much younger, more innocent Joshua Reed. I couldn't look away. It was a complete transformation. I don't know whether Momma bought it, but she shook her head and left the room. Once she was gone, Joshua's face returned to normal—or to the sour version of normal he'd worn from the moment he'd walked into our house. He took a bite of pancakes and turned back to the paper.

"I want to ask you," Joshua said. Breakfast was over. Beau Ray had gone to take a shower, and Momma had left for work. "What's the deal with the TV?"

I didn't know what he was talking about. "Is there something wrong?"

"Well, I couldn't figure it out. Where's the cable box? How does it work?"

I cringed. I'd forgotten to mention it, because it had never been a big deal before. But I had a feeling that it was about to become one.

"We don't have cable," I told him. "It hasn't come up the road yet."

Joshua blinked at me. "You're kidding," he finally said. "You're not kidding?"

I shook my head. "There's cable in Charles Town—but that doesn't help you," I said.

"You can't get cable? Who can't get cable?" Joshua seemed confused. "Then what about satellite? You could get a dish. Satellite."

I shrugged. Sandy's parents' new house in Charles Town had cable, so I'd always gone there if I wanted to watch something that didn't come in on one of our five stations.

"Maybe," I told him. "Momma has this thing about TV. You'll have to ask her." I left it at that.

"Jesus. You live in the absolute sticks," Joshua said. He sounded amazed, but not in a good way.

"You act like someone told you Pinecob was a big city," I said. "No one told you that. I know I didn't tell you that. Besides, you know what a small town is like. You grew up in Rackett, Texas. Population three thousand." I knew this from his fan club biography.

"Don't talk to me about Rackett. I left that rat hole as soon as I could," Joshua said.

I swallowed hard. "Some of us haven't had that luxury," I said. I hated that I felt so shaky.

Joshua looked around the empty room, then calmly back at me. He didn't look at all ruffled.

"Apparently everyone else had the good sense to leave," he said. "I'm going to call about getting satellite TV." He left the room. Me, I left the house and didn't come back again until after dinner, if only because I could.

When I came back—I would have caught hell from Momma had I stayed out any later—Joshua was up in Vince's room, reading one of the ten scripts Lars had left with him. I walked down the hallway and saw Joshua glance at me before he kicked his door closed. Momma was in her bedroom, lining up square after square of calico cotton.

"We're not getting no satellite TV," she told me, before I could say a thing.

"Okay," I said.

"Joshua asked, but I just…" She paused. "I don't think it's a good idea. Even if he pays, you know television is addictive. I don't want Beau Ray watching more than he already does."

"Okay," I said. "It wasn't my idea. I don't care."

"Okay, then," Momma said. "Beau Ray said you were out all day. You told me you'd already cleaned things up at work."

"I just had a few more things to do there," I told her. It was a lie. I'd gone and watched the same movie twice at the Charles Town Cinema.

Momma nodded. "I'm going out Thursday night, so I'll be wanting you around here then," she told me.

"You're going out? Who with?" I asked. Momma almost never went out. I tried to think of the last time she'd socialized and who it had been with. "The Williamses?" I guessed.

"No."

"Church potluck?"

"I'm going out to dinner with Bill Weintraub," she said. I didn't recognize the name at first, and then it hit me.

"*Judge* Weintraub?"

"He seems like a very nice man," Momma said.

"You have a date with Judge Weintraub?" I asked. "Or is it some sort of meeting about Joshua?"

"I'm going out to dinner with him," Momma said. "That's all." And I could tell that she wasn't going to say anything more.

On Wednesday, day three of the ninety, there was a knock at our front door. I was doing dishes in the kitchen, so I pulled off my gloves and went to answer. A tall, skinny woman was waiting outside. She wore sunglasses even though our porch was shady and it looked like a storm was about to blow in. Behind her, in the driveway, a big black car sat idling.

"Is Joshua here?" she asked. She took off her sunglasses then and blinked. "I mean," she continued, "I know he's here. Can I see him?"

I stepped aside and let her into the house. "I think he's sleeping," I told her. "Come on up. You're his girlfriend, right?" I asked.

I knew who she was. She was the model for All-American Cosmetics, among other things. I'd seen her in magazines. Her name was Elise.

"And you are?" Elise asked, following me up the stairs.

"I'm Leanne," I said. "I live here."

Elise nodded. "Oh right. I heard about you," she said. "The fan."

"Fan *club,*" I said. "Here's his room." I knocked lightly. Elise stood beside me and knocked hard.

"What?" Joshua snapped from behind the door. He opened it then, looked at me, then at Elise. He smiled when he saw Elise. "Hey, baby!" he said.

Elise stepped into Vince's old room, and Joshua closed the door. I stood in the hallway for a moment, feeling even more stupid when I realized I still had a dish sponge in my hand. Then I walked back downstairs and sat at the kitchen table.

They were in his room for about an hour. After that, I heard the door open and the stairs creak as they came back down.

"You want some lemonade?" I heard him ask. She must have nodded because he called out, "Leanne, bring us some lemonade, would you? We'll be on the front porch."

I went to the refrigerator, then stopped. I didn't open it. Instead, I walked to the kitchen window and listened. Joshua hadn't been in our house long enough to realize that where I stood was perfect for overhearing any porch conversation. I'd discovered that in high school—my mother would listen to all my dates as they were ending, so I'd learned to give kisses in the car, beforehand.

"Are you kidding me?" I heard Joshua say. "You're just telling me this now?"

"Sorry," Elise said. But she didn't sound sorry. I heard her sigh.

"I can't believe I'm hearing this, Leesie," Joshua said. "I thought you of all people would stick around. We talked about this!"

"It's clear that you have some work to do on yourself right now," Elise said. "And I need to focus on my career. I'm the All-American spokesmodel. I've got a responsibility there."

"You're not even American," Joshua said.

"That's not the point," she said. "I'm sorry, Josh. It was good to see you, but I have to get going."

"You kept the car running?" Joshua said.

"Of course. It's hot out here," she said. "Oh, don't pout. It's not like you and I were going anywhere long-term," Elise said. "And you *can't* go anywhere short-term."

From the kitchen, I could hear a car door close, then the crunch of tires on the driveway. I could hear Joshua's footsteps, back and forth across the porch. I went to the refrigerator and got out the pitcher.

He was sitting on the porch, staring out toward the street. I handed him a glass of lemonade and he took it, absentmindedly. He didn't say anything.

The next day was Thursday. In the evening, Momma got to go out to dinner with Judge Weintraub, Beau Ray got to go to "Life Skills Training" at the Charles Town Community Center and I got to drive Joshua to his first AA meeting. He didn't talk to me on the way there, and when I asked if he knew where to go and what room it was in, he handed me a piece of paper: Room 220.

"I'll walk you there," I offered.

"Suit yourself," he said.

Room 220 was where I'd taken French in eleventh grade. It looked like it was still being used for language study— on the walls were posters of L'Arc de Triomphe in Paris and Los Rambles in Barcelona. There weren't any other languages offered at Potomac Springs Senior High. When I was in ninth grade, you could take German, but by my sophomore year, the teacher had left and hadn't ever been replaced.

Chairs were arranged in a circle, with the student desks pushed back against the chalkboard. There were a few other people in the room when we got there. Joshua walked in ahead of me and dropped into a chair close to the door.

"So how does this work?" I asked him. It was seven twenty-five, and all I knew was that the meeting would last from seven-thirty until nine.

"How should I know?" he snapped.

"Is that you, Leanne?" The voice came from behind me.

I turned around and said hello to Mr. Pearson. Grant Pearson had been my gym teacher during high school, and I still saw him around Pinecob every so often. He always seemed too thin to be a gym teacher, but that was probably just compared to Coach Frawley, who was gigantic.

"What are you doing here?" I asked him. It made sense enough to see him at the school, but not on a summer evening.

Mr. Pearson eyed me like he wasn't sure I'd meant to ask that question. He nodded good evening to a woman just coming in.

"I'm a group leader," he said. "For the Tuesday-Thursday meetings."

"I'm not, I mean, I had to bring," I said, knowing I wasn't making sense.

Mr. Pearson smiled at me. "I understand," he said. Then he turned to Joshua. "We were told to expect you," he said. "Grant Pearson. Welcome."

Joshua looked up and shook his hand.

"I'll have a couple of forms for you to sign at the end of things tonight." Mr. Pearson turned back to me. "This isn't an open meeting," he said. "The second and fourth Thursdays of each month are open, and you're welcome—in fact, encouraged—to take part then."

I nodded. He told me I should come back at nine to pick up Joshua.

"I guess I'll see you then," I told Joshua. He didn't look up.

Mr. Pearson smiled again. "Good to see you, Leanne," he said.

On Friday, day five of Joshua Reed's stay, I got mad. What happened was this: I'd been down in the basement trying to organize my fan club materials. I'd gotten a little lazy in the previous few weeks, with all the other stuff going on, and the Ping-Pong table had turned into a sort of staging area, covered with different piles of papers I hadn't filed. I was determined to clear it off, for neatness sake mostly, since we hadn't used it in ages. So I'd been working on that for a while, and was bringing upstairs an overdue library book of Beau Ray's when I heard Joshua on the kitchen phone. I don't know who he was talking to—I still don't—but I heard him say, "surviving, barely." And then he laughed.

I remember pretty much to the word what he said next.

He said, "No man. No way… I don't know, she's twenty-five, I think. Something like that."

I thought, he's talking about me.

And then he said, "Because she's a fucking hick for one… And it's not like I could leave before she woke up, if you catch my drift. Maybe she's got some decent friends, but I haven't met them… And Jesus, you should see the room they've got me in. It's like a fucking all-American shrine…very funny, not *that* All-American… No, like trophies and shit… No, that's the one who hit his head. This one disappeared or something… How should I know?"

I stopped listening after that. My cheeks were hot, and I felt this little, dull pain in my stomach. I went back down to the basement and stared for a minute at all my fan club files.

Then I found a box, and before I'd really thought about it, I had pulled out all of my out-of-date headshots of Joshua—the ones from the Colin Ashcroft days and the ones from the Stormy days and from when he was Nate. I threw them into the box, and also extra copies of old newsletters, print-outs of e-mails I'd been sent, and a whole stack of news clippings that dated back nearly eight years.

I clomped up the stairs so that he could hear me coming, and kicked open the basement door. By then Joshua was off the phone and reading a script at the kitchen table. He watched me without saying anything.

"I don't know if you want any of this, but I'm throwing it out," I told him.

Joshua shrugged. "Probably not," he said, but he glanced over at the box, and he must have seen some corner of a photograph, or something else that caught his eye, because he sat up taller. "What's in there?"

"Garbage," I said.

He got up from the table. "Like what? Hey, I haven't seen that picture in years. What's…oh my God, that's my first *Teen People* interview!"

"You want it?" I asked him. "Take it."

He started to dig through the box. "You're throwing this out? Oh my God—look at me, I was so young!"

I did look at him. I looked at him looking at the picture of himself, five years earlier.

"Wait, wait, look at this one—this is that article where the guy compared me to Gregory Peck." He pulled out another clipping. "I loved this article," he said. He sounded almost sad. "I can't believe you have all these. Leanne, this is great!"

"Part of the job," I said. I pushed the box at him. "Take it if you want. Like I said, it's garbage to me."

Joshua took the box and wandered back to the kitchen table. I went upstairs, opened the door to his room, and walked in without hollering down to ask permission. One by one, I took all Vince's trophies from the shelves. I took his cleats and his football helmet. I took his shoulder pads and his yearbooks.

"Hey, Leanne!" Joshua called up from the kitchen. "You've got to come down and see this one! Oh, my God—it's hilarious!"

"In a minute," I yelled back. But I knew that I wouldn't. I heard my voice crack when I said it, and then I was crying. There in Vince's room, with his trophies poking into my arms. I made it as far as my own room, then sat on my bed and really started to bawl. After a while, my hands hurt from holding on so tight, and I dropped Vince's stuff to the floor and kicked it under my bed. That was day five. I remember wondering how I was going to get through the next eighty-five days. I hated him.

Chapter 5

The Press

Like the press wasn't going to find him. I mean, Joshua Reed got stories written about him when he was sitting still, when he was eating fried chicken or showing up at some new club in New York or L.A. I would know—I searched fan magazines and newspapers and the Internet for stories like that each week. And whenever there were good pictures or sticky situations, the same stories would usually end up in *People* and *Teen People,* so I'd read about him there, too.

Starting a few days after Joshua's run-in with the cow, Judy's phone started ringing practically nonstop. She said mostly it was people wondering why they hadn't heard from her, or hadn't heard about Joshua in almost a week. Sometimes, people called who'd heard a rumor having to do with him. Sometimes, she'd say "No comment" or "Honey, you know I'm not going to get into that," when she knew the person doing the asking. Sometimes she'd say, "Don't you want to ask me about *Musket Fire?*" But in that first week, no one was asking about a film that hadn't even started shooting yet. It was like they could sense that she was hiding something.

A few days before the big meeting between Judge Weintraub and Lars and the lawyers from both sides, when it was clear that a plea bargain for house arrest would likely work out, Judy sat me and Momma down and talked to us about what to expect if everything did happen as planned.

"To be honest," she said, "I'm not quite sure what to expect. I've been through a few scrapes with J.P. before, but we've usually been in L.A. and known people to go to and could head off the press. Or we pretended that there wasn't anything to say. But this is different. This is going on his record, and that's going to become common knowledge before you know it. We've been lucky so far—and I've been promising exclusive interviews, you know, down the road, and that's kept the dogs at bay. Plus, we're in West Virginia. Can you believe that neither of the arresting officers recognized him? That works out great for us, but sheesh! They gotta get out more!"

I saw Momma frown. It was clear to me that she didn't much cotton to Judy.

"Anyway," Judy went on, "once the real story breaks and people know that he's holed up in your house for the summer, someone's bound to try to get in there to interview him—"

"You're saying people's gonna break into our house?" Momma asked.

"Oh, no. But that reminds me—I'll tell the police to keep a closer eye on your street, to be sure. I'm only saying that people can get weird. You know, if they can't get to him, sometimes they can go a little crazy."

"What sort of crazy?" Momma asked.

Judy turned to me. "I don't know. Like climbing up to his

bedroom window to get pictures of him sleeping. Leanne's guess is as good as anyone's. She's been sending me stories and rumors about J.P. for years now. What do they tend to focus on?"

I tried to remember. "Who he's dating, mostly. Whether he showed up drunk somewhere. Girls trying to break into his hotel room. Whether he's gay. There was that rumor about him having the snake tattoo that turned out to be ringworm. And there was the one about him getting into a bar fight in Houston," I said.

"Unfortunately, that one wasn't a rumor," Judy said.

I frowned because I remembered clear as day her telling me that it had been someone who only looked like Joshua. I said as much.

"Right. I did say that. Repeatedly," Judy admitted. "I told a lot of people that story. Luckily, most everyone at the bar was seeing double."

I was surprised to hear that. I thought back to when it happened. Lots of people had written to ask about it, and Judy sent me a paragraph to post in the newsletter as an explanation. The paragraph said that Joshua Reed had been at a friend's house in Dallas at the time of the alleged incident. I'd taken her at her word.

"I don't want no people rooting through our garbage," Momma said. "I won't stand for it. I don't want them kicking up our lawn. And I don't want them coming to our door, pretending like they've got some business being there."

Judy nodded. "I'm going to do my utmost to see that none of that happens. But I did want to tell you what you might expect. We'll keep as low a profile as possible. And we're planning to spin it as part of a rehab deal, so they'll probably grant us some space. People hate when the press hounds someone who's trying to get his life back on track."

"But you expect something?" I asked.

"I'm sure there will be something," Judy said. "I imagine

we'll arrange an interview at some point, to open it up a little and cool things down. At the very least, since he'll be staying with you, people will want to know who you are. We'll probably say that you're old family friends. It'll be easy to link you to the fan club, but we can say you've been running that as a favor. Something like that."

"I have," I said.

"Oh, I know," Judy said. "I'm only thinking out loud."

"Anything else?" Momma asked. She looked at her watch. I could tell that she'd had about enough of "the California Crowd" as she called them, and this was before she'd even met Joshua.

"There'll be fans," Judy said. "Sometimes, they're worse than the press. Again, I'm going to try to keep a low profile, keep your names out of it, your address hidden. But you know how it is. You live in a small town."

"I don't want my son Beau Ray nowhere near this," Momma said.

Judy nodded. "Although that could play pretty well, if they get along," she said.

"Nowhere near, you hear me?" Momma said.

Judy sat up a little straighter. "I'll do my utmost," she said.

Judy did do a lot, there's no question. I only saw two local journalists when Joshua went into the courthouse that day, and they were the same ones who always hung out there—bored-looking stringers for the *Charles Town Register*. Of course, the name on the notice was still Polichuk, and Judy had Joshua wear a mustache and glasses and then leave out the back door. I think Judge Weintraub helped—the day of the arraignment, he gave everyone who worked at the courthouse a refresher talk on privacy and what it meant to be a private citizen and how everyone deserved a little peace, especially people who were trying to get their lives straightened out. Still, someone must have recognized him or put two and two together. There were three messages on our answering machine when we got back to the house, from people around town who'd heard a rumor that Joshua Reed got house arrest somewhere in the county. They figured that I'd know, if anyone did, whether the rumor was true.

I don't know who finally told whom. I'm not even sure that it wasn't Judy who tipped people off, tired of sticking to her official story, that Joshua had been remanded to a private home for ninety days and would be undergoing alcohol counseling. Maybe it was the announcement from Elise's publicist that the couple was no longer dating but had "nothing but deep respect and affection for one another." Whatever the reason, the reprieve was over on Saturday morning, day six of Joshua Reed's house arrest.

When I raised my window shade that morning—around six—our driveway looked different. There were two white vans parked behind Momma's station wagon, with television station lettering along their sides and antennas and what looked like satellite dishes on their roofs. And there were cars, many more than usual, parked along Prospect Street.

I pulled my shade back down and got dressed as quick as I could. My mind was racing like I'd done something wrong, like my hobby had just spilled from the basement all over our lawn and neighborhood.

Even though I knew that Joshua was surely still asleep, I tapped lightly on the door before opening it. Joshua hadn't rearranged anything in Vince's room, hadn't moved a chair or a lamp or I doubt even a book. But for the first time since I could remember, the space no longer felt like my brother's.

Vince's room had always smelled like Vince, even as the years passed, a smell somewhere between leather and grass. Maybe I'd changed that by pulling his sports paraphernalia from the shelves. Maybe Joshua had changed it, in the way he piled his clothing around the room. However it came about, the room now smelled only of Joshua, a mix of spicy aftershave and limes.

It was a surprisingly soft smell, and I stood at the threshold and breathed deep. The low sun through the window shade colored everything rosy, and in that early morning light, Joshua was unbelievably beautiful—with his eyes closed, it was hard to remember that he wasn't the sweetest soul in the world. I put my hand lightly on his shoulder— the first time I'd actually touched him since he kissed me on the cheek before the Harper's Ferry dinner—and he made a little purring noise. I shook him a bit and he opened his eyes. He looked up at me and gave a slight frown.

"What are you doing?" he asked.

"Sorry to wake you up," I said.

"What time is it?"

I told him that it was early and he asked why I was there then, if it was so early. I told him about what I'd seen out of my window.

"Oh," he said. "Huh." He yawned.

"Momma doesn't want them messing with Beau Ray or going through our garbage or any of that. What should I do?"

"Did you call Judy?"

"It's three-thirty in the morning out there," I told him.

"That's what she's paid for. Go and talk to them if you want, if you're so worried about the garbage."

"But they want to talk to you," I pointed out.

"But they don't get to. At least not until I've showered." He squinted up at me. "You should shower, too. You don't want to look like that on television."

So I did—shower, I mean. And then I made some coffee, and it was not yet seven. Out the kitchen window, I could see a few people milling around. Just beyond our driveway, I made out a police car, which probably had a hand in keeping people away from our doorbell. I took the pot of coffee with me when I walked out onto the porch. As soon as one person saw me, everybody did, and there was a clattering of sound—camera equipment, I guess, and microphones and car doors. I put a finger to my lips to say, hey, keep it down. I explained how my brother was still sleeping.

"Are you saying that Joshua Reed is your brother?" one of them asked me.

I almost laughed.

"No. Beau Ray. Beau Ray's my brother, and believe me, you don't want to mess with my mother if you wake him up."

"But Joshua Reed is also inside, isn't he?"

I said that yes, he was. One of them asked if Joshua would be doing interviews. Another wanted to know which bedroom he was sleeping in. Another asked for "the real reason" he was there. They kept talking at me, asking questions, and every once in a while, a bright light would shine in my eyes, and awfully quick, I found I didn't like being the center of attention in that way.

So I offered to make more coffee, and I said I didn't know much, but that I would try to find out when Joshua might be available. I also told them to get in touch with Judy, and said that she'd be able to answer more of their questions than I could. Then I went back inside. I was glad that Momma had locked the shed where we kept our trash cans and that she'd nailed Posted: No Trespassing signs around our property, front to back. I realized that maybe she'd been right to be so cautious.

Judy called that afternoon. It was the first time we'd spoken since she and Lars had left West Virginia, and maybe even the first time she'd spoken to Joshua in that time. His cell phone didn't work at all in Pinecob and he never answered our home phone, so unless she'd called when I was at work, they hadn't talked. Still, Judy seemed to know everything about the press, and even that Elise had come by the house a few days before.

"It was in her best interests to cool things off," Judy said. "She's got her career to think of and her position in the industry."

The way she said it made me wonder whether Judy had spoken to Elise before or after the breakup visit.

"How's he doing?" Judy asked.

"I guess fine," I said. "He's been busy reading those scripts that Lars sent. I haven't talked to him that much," I admitted. I didn't tell her that it was because Joshua seemed to be avoiding me.

"Good for you," Judy said. "Don't let him charm you."

I told her that he'd gone to AA. How Momma wouldn't let him install satellite TV. How Momma had refused to keep the phone's ringer on after 10:00 p.m. How I'd gotten a flurry of e-mails that day about the house arrest story.

"So the news is out," I said.

"And people in town?" Judy asked.

I said that we hadn't told anyone about him being in the house, but now with the press vans clogging Prospect Street, a lot of people probably figured. When I'd gone to pick up Beau Ray from his class at the Y earlier in the day, the mother of one of his friends had asked me whether the rumors she'd heard were true. But Beau Ray had gotten a mini-seizure right after that, so I hadn't been forced to answer. It was the first time that one of his seizures could actually have been called convenient.

"Is he okay?" Judy asked.

"Joshua or Beau Ray?"

"Beau Ray. Is he going to be okay?"

"You know," I said. "It happens. Ever since the fall. We don't really know. Sometimes, they're practically nothing and he feels them coming on and has learned to lie down. A couple times, we've had to bring him to the hospital."

"I didn't realize," Judy said. "I didn't realize there were still...aftershocks."

"That's why someone ought to be with him most of the time," I said. "Actually, Beau Ray and Joshua are getting along fine, and he loves the television vans," I said.

"Joshua's always been good with the press," Judy said.

"I mean Beau Ray. He's been out talking to the technicians since we got back from the Y. I'm not sure they'll be able to shake him."

"Your mother's not going to like that, is she?"

"So long as he's happy," I told her.

Chapter 6

Sandy

The next day was Sunday, and finally Sandy was back. It seemed amazing all that had happened while she was with her family at the beach. She called in the morning, said she'd made it home safe and when would be a good time to come by? I knew she wanted to meet Joshua, but she also said she wanted to talk to me about something, and it sounded important. I said to come by whenever. I told her to slip in the back way though, through Brown's field and into our backyard, unless she wanted to deal with the reporters. She said that she didn't think her vacation update was front-page news.

Momma was at church and then meeting Bill Weintraub for lunch (which she hadn't told me directly, but I knew all the same), and Beau Ray was out front with the television guys. Sandy and I sat on lounge chairs in the backyard, sipping iced tea. She had always looked like a cat to me, like a lion, especially in the summer after she'd worked on her sun.

That day, Sandy was very tan, golden brown all over, from her hair to her toes. Even her eyes.

Every year at the same time, the Wilsons closed their service station for two weeks and went to stay with Mr. Wilson's brother who lived at Dewey Beach, in the Delaware part of the Delmarva Peninsula. Basically, it was a time for playing Chinese Checkers and Yahtzee, eating crab dinners and practicing putt-putt golf. I'd gone with her a few times when I was growing up. Her brother, Charlie, would bring his best friend and Sandy would bring me, and we'd spend the two weeks fighting, boys versus girls. Sandy and I would usually lose.

That year, only Sandy and her parents had gone. Charlie's boss had refused to give him time off, so Sandy had hours to kill by herself. She told me how she had explored Ocean City and Fenwick Island and Bethany Beach to the south, and Rehoboth to the north. In Rehoboth, she'd met Alice, who was around our age and also stuck with relatives on an extended family reunion. Sandy said that I really had to meet Alice one day. She was fearless, is how Sandy described her. Alice had wanted to break into the go-kart speedway after hours. She had tried to teach Sandy to surf. I said that, yeah, of course I wanted to meet her sometime.

Sometimes, people give you big news—like, "I'm moving to Nebraska" or "I'm having an affair with my boss"—and you're caught utterly unawares. You think, how is that possible? Do I even know you at all? And maybe the point is that you didn't.

But sometimes, what seems like it would be a surprise hits on the quieter side. Like a puzzle piece, missing for so long that you'd accepted the incomplete picture as finished. Click the piece into place, and you can finally see all you were meant to see.

Sandy talking about the beach got me thinking. It got me thinking about all the fries with vinegar we had eaten on the boardwalk, the bikinis and sunglasses we had tried on, and the skeeball we'd played, trading in our winning tickets for sawdust-stuffed plush bears. It got me thinking about Barton Albert who had been Sandy's boyfriend for three years, up until the year before. About the bars we'd gone to and the guys who'd bought us beer, and how she had always thanked them politely, then looked away. I'd always thought that was her version of hard-to-get.

Now things were different. Or rather, something that had always existed had at last been revealed. Sandy said that she didn't want anything between us to change, and neither did I. I felt closer to Sandy than I did to my blood sister, Susan. I didn't want to lose that. I was about to say so when Joshua slid open the screen door and walked outside.

"So you're the famous Sandy," he said. He was wearing sunglasses and shorts and the ankle sensor, of course, but that's all. His hair curled around his ears and jawline. "Leanne talks about you a lot."

"Yup," Sandy said.

Joshua looked over at me. I thought about what he'd said on the phone two days before, how he'd described me to someone as a "fucking hick." I hadn't told Sandy all of what he had said. I felt too bad about it. It made me hate the sound of my voice and the look of everything I wore. It made me hate our house and the marigold planter made from a tire and our cars that both could have used new shocks and upholstery. Everything. It even made me hate Pinecob, and it seemed like a cop-out to hate my hometown, so long as I was still living in it. So with all this running through my mind, I'd hardly spoken to Joshua since, and if he had even noticed, he hadn't asked why Vince's things were suddenly gone from his room. I picked up the magazine lying beside my chair.

"You've sure got a nice tan," Joshua was saying to Sandy. "I need to work on mine." He looked at his arms and flexed his triceps. I looked away.

"I've been at the beach," Sandy said.

"Right. I guess that's why I haven't seen you around. You should come around. I get so bored during the day. I need to have some stimulating company," Joshua said. "And a wading pool would be nice."

"Sorry, sweetpea," Sandy said. "This nurse is working days until the end of the month at least. But if you lose an appendage and end up in the hospital, I'll take real good care of you. Besides, you got Leanne," Sandy said. She patted my hand. "She's stimulating."

"Of course she is," Joshua said quickly. He smiled. "But she's got to be sick of me by now. Aren't you, Leanne?"

I looked up from the magazine and nodded.

"See?" Joshua said.

Sandy looked at me like she was trying to talk with only those golden eyes of hers. I raised my eyebrows and shrugged. I nodded, just enough so that she could see. Sandy had a very seductive smile. Her patients, men and women, were always falling for her. The Nightingale Effect, she called it, but I thought it was Sandy's smile, and maybe the way she looked in her nurse's uniform. She turned back to Joshua.

"Okay," she said, smiling at him.

"Okay, what?" he asked.

"It's way too hot out here," Sandy sighed, suddenly all girly. She gazed at him with her lion eyes. "I've got to get inside, where it's dark." She rose from her chair and stretched.

I watched Joshua watch her.

"And cool." She smiled at him again. "You're game, aren't you?" she asked him. "I know you want to get inside."

Joshua smiled. "You know I do," he said. He was looking at her like he couldn't believe his luck.

Sandy turned back to me for a second. "Leanne, you want anything?"

I shook my head and watched them disappear into the dark of the house. I looked back at my magazine, but I couldn't concentrate, so I sort of stared around the yard. I found myself staring at the trees behind the shed, the stand of dead oaks stripped bare by a gypsy moth hatch a few years earlier. There were maybe ten of them, all old trees and tall, and their craggy limbs still reached out, reminding me of the evil apple trees from the *Wizard of Oz,* grabbing for living creatures to hold onto.

I sipped my iced tea and listened hard, but I couldn't hear anything from inside the house. Most of me really trusted Sandy, especially now. But a lot of me was still jealous and itchy. I didn't think I'd ever heard her so determined to charm. The way she had dropped her voice to a purr. The way she had stood there, waiting for him, her tan legs just a little farther apart than they needed to be. She'd never acted that way with any of the guys who crossed bars to offer her beer. I doubted that Barton Albert had ever received such treatment. Had Alice taught her this?

A few minutes later, Sandy slid open the screen door and stepped back outside. She sat down at the end of my lounge chair and put her hand on my foot.

"So?" I asked. "Did you? You know, anything?" Anyone else, it would have been hard to ask. But this was Sandy. We told each other everything and always had. Just about.

"Are you kidding?" Sandy asked. Her voice was back to normal. "Do you actually think I'm different now than two weeks ago? I'm not different. I'm just more me now."

I was half embarrassed for being worried.

"All I did in there was sit him down and point out a few relevant facts. Things he needed to hear and a few things I knew you'd never say yourself," Sandy said.

"What things?" I asked.

"Just some things. He doesn't know how good he's got it here. Damn whiner."

"No, really, what things?"

Sandy rolled her eyes. "I said that you were the best damn

fan club president a guy like him could ever hope to have. And that if he didn't behave, I'd tell you to quit. I said that you were exceptionally talented."

"At what? Talented how?"

"I don't know. Just talented. Make him guess." She smiled at me. "Oh, and I told him that you were the valedictorian and the star of our tennis team and also the prom queen."

"What? I don't even have a tennis racquet. Why?"

Sandy looked a little embarrassed. "It just sort of came out. I wanted him to think you're cool."

"So you had to lie? Am I that uncool?" I asked her.

"No, no—I mean, that you've *always* been cool," she said quickly. "Besides, the rest was all true."

"Great."

"Listen, I gotta go," she said. "I got laundry. Talk to you tonight, okay? You sure you're okay, about everything?"

"I'm okay. We're good. Let's talk tonight. I do want to meet Alice."

Sandy nodded and left, walking out the way she'd arrived, through the trees at the edge of the backyard. She was gone by the time Joshua came back outside.

"So," he said. He sat down on Sandy's lounge chair. I pretended to read my magazine. "She called me a butthole," he said, and laughed a little.

"She's my best friend," I said. "What did you expect?"

Joshua nodded. I watched him out of the corner of my eye.

"Anything else?" I asked. I realized then that it didn't matter what sort of résumé Sandy had given me. He'd forget it, or hadn't listened to begin with. It didn't affect him.

"That Sandy's a little scary," Joshua said. He turned to me like he was about to ask something, then he looked away. Then he looked back. "So is she really a lesbian?" he asked. "She told me she's a lesbian."

I looked up from the magazine. "Yeah. She told me that, too." I said. "She met someone when she was at the beach. I guess it all clicked."

"Huh," Joshua said. "It's a good thing they don't all look like her. Life would be harder than it already is," he said. He looked over at me. "You're not one, are you?" I threw him the *Cosmopolitan* I'd been reading.

"Fuck you," I said, and got up to go inside.

"Hey, I thought we weren't supposed to swear around here!" he said right before I slid the glass door closed.

Chapter 7

Sunday Shopping

I think I already mentioned how I went to the Winn-Dixie pretty much every Sunday afternoon to buy groceries for the week ahead. That Sunday, Joshua's seventh day, the first day of Sandy being back and me hearing that she was in love with a woman named Alice, just a day after all those vans started hanging around our driveway making noise and asking questions, that Sunday, maybe I was just a little pricklier than usual. It seemed a lot to take in a week. Momma and Beau Ray were apparently able to go on like nothing had changed. Maybe for them, not much had. I was the one who was only working half time, but couldn't take any classes in my free hours. I was the one who was supposed to play hostess to some guy who alternated between wanting nothing to do with me and wanting me to run his errands or fawn over an old interview in which some geezer said he looked like Gregory Peck. Pretty as Joshua was, I can tell you, he didn't look much like Mr. Peck.

So maybe I was a little distracted that afternoon, because I didn't even consider that anyone might follow me to the Winn-Dixie, or want to interview me about Joshua and what he liked to eat. But of course, that's what happened.

I'd gotten my cart and pulled out my shopping list. I always worked from a list, so it wouldn't take me too long to buy everything for the week. Joshua had added a few requests, but for the most part, seemed content to eat whatever we put in front of him. I was surprised by that. I'd heard all these stories about L.A.-types wanting bottled water ice cubes and special nonfat bacon. Being from a small town himself, maybe Joshua had low expectations. Or maybe he just didn't want to ask me for anything.

Beau Ray's old friend Max Campbell generally worked Sundays, so before I started shopping, I rolled my cart over to the door of the managers' office and poked my head inside.

"Hey, Max," I said.

He was watching TV with one of the guys from the butcher department. "Hey," Max said. He stood up and came to the door. "Got the Gitlin Sunday list?"

"Got it," I said.

"Well, come on, girl. Let's get a move on then," he said, stepping out into the store.

That might make it sound like Max and I were good friends, but we weren't. Most Sundays, he would simply wave from the office, or talk with me for a few minutes before I wandered off to start filling my cart. To be fair, in the past few months he had walked with me more often—a few times, maybe four. I took that as a sign that Max was getting bored with the Winn-Dixie, even though he never said one negative thing about it. I could have asked, I suppose, but I didn't want to draw attention to the increased frequency of his company—in case it would have scared him off. Part of me always felt like I was walking beside a rare deer that stayed nearby so long as you pretended not to notice it. Look at it straight on and it would startle and disappear forever.

"I need to get sardines," I said.

Max wrinkled his nose. "Since when do you buy sardines?" he asked.

I shrugged. "They're on the list," I said. I didn't like to be cagey around Max but I'd promised Judy that I wouldn't go around spouting off facts and stories about Joshua Reed. Turns out, I didn't need to be half so cautious.

"I hear you've got something of a houseguest," Max said. He looked me straight in the eyes, and when I tried to look away, he held my chin so that I couldn't. Not that I minded having to look at him.

Here's what I saw when I looked at Max Campbell: I saw the guy who once ran into the middle of traffic to save a dog that had been hit by a car. I watched it happen, and I screamed for him, because by that point, I'd had some experience with death and didn't want any more. I watched it happen and even as I watched, I knew that the dog wouldn't make it, but Max ran out into the road anyway. Later, after the vet had put the dog down and Momma had given Max a new T-shirt to wear, since his had been ruined by blood, Max admitted that, yeah, he'd figured that the dog was too broken to live. "But I couldn't let it die all scared like that," he'd told me.

When I looked at Max, I also saw the gangly, twelve-year-old boy my brother Beau Ray brought home after school one day, soon after the Campbells moved to Pinecob. Max, who already had a job by then, helped his dad sell peanuts and popcorn at the minor league baseball stadium. That was a forty-five minute drive, each way, twice a week, and he didn't even get to keep what he earned.

And of course I saw the guy I'd dreamed of marrying, all through those silly middle-school years, trying out "Leanne Campbell" and "Max loves Leanne" and "Leanne-n-Max,

TLA" (meaning "true love always") in my best cursive. I learned quick to rip out those notebook pages though, what with Beau Ray always grabbing a sheet for his paper football games.

Most people looking at Max wouldn't see the things I saw. They'd see straight off that he was good-looking, with these crazy blue eyes, the color of brand-new jeans. And a sort of heavy, brown hair that faded gold in the summer sun, and a perfect smile, like Robert Redford, almost. People also noticed, after a while at least, how he was missing most of his right earlobe, from when a dog (not the one he tried to save) bit him when he was three.

And now here he was, holding my chin and asking me about my "houseguest." Max looked amused, like he was in a real light mood—which didn't seem fair, given all the heavy things I was dealing with.

"Someone at *my* house? What do you mean?" I asked. "What did you hear?"

Max dropped his hand. He leaned in as if to tell me a secret. It was probably as close as he'd ever been to me, at least since I was twelve and started needing a bra and Momma said I shouldn't play touch football with Beau Ray's friends anymore. All of my nerves set to tingling at once. I could feel the heat of his cheek almost touching mine. I caught the barest scent of him and wanted more. But I knew that Max likely had no conception of this, of any of this. He was just leaning in so as to seem all hush-hush.

"I heard he's going to be there for ninety days. Did you actually think there was such thing as privacy around here?" He stepped away again and looked all satisfied with himself.

"I hoped," I said. "I mean, we can't get cable or California Red Ale, but heaven forbid, you try to keep something quiet or personal." I knew as I was saying them that the words were coming out more snappish than I meant—or rather, I was snappish about those things, but Max was hardly to blame (even if he was associate manager and could probably have ordered the California Red Ale that Joshua, the night before, had mentioned he favored).

"Didn't mean to get you riled, Leanne. Honest," Max said. "I only wondered if it was true." Max dropped a bag of carrots into my shopping cart. Beau Ray went through a bag each week.

I looked at the carrots and felt guilty. Why shouldn't Max be allowed a little satisfaction?

"You didn't upset me," I said. "I was there already. It's not like he wants to be with us. Tell the truth, he's not very nice," I said.

Max frowned. "Ain't that a wonder. You want me to kick his ass?"

I knew he wasn't serious, but it was nice to have the offer. "You wouldn't really, would you?"

"Not without a pretty big reason," Max admitted. "Do you think I could take him?"

I tried to imagine Joshua standing right beside Max. They were probably pretty evenly matched, Joshua maybe a hair taller, but I knew what the right answer was.

"No question about it," I said to him. Max smiled again and I felt like I'd paid up.

That's when the camera crew came up to me, right there in the middle of the Winn-Dixie produce department. There were three of them—a man with a big news camera, another with headphones and cords and a woman with a microphone. The woman wore really red lipstick and had blond hair that did the sort of perfect flip I could never get my hair to do.

She smiled at me and said something like, "Excuse me, Leanne, Marcy Thompson from ABC's *Hollywood Express*? I was wondering whether I could have a minute of your time. That okay? Great!" A light flicked on above the camera, and it felt as if a laser beam had pinned me into place.

"What are you doing?" is what I heard myself ask, but Marcy Thompson didn't reply. I think she had a list of questions she wanted to get through, whether or not I answered them.

"I understand you've got a special visitor in your house," she said.

I nodded.

"Is it true that Joshua Reed, the actor, was remanded—"

"It's true," I managed to say. "He's there." I looked for Max, but he suddenly seemed far off. I tried to catch his eye, but he just stared at the camera and the light and the woman with perfect hair.

"That must be very exciting," Marcy said. "Are you getting some special foods for him today? Is there anything in particular he likes to eat?"

"I'm only getting what's on my list," I said, and held the paper up like a shield that might protect me from Marcy and *Hollywood Express.* It didn't.

"What's it like waking up with Joshua Reed in the house?" Marcy asked me.

"Are you kidding?" I said.

She blinked at me and bobbed her head a little bit and held the microphone still. I'm not sure why, but I felt obligated to tell her.

"Imagine you're at breakfast and some stranger walks in, asking where's the coffee. That's pretty much what it's like. In the morning at least."

All the while, I'd been backing slowly away from her and the camera, and right at that moment, I'd backed up against a pyramid of apples and couldn't go any farther. I must have bumped it a little hard, or in the wrong place, because I felt the pyramid shift, and a tumble of apples roll down behind me.

"Ooh!" Marcy Thompson said. "Watch out!"

I spun around to try to catch them.

"It's okay, Leanne," I heard Max say. "Don't worry about it." He was suddenly next to me again, and put his arm out to stop the apples from careening every which way. "Sorry, ma'am, but we've got a bit of an applelanche here." He said this to the woman with the microphone and the perfect hair. She laughed.

The man with the headphones suddenly pulled them off and took a cell phone from his pocket.

"Yeah?" he said into it.

"Cut here," Marcy said to the camera man, and the bright light went out. I could see purple and yellow spots when I blinked.

"There in ten," the man on the cell phone said and hung up. "We've got Reed, back at the house. Exclusive."

"Yes! Psych!" Marcy said. She turned back to me and Max. "Thanks guys. See you later."

I turned to Max. "I'd better get back to work," he said. An apple fell onto my left foot and bounced away.

That night, Beau Ray and Joshua and I sat in the living room and watched ABC's *Hollywood Express* exclusive interview with Joshua Reed. It had been taped in our backyard while Momma was out of the house. Joshua looked relaxed and friendly. He laughed with Marcy, and sounded serious and remorseful in all the right places. He talked about "the pressures" he'd been under and how "the experience" had taught him so much and how he was just trying to get back on track and how much he appreciated the good wishes from Marcy and her staff. By the time he stopped talking, Marcy looked like she would have been willing to curl up with him in Vince's room for the rest of his sentence. Part of my interrupted interview also made it in. The stranger at breakfast part. And also the apples, and Max calling it an "applelanche."

"I get my own coffee," Joshua complained. "Some of the time at least."

"Whatever," I said. Ending the day with a national news report that showed me wrecking apples at the Winn-Dixie seemed right on target. "I'm going to bed," I said.

But the phone rang as soon as I got upstairs. It was Judy.

"I just finished watching the *Hollywood Express* interview," she said. "Next time, try to sound a little more enthusiastic, okay?"

I told her that I was sorry. "They followed me. I didn't expect it," I said.

"Of course. I forget that you're not used to this," Judy said.

"But Joshua sounded good," I said.

"Didn't he though? That's my boy. *Hollywood Express* doesn't have the highest rating, but it'll still do a lot for us. I told you he's a great actor. So listen, who was that guy with you, the one with the apples?"

"Who?" I asked her. "Max?"

"Is that his name? Is he a friend of yours or does he just work there?"

I told her that Max was a friend—or rather, how he and Beau Ray had been good friends, and how I saw him every now and again, and most Sundays.

"He looks good on screen," Judy said.

"And off," I told her. "In high school, he was voted most photogenic."

"Oh really?" Judy asked. "Do I sense that you harbor a crush?"

I felt my heart start to race. I regretted being so obvious. "I don't know. I shouldn't. I don't really want to talk about it," I said.

"I didn't mean to pry," Judy assured me.

"It's just," I tried to explain, "Max is great, but everyone will tell you that he's still got a thing for his ex-wife. It seems like a lot of uphill."

"Ah, the old ex-wife," Judy said. "Why don't you ask him out and find out?"

"God, no!" I said.

"Why not?"

"Because I've known him since I was eight, for one."

"That's a long time to harbor a crush," Judy said.

I wanted to change the subject. I didn't want to get to the second reason. I asked her why she'd given an exclusive interview to *Hollywood Express,* if it didn't have a high rating.

"It's the highest-rated show on ABC," Judy said. "And I understand that's the clearest of your five channels."

That's how the first week ended and the second one began. Judy was right—after Joshua's Emmy-worthy performance with Marcy Thompson and her perfect hair, the press backed off. For the next couple weeks, there was often a news van nearby during the daylight hours, but rarely more than one, and after that, they left altogether. I didn't much care for the on-camera types, but the sound guys and van technicians all seemed decent, and a few of them let Beau Ray hold cameras, look at monitors and listen in their headphones. He even got one crew to drive him to his "Move Your Body, Move Your Mind" class on a particularly slow day. Nothing had held his attention that long since his accident.

Even Momma didn't seem to mind the press after that. "So long as they stay out of our garbage," she said. (She'd become sort of obsessed with the vision of someone digging through our trash cans.) I wasn't sure if it was because of Beau Ray's enthusiasm or because things had continued with Bill Weintraub. She didn't say, and I was afraid to ask. Part of me thought that she was actually enjoying the attention her legal guardian status brought. Susan had called home more regularly since Joshua moved in—to check in with Momma, officially, though I figured she was hoping Joshua would answer the phone. Even Tommy called a few times after the *Hollywood Express* interview aired, though I could have done without his "way to go with the apples" commentary.

That Tuesday, when I dropped Joshua at his AA meeting, there were fifteen people in my old French classroom. That Thursday, maybe twenty-five. It was so crowded that Grant Pearson had to move the meeting to the small lecture hall, and the following week, to the gym. Such is the power of television, or at least, a well-placed interview on *Hollywood Express*.

Friday night marked the end of day twelve. I was up in my room reading when I heard a car in the driveway. It was getting late—I figured it was Momma back from her date, until I heard a girly shriek, and then a giggle.

I opened my window shade and looked down at the front lawn. A woman I didn't recognize stood on the grass. The motion-sensitive lights that Momma had set up lit her from above, so I couldn't tell how old she was, maybe twenty, maybe older. She had long brown hair, and looked kind of pretty, what I could see of her face. I noticed right away that she was stumbling around, squinting in the light, and that she was trying to undo the buttons on her blouse. She looked up at my window.

"Joshua Reed!" she called out. The car in the driveway flashed its lights and honked. "Joshua Reed!" she called again. "Come out and play! I got a present!"

"Hey, Joshua," I called across the hall. "You've got a visitor."

"I'm sleeping," he said, even though I could see that his light was on.

So I told him that his visitor was taking off her shirt, and he jumped out of bed and came into my room. He looked out the window, down to the girl in the yard.

"Yoo-hoo!" she called up. "Hey there, is that you? Come out and play!" She looked like she might topple over.

Joshua shook his head and turned away from the window. "At least in L.A., the freaks are good-looking," he said. He wandered back to his bedroom.

I didn't know what to do, but I knew that she couldn't be on the lawn when Momma did get home. I went downstairs and out the front door. The girl was still weaving on the grass, her shirt halfway off. I was glad she was wearing a bra. I could hear giggles from the car.

"Hey," I called out to get her attention. I told her that Joshua would not be coming down.

"Then I'll go up," she said, and lurched in the direction of the front door.

"You can't."

"I can't?" She looked confused. When I saw her up close, I could tell that she wasn't so young. She looked older than I was.

"No. Besides," I said. "I'll tell you a secret."

The woman leaned in. She smelled strongly of alcohol.

"He's good-looking and all," I told her, "but he's a real asshole."

The woman teetered a bit, frowned, and nodded. "That's okay," she said, slurring a little. "I don't mind."

"No, really. A real asshole. He doesn't deserve it."

"I don't mind," she said again. "It's Joshua Reed."

"Jesus," I said. I yelled toward the car. "Take her home or I'm going to have to call the police. This whole area is posted no trespassing."

I heard the car door open. By the time I was closing the front door, her friends were pulling her off the lawn. By the time I was back upstairs, the car was out of our driveway.

"Is she gone?" Joshua asked.

"Yep," I said. "I told her that you were an asshole, but she wanted to sleep with you anyway."

"Fame's amazing, isn't it?" he said.

Chapter 8

The Guys

The next Sunday when I was back at the Winn-Dixie, no one followed me. Max was there, and he walked with me again, and told me that their distributor was checking to see if they could get California Red Ale. That's the exact sort of thing Max did that made him hard to forget about.

We filled up the cart—milk, dry cereal, apples, pasta, hamburger, eggs, bread, cheese, carrots. The usual stuff. Max walked beside me and passed along gossip he'd heard in the previous week about people we both knew. He said that Loreen (the skank that Howard Malkin once cheated on me with) had come in and bought a home pregnancy test. He said that Brennie Critchett had hauled out four cases of Budweiser.

"She's stronger than she looks," Max said, sounding impressed.

"I thought what people bought was confidential," I told him. "Isn't the Winn-Dixie associate manager like a priest or something? You know, cone of silence? Manager–shop-per privilege?"

"That's the manager you're thinking of," Max said. "The associate manager can be a terrible gossip." He grinned at me.

"Makes me nervous, you watching things so close," I said. "I hope you're not going to start telling people how I bought sardines for some strange man."

Max laughed. "Sometimes I watch close and sometimes I can miss everything, if you hadn't noticed. But I wouldn't rat you out, Leanne," he said. I wanted to believe him. "Though you can bet that people are asking."

"Asking?"

"Well, duh. That interview on television. It's all everyone's been talking about. Your movie star is the biggest thing in Pinecob since…for a long while."

"He's not *my* movie star," I said.

I'd either been in the house or at work all week, or with Sandy, so I guess I hadn't noticed. But I didn't like the sound of what Max said. I asked him what people were looking to know. And why they were asking *him*.

"Everyone knows that Beau Ray and I go way back. So they ask. You know, what do I think is really going on."

"And what do you tell them?" I looked hard at him. I didn't want him to turn it into a joke. I needed him not to. This was my family, after all. And me. And he didn't.

"I say I don't know. I tell them I don't know you well enough to hazard a guess about something like that, but that in my opinion, your family has gone through enough to have earned a little privacy."

"You *know* me," I told him.

"Not really," Max said, like it was just another fact and not something he felt one way or another about.

I winced at that a little, on the inside, because it wasn't as if he hadn't had the opportunity, in such a small town. And there *I* was, able to recollect exactly how close I'd stood to

Max and when. Able to recall entire conversations we'd had—what he'd said, what I'd said, what I'd been wearing, how his expression had changed with the topic. And after certain run-ins, I'd spent hours wringing out every bit of potential meaning, and then again with Sandy. I used to map out conversations with Max in advance, just in case—the hints I would drop, cute stories I would tell that showed me in a good light, sounding funny, sounding witty, sounding charming. But apparently he'd missed all of it. Like he claimed he could.

"Think I'm done," I said, rolling my cart up to one of the check-out aisles. Isn't there a point at which the mind should be able to surrender on behalf of the heart? Or check it in to an asylum, somewhere safe and locked, if the heart keeps refusing to see a landscape for what it is? Yet with some people in life, it seems you just can't loose yourself, even when you should. "Thanks for walking with me," I said.

"A pleasure as usual, Ms. Gitlin," Max said. He pulled a box of cereal bars from my cart and put it on the conveyor belt. "So, what have you got going tonight?" he asked.

The cashier looked up like she hoped he was asking her, but Max was looking right at me. Right at me. I could see the cashier give me a once-over before going back to ringing my groceries. I hoped she wouldn't overcharge me.

"Tonight? Nothing, I don't think. Why?" I was really working to sound casual.

"Lionel's renting *Die Hard* and *Die Harder* and we were all going to watch them over at his new house. You want to come?"

I considered it for about a second. Max Campbell was asking me out. Not on a date, but still. It was the flip side of oblivious.

"What time?" I asked, like it mattered, like I might have other options more pressing, like I wouldn't automatically go anywhere Max asked me to go.

"We were going to order pizza in about an hour and start after that. I'm about to get off work. You want me to come by and pick you up? Or better, I could go with you now, and come back for my car later." He glanced at the big Winn-Dixie clock over the row of check-out lanes, then back to me.

"Well, if you're ready to go now. Whichever you want." I figured the more time I could spend with him, the better, although I wouldn't have minded the opportunity to wash my face and look a little nicer. But I got the distinct impression that Max wanted out of the Winn-Dixie then and there. So I waited in the car as he clocked out, and we drove back to Prospect Street.

As soon as I'd parked the car, Max got out and started pulling grocery bags from the back seat. I watched him and thought back to when he was sixteen and Winn-Dixie's newest bag boy. Here he was, nearly twice his life later, still holding grocery bags. It figured he might be getting restless.

"So will I get to meet the mystery man?" Max asked, heading toward our front door. I felt a little ping in my stomach. Of course that was why he wanted to help with my groceries. He wanted to meet Joshua Reed. Why wouldn't he? He'd said it himself—this was the biggest thing going in Pinecob.

"You can be sure he's around," I said.

Max followed me into the house.

"Beau Ray!" I called out. "Look who's here." No one answered.

Max and I put our bags on the kitchen table, and I walked through the dining room and into the backyard. Beau Ray and Joshua were sitting in the lounge chairs, playing cards.

"No," Joshua was saying. "Remember? You need to get three of one number, or else three in a row of one suit, like all diamonds or all hearts, but in a row, you know, like eight, nine, ten."

Beau Ray nodded.

"Hey there," I said. "Beau Ray, look who's here."

Beau Ray looked up at Max. "Hey, Smax," he said.

"Yo, Bobo," Max said. That's how they had greeted each other since the seventh grade.

"Max, this is Joshua. Joshua, Max. Max is an old family friend."

"Nice to meet you," Max said.

"Likewise," Joshua said, lifting his head. "Call me Josh." He looked back and forth, from Max to me.

"Max, you know how to play Gin?" Beau Ray asked. "Josh is teaching me Gin."

"That's a good game," Max said.

"We'll deal you in the next hand," Joshua said.

"Sure, cool," Max said.

"So what time are we supposed to be at Lionel's?" I asked.

Max spun around and looked at me, and it seemed that he'd forgotten I was there until I spoke.

"If you still want to go," I said.

"No, I do. I do," he said.

"I need to get the rest of the groceries from the car," I said, heading back into the house.

"I'll help," Max said.

"I'll help," Beau Ray said and stood up. The cards on his lap fell to the lawn. Ever since his accident, Beau Ray had liked putting the Sunday groceries away. In the economics course I'd taken at night school, my teacher called something like that a "positive externality." A good thing, unexpected.

"I guess we're not playing then," Joshua said. He stood, too.

"Bobo," Max said. "Lionel's renting movies tonight. You want to come out and watch?"

Part of me dropped down a little. If Beau Ray came, I knew that Max and I wouldn't be alone, not in the car, not ever. The other part of me knew that this was the same guy who had run into traffic after a dog—the generous side of him, and I'd always liked that side.

"I want to go!" Beau Ray said.

"Why don't you guys watch them here?" Joshua said. "It would be cool to get to know some more people in town, and have a little company. That is, if it wouldn't screw up your other plans."

I stared at Joshua. He was so friendly to everyone but me.

"Here?" Max asked. "You sure you want to? It's just a bunch of guys we went to high school with. I mean, if you're cool with it, that's cool."

"I should probably call Judy, to ask," I said. "She didn't want—"

"Fuck that, Leanne," Joshua said. "Sorry, but why can't I watch a few movies with some of the guys? What's the harm in that?"

I shrugged. Any hope of the night turning into a date with Max was already blown, so I didn't see how having the guys over to my living room would matter much. I'd dated Lionel for a time anyway, the year before, and it had been a while since I'd seen him.

"If you think Lionel wouldn't mind switching locations," I said to Max. "I could order the pizza."

Of course Lionel didn't mind. Not when he heard that he'd be watching the *Die Hard* series with Joshua Reed, who had actually met Bruce Willis. And the other guys—Paulie and Scooter—didn't mind either.

"Hey, Leanne," they all said, as they walked in with their beers and dug into the pizza I'd had delivered. Joshua and Beau Ray and I drank lemonade.

"So, Leanne," Lionel said, later, when we were in the kitchen at the same time. "How freaky is it you've got Joshua Reed living here? Crazy cool though."

"Just for ninety days," I reminded him. "Or seventy-six, after today."

"So he's what, staying in Vince's old room?"

I nodded.

"And you're still in your old room?" Lionel asked.

"Nothing's changed," I told him.

"I like that room," he said.

Lionel was tall and big at the same time, like a bear, and because of that, I'd always felt sort of dainty in his company. Maybe it was being the youngest of five that set me up to be taller than most girls. Vince used to say it was because I had more room to stretch from the outset, and my body had grown used to it, way back in Momma's belly. My dad would always tell me that being a little above average was generally better than being a little below, but there were times— around my sister Susan and other petite types—when I felt more galumphing than girlish. Women are supposed to be strong, sure, but they're also supposed to be delicate, like filigree made of steel. One of the reasons I'd first been drawn to Lionel was how his very size let me feel nearer to delicate.

He took a step toward me and I smiled. Lionel and I had more drifted apart than broken up. He'd wanted someone who could stay out all night, playing pool and drinking beer, and I'd always had to be home for one thing or another. But there was nothing wrong with him, and even less when he was right there in front of me, looking at me like he was remembering a song he liked the sound of.

"It does the job," I said. "It's a good room."

"What is?" Max had wandered into the kitchen during my last sentence. He looked from me to Lionel.

"My bedroom," I mumbled. "It's nothing. We were just talking. Have you guys started the second movie yet?"

Lionel was still looking at me with that look of his, and I suddenly wished he wouldn't.

"We just did. I was coming in to tell you," Max said. "You done in here?"

"Sure," I said, and Lionel and I followed him out of the kitchen.

In the living room, the guys were sprawled on our two couches. Joshua was in Dad's old recliner, and Beau Ray lay on a floor cushion. I sat on the floor in front of the long couch. Lionel sat behind me, and at some point in the middle of the second movie, he started twirling his fingers through my hair. It would have felt good had we been alone, but there were five other guys in the room, and since Lionel and I weren't a couple, it mostly felt like a possession thing.

By the time *Die Hard 2* was over, the beer and pizza were long gone and Joshua was calling all of them "Man" and "Dude," the way guys do when they're familiar past first names. Lionel talked about coming over the following week with another movie rental. Scooter suggested that Joshua join their standing Tuesday night poker game, with Paulie pointing out that, of course they could relocate to our house.

"I'll have to see about that," Joshua said. He glanced over at me, because both of us knew that Tuesdays were AA nights.

"Tuesdays aren't so good around here," I said. "My mother…" I left it at that, and Scooter and Lionel nodded. Momma had a long-standing reputation for being strict about her house and what went on inside of it.

"That's cool," Paulie said. "Another time."

I walked Lionel to the door, and he kissed me on the lips. Lightly, but still on the lips.

"Good to see you, little lady," he said. "A right pleasure."

"Yeah, you, too," I said. "Drive safe, all of you."

"Thanks, Leanne. Say hey to Sandy for me," Scooter said as he was leaving. "Max, don't you need a ride?" he asked.

"I'll be right there," Max said. He stood in the doorway

like he didn't know where he wanted to go. He looked at Joshua and Beau Ray, who were still lounging in the living room, poking at each other. He looked at the idling cars in the driveway, and waved to Scooter. He looked at me.

"Thanks for letting us locusts descend on your house," he said.

"It was Joshua's idea," I reminded him.

"Yeah. Change in plans," Max said. "Fun though. So I guess I'll see you around."

"Probably next Sunday," I said. "Now at least you'll have more to say, if anyone asks."

"Oh, yeah," Max said. "Nah."

"Or stop by, if you want to. You know there's always going to be someone here." I motioned with my head to Joshua.

"Hey," Joshua said. "I heard that."

I looked over and saw that he was smiling. It was the first time he'd been anything on the positive side of blank to me. I smiled back. If he didn't think these guys were hicks, I thought maybe he'd stopped thinking of me as one.

"I'd better go," Max said, and I looked back at him.

Maybe he wasn't so obviously handsome as Joshua, but to me, he was almost. And to watch him stand in front of me, looking straight at me, I could feel that crush of mine rising up again. I wished I could squash it. I thought about Charlene, the ex-wife. I wondered about the torch he carried. I wondered whether his *Die Hard* invite was more about me or about Joshua.

"So, thanks again for tonight," I said.

"Sure." Max turned and walked to Scooter's car.

I closed the door.

"Leanne has a crush," Joshua said in a singsong voice. Beau Ray sat up and looked toward the door.

"Shut up," I said.

"Leanne and Lionel," Beau Ray sang. Joshua looked at

Beau Ray and then back at me, then shook his head and shrugged.

"I'm going to bed," I told them, and started up the stairs. "Don't forget to put all those bottles in the trash before Momma gets home, okay?"

"Sure, sure," Joshua said, waving me off.

"You know who she's out to dinner with," I reminded him.

Joshua sat up straight. "Oh, fuck," he said. "Shh, Beau Ray. I didn't say that." There were beer bottles everywhere, and though I hadn't seen Joshua drink from one, Judge Weintraub would not likely have approved. "Hey, Bobo, help me get these into the garbage, okay? Will you please?"

Watching them start to straighten up, rushed but laughing, reminded me of having Vince back.

The next morning was one of those early summer mornings that gets hot early, a reminder that the real heat is about to start beating down. I don't mind those days. I'm good in the heat, and I've always loved summertime evenings in West Virginia, after the sizzle of the day has broken, and the breezes drift through like the whole sky exhaling relief. At just six in the morning, you could tell we were in for a scorcher. I got up and walked out into the hallway. Joshua's door was still closed. Momma's door was still closed. I was starting to get used to the closed door routine.

I was almost at the bottom stair when I heard something in the kitchen. I figured it was Beau Ray, rooting around for some of the cereal bars I'd brought home the night before. But when I walked into the kitchen, the man I saw wasn't Beau Ray and it wasn't Joshua either. I must have yelped, because he turned around and jumped. He was in boxers and a T-shirt and black socks, and when he jumped, his feet slid on the wooden floor a little, so that he had to grab the counter to steady himself.

At that point, I wasn't scared anymore. There's only so scared you can be by a man in boxer shorts and black socks. Mostly, I was shocked. And surprised I hadn't heard anything earlier on. And relieved, too.

"Leanne!" Judge Weintraub said.

I think I stuttered a little and tried to back out of the kitchen. I told him to finish whatever he was doing. I told him I'd give him some space.

"Leanne," the judge said again. "Let me apologize. I was sure no one would be up yet. It's so early." He had a surprisingly dignified presence, given what he had on. "I wanted to make Lenore breakfast before I got going, but I can't find where you keep anything. Can you lend me a hand? Hell, you've already seen me."

I nodded. He was right, and I figured that was probably the most uncomfortable things were going to be. So long as Momma didn't show up in the kitchen without a stitch.

"Coffee's in that canister. Bread's in that drawer," I said, pointing. "What did you want to make?"

"How about coffee and toast?" he asked. He smiled. I'd always thought he had a nice smile.

"We've also got cereal bars," I told him. "You spent the night?" It just came out. I didn't know if that was a rude thing to ask, but he was in our kitchen and it was early.

"We got in late," he said. "Your mother suggested…"

He didn't finish, and he didn't have to. As soon as I heard him start that sentence, I knew we'd made it somewhere new. Like the whole Gitlin clan of us had been climbing a mountain for years and didn't realize we'd reached the top. Up, up, up, slog, slog, slog, until someone says, "hey, great view!" and you see that it's time to stop trudging, at least for a little while. And even if it's not a great view, you're looking at something other than the path ahead. My eyes welled up and I plopped down in one of the kitchen chairs. Judge Weintraub hurried over and sat beside me.

"Leanne, I didn't mean to upset you. I hope I didn't scare you," he said. But that wasn't it.

Who would blame my mother for hunkering down after Dad died? There she was, forty years old and she'd had me to take care of—I was only fourteen—and Vince, who was sixteen, and Beau Ray, who was still finding his way to a new version of normal. And sure Tommy and Susan were out of the house by then, but you don't stop being a mother and feeling partly responsible for your kids' success or failure or happiness with an address change.

After Vince left, in the middle of the night with little more than some money and his class ring, Momma really started to clamp down. My curfews turned strict, as if everything bad in the world happened after eleven-thirty at night. My chore list filled up and my weekends clogged with housework and chaperoning Beau Ray. But that was good training, as it turned out, for when the deepest of Momma's blues hit a few years later and I actually thought she might disappear into them.

I'm not saying she couldn't have done better—that's beside the point. She made her decisions, and then I think she started believing that those decisions were the only ones out there. It's not like she was unattractive, just weighed down by a lot, and after a time, I think she got used to the weight and forgot what life had felt like before.

But here was Judge Weintraub, in our kitchen, after almost ten years of time passing. Here was Judge Weintraub breathing in deep and saying, "Hey, would you look at that view." I wanted to explain this to him, but all I could manage to say was that I was glad he was making my mother breakfast.

"Be nice to her, is all," I asked him.

"I intend to," he said.

"You want me to help with breakfast?" I asked, standing again. I was a little embarrassed for getting all heavy at such an early hour. "She likes things barely toasted."

"You sit," he said. "You do enough. Come to think, why don't you sleep in a little? It's awfully early."

I didn't know if I'd be able to fall back asleep, but figured I'd give it a try. Besides, I suddenly felt sort of shy. "So I guess I'll see you around," I said.

"I hope so," the judge said.

I went to my room and crawled back into bed, this time leaving the door open. I must have been sound asleep by the time the judge came back upstairs. I didn't hear a thing, didn't hear him leave, didn't hear Momma get up. I woke to the sound of Joshua opening his door. He was looking across the hall at the tray that had been left outside my doorway, set on the floor, a cup of coffee, a plate with two slices of toast, a glass of juice and an azalea flower from the bush in the backyard. It was all cold by the time I woke up, but that wasn't the point.

"Why don't I get breakfast in bed?" Joshua asked, and shuffled off to the bathroom.

"So you and Judge Weintraub," I said, later, after Beau Ray and Joshua had eaten breakfast. Joshua was watching a talk show in the living room, and I'd followed Momma into the kitchen. She took a sponge from the counter and started scrubbing the sink. "You know, I ran into him this morning."

"He said as much." She kept scrubbing, her back to me. "You got a problem with that?"

"Of course not," I said.

Momma put down the sponge and turned around to face me. She eyed me with the squint she always used when trying to suss out if one of us kids was lying. But I wasn't lying.

"Don't you?" she asked me.

"Why would I?" I asked her. "I like him. Hell, I would have introduced you two, you know, earlier on, if I thought you might—"

"I wasn't looking," Momma said, snap like a door closing.

"He asked me to dinner and I figured it would be polite to go. We got things in common."

"Okay," I said, although by that point I had remembered how she'd been humming all the way home from the courthouse that day.

"I thought it would do well for Joshua. Figured it might help his situation," she told me.

"I hope you didn't invite the judge in last night on account of the California crowd," I said.

Her eyes got wide. "Leanne!" she said. She turned back to the sink and stood there, not talking but not really cleaning either.

"Are you mad?" I asked, after she hadn't moved for a minute or so. "I didn't mean it like an insult."

"Not mad," she said. "I'm just—" She petered off and stood up very straight. I knew what it was. Of course, I did. You don't live by a river without learning its banks and curves and how to read flood signs.

"It'll be ten years in November," I said. "That's a long time."

"I know," she said.

"And I think Dad would have…"

I watched her turn ever so slightly toward me, and it scared me a little. I could see that she was listening hard for an answer, and I knew I didn't have one. I knew my own mind, but that was all. I guess with the dead, that's all you're left with—the minds of those left behind.

"You don't need to decide anything right now," I said. That's what Sandy always told me, whenever I was wondering what to do—with a guy, or a job, or my life in general. It was like the chorus of our friendship, and when she said it, it always sounded true. I hoped it would then, too.

"I don't, do I?" Momma asked. She turned around again. I was surprised to see that she'd been crying. "It's a little scary," she said. "It's so different." She wiped her eyes and managed a smile. "When did you get so smart?"

★ ★ ★

That was Monday. Tuesday was one of my work days—
Tuesdays, Wednesdays and Friday mornings. I went in at
nine like always, and spent the first part of the morning answering Mr. Bellevue's questions about Joshua. He'd taken
to starting Tuesday mornings with, "So, tell me everything," and he meant it. He wanted to hear everything
Joshua had done or said or eaten since I'd left work the Friday before.

That day, I told him how I thought that Joshua was growing addicted to morning talk shows, especially Ricki Lake.
How he and Beau Ray had played hide-and-seek in the
backyard, but Beau Ray had hid back by the ditch, farther
than Joshua was allowed to go, so that particular round ended
up lasting near an hour, until Beau Ray wandered out again.
I told him that I'd finally managed to send out new membership packets to the one hundred and forty-three people
who'd joined the fan club in the previous month.

"You do live an exciting life," Mr. Bellevue said.

I wondered what Mr. Bellevue had done in the past three
days if typing out one hundred and forty-three membership
cards qualified as exciting.

I had meant to grab a hamburger for lunch, but I got a
call from the courthouse secretary asking me to come to
Judge Weintraub's chambers soon as I had a moment. So instead of the burger, I made my way over there. I didn't know
what he wanted. First, I worried that maybe Joshua had
wandered past our mailbox and was headed straight for jail.
Then I worried that some crazy fan might have broken into
our house. Then I realized that it was probably something
to do with Momma. I was afraid he was going to tell me that
he'd changed his mind, that he'd realized it was a mistake—
or worse, that my mother had called the whole thing off.

It put knots in my stomach as I got closer to the courthouse wing. Momma was probably too scared of the change,

I figured. It felt too different, and she'd decided to run back to the frozen-in-time way things had been for the past nine, almost ten years. I hesitated knocking on his door for that reason, but he'd called me over and he was a judge, which tops the county courthouse food chain. So I knocked and when I heard him say, "Come in," I did.

"You got my message," the judge said. He was sitting at his desk.

I nodded.

"Sit down," he said.

I sat down.

"Leanne, communication is very important to me. As we go forward, I want to make sure that we're clear with each other," the judge said.

"Is there something we need to be clear on?" I asked him. I wanted to close my eyes.

"How are you feeling about me dating Lenore? Your mother?" he asked. "Are you uncomfortable? Does it make you angry? Or upset?"

"Are you still dating?" I asked him.

"Aren't we? Do you know something I don't?" he asked. He sat up a little higher. As soon as I saw that he looked worried, I knew I didn't have any reason to be.

"Oh," I said. "No. It's fine. I feel fine about it. I think it's great." He nodded, but looked like he wasn't sure whether or not to believe me.

"And if I were to come for dinner during the week—or, say, if your mother were to spend time at my house, how would you feel about that?"

"Fine, I guess. Only it would be better if you were at our house, because then you could help with looking after Beau Ray."

"I see your point."

I was so relieved that I thought I might start giggling for no reason.

"How often do you look after your brother now?" the judge asked.

"Most of the time I'm not here. Since I'm not signed up for any classes just now."

"You were taking some courses, weren't you?" the judge asked. "How were those going?"

"Great, when I can manage it."

He nodded. "Your mother was worried that you might be having a hard time adjusting to our relationship. Hers and mine," he said.

"I told her I was fine," I said. "I think she's the one having a hard time adjusting. It's been a long time since my dad died. I'm sure you know that."

The judge smiled. "And how are things with the criminal element?"

"Joshua? They're okay, I guess. He sees it as a punishment, that's for sure."

"I prefer education to punishment. I hope he takes the opportunity to think about the consequences of his actions and to learn something. That's all we can hope for."

I was actually hoping for more than that, but I didn't say so. I was hoping he'd turn out to be a decent guy, that he'd stop looking at me like I was some common hick, that I wouldn't look back on that summer with a big load of regret on my shoulders. But I worried that maybe I was hoping for too much.

Chapter 9

Enter Alice

So I finally met Alice, Sandy's Alice. It was a Wednesday, I remember, because it was midweek but there was no AA meeting. Alice drove over from Hagerstown, in Maryland, and the three of us went to dinner at the Chili's in Charles Town. She wasn't anything like I'd imagined. She had short blond hair and light skin and little girl features, like an old-fashioned doll. She looked like she'd be quiet and dainty, but instead, she laughed loudly, didn't seem to worry much over keeping to polite topics and said whatever she felt like saying. She was more of a city girl than I'd expected. I liked her right off.

I'd been a little nervous about meeting her. I was worried it was going to feel weird. But right off the bat, Alice blurted out how she'd been nervous about meeting *me,* how she'd kept changing her clothes over it. She said she felt a little jealous—in a friendly sort of way—of how far back Sandy and my history stretched, of how one word could prompt a year's worth of recollections. That made me feel better. Plus, I could tell that Alice really liked Sandy, and more important, how much Sandy liked Alice. Of course, I'd seen Sandy with boyfriends, but I hadn't seen her as happy, ever, not even when she was talking about marrying Barton Albert. I figure, that's what you want for your friends, that they find people who help them smile more.

Funny thing—Alice had also had a crush on the Colin Ashcroft character on *General Hospital,* way back when. To be accurate, she'd had a crush on Colin, then said that she found herself distracted by the Helen and Bart affair, and then by Helen.

"It was one of my early clues to myself," Alice said. "But what a coincidence that you've got Colin Ashcroft sleeping across the hall. Have you messed around with him yet?"

Sandy must have nudged her under the table because Alice jumped a little, then turned to her.

"For God's sake, what?" she asked.

"He's a butthole," Sandy said. "I told you that. I told you what he was like when I met him."

"Maybe Leanne has decided to overlook his butthole tendencies, annoying though they may be. Hell, he's all sorts of good-looking. And in that interview, he came across like a decent guy, all repentant and sensitive."

"The thing is," I told them, "he thinks I'm a hick."

"Oh, please," Sandy said. "Why would he think that? I told him you were prom queen."

I shook my head and told her how I'd heard him on the phone.

"What a fucker," Alice said.

"I can't help being from Pinecob," I said. Alice nodded.

I wanted to explain, but I wasn't sure where to start. Sandy could vouch for me, how I had long planned on living somewhere else. One of the first things I remember doing with Sandy, right around the time we met, was making lists of where we were going to live, who we were going to marry, what we were going to be when we grew up. Some of the items never changed. For Sandy, it was living in New York City. From the time we were both eight, she swooned over the shiny Chrysler Building, even though she'd never been there. For me, it was Max Campbell. He always topped my list of whom I'd be willing to spend years with.

It grew to be a tradition of ours. At the end of each school year, Sandy and I would make new lists, without looking at the ones from the year before. One summer, I was crazy to see Nova Scotia. The next, I remember being certain that I would move to Colorado and become a large-animal veterinarian. Another year, I wanted to live in London and write devastatingly romantic folk songs. Then, the year we were both fourteen, we skipped the tradition. Other events had taken over my family, and I remember Sandy saying that we could always do it the following week. We didn't, and we hadn't.

I knew that working at the county courthouse hadn't ever been on my list. I knew that living in Pinecob hadn't been there, either. And I don't think that Sandy ever planned to be a nurse. Not back then. But when the time comes, you work with the available choices, and some choices seem more available than others.

Alice reached out her hand and touched my hair. "You've got such beautiful hair, Leanne," she said. "I love the color. I really do. But could I make a tiny little suggestion?"

I shrugged. "About my hair?"

"It's just…well, I think, but it's only my opinion of course, that you could do with a slightly different cut. Hell, you've got a great face—I'd kill for your cheekbones—but your hair's maybe a few years back. What do you think, hon?"

"Maybe," Sandy said, nodding. "Remember how Brennie used to do hers?" she asked me. "Sort of sleek and out of her face, but not feathered."

I suddenly felt self-conscious.

"I'm not talking about anything drastic," Alice said. "Your natural color is great. Just a little polish. Next time I come down, I'll bring some magazines I got when I was in New York last time. They might give you some clothes ideas."

"Clothes, too?" I asked. "I can't afford anything new. He's still going to think I'm a hick."

"Why? Because you live in Pinecob?"

"Because I've *only* lived in Pinecob. And I can't change that," I said to Alice. Then I turned to Sandy. "At least you got to leave for nursing college."

"Maybe it's time you looked around again," Sandy said. "You don't want to be at the courthouse forever, do you? So there's no reason to act like you do. Sometimes, you sort of act like you do." Sandy looked sad as she said it, and I'm sure I didn't look thrilled to hear her. You want friends to look out for you, but it still stings when they notice the exact things you'd prefer to gloss over. No, I didn't want to be at the courthouse forever.

"He's probably harping on you for, well, like you said Leanne—for being sort of grounded here," Alice said. "Maybe focusing elsewhere isn't a bad idea—just in general."

"I focus on things outside of West Virginia," I said.

"Like what?" Sandy asked. "Besides the Joshua Reed Fan Club, which you don't need to talk to him about, that's for sure."

I just stared at my plate.

"Something to think about anyway," she said, more gentle.

"I'm so bummed that he's an ass," Alice said. "Colin Ashcroft was so nice."

"He's a good actor, I guess," I told her, glad to turn the conversation away from me and my flaws. "He can pretty much sound how he wants to sound. It's creepy."

"I wish there was something we could do," Sandy mused.

"What, to fuck with him?" Alice asked.

"Not necessarily. I mean, I told him how cool you are, Leanne," Sandy said.

"Why not fuck with him?" Alice wanted to know.

Sandy and I looked at each other. Sandy shrugged.

"Well, how do you mean?" I asked Alice. "I mean, it can't be anything illegal. This is a legal situation, him being in our house. I wouldn't feel right about tricking him into going past his house-arrest boundaries so he'd be thrown in jail or something."

Alice and Sandy looked surprised.

"What?" I asked. "Well, of course I've *thought* about it."

"What were *you* thinking?" Sandy asked Alice.

"I don't know. Just showing up, like I'm some crazy fan."

"We had one of those already," I told her. "It didn't faze him."

"Then what about a prank call? From his agent or something?" Alice suggested.

"Alice did a lot of acting in high school," Sandy said.

Alice nodded. "I was quite the drama queen."

"He never answers the phone," I said.

"Then," Alice said, still thinking, "what if you said that his agent had called? While he was in the shower or something."

"And then what?" I asked.

Alice frowned. "What does this guy really want?" Alice asked. "What are his motivations?"

"To be somewhere other than my house, mostly. To get away from me," I told her.

"But that's not an option. What else?" Alice asked.

I thought about it. "I don't know," I said. "He likes people from L.A. And New York. People who think they're cool, you know? And people in the movies—but not just anyone, not the extras or the assistants. Just the bigger names."

"I'm getting an idea," Alice said. "Someone from the movie set, maybe? What's it called?"

"*Musket Fire,*" I told her. "Maybe."

"Oh, my God, Alice, that would be perfect!" Sandy looked delighted. "Leanne, can we? Can we at least try? Why not, right?"

"Sure," I said. "Why not?"

We did it the next day, and it started out pretty funny, I have to admit. I told Joshua that someone from Judy's office had called and said that a new cast member from the movie was dropping by the house.

"I don't know who," I said, when he asked. "Just that some actress was coming by who's the new romantic lead, you know, that your character falls for."

"But I thought Sarah Powers was playing Elizabeth," Joshua said.

"Who?"

"The girl in *Bottleneck Junction?* Really hot."

I shrugged, even though I knew who Sarah Powers was. I thought it would make me seem less suspect.

"When is she coming by?" Joshua asked.

"Soon, I think. Sandy and I are making cupcakes for the hospital bake sale. We'll be in the kitchen if you need anything."

So Sandy and I were there when Alice rang the doorbell.

"Golly day, this is so exciting! It's really you! Joshua Reed," we heard her say. "I'm Nicolette Menderhutt. The new Elizabeth? Judy said you'd be here. You're so cute!" Alice was wearing a wig that gave her long brown hair, and she'd put on what looked like a ton of mascara.

"You're in *Musket Fire?*" Joshua asked.

"I still can't believe it. Golly, well, I can but I can't, you know?" she said. "That was some trip. I took a plane and then a train and then a taxi to get here. It's like that movie!" Alice giggled.

"Come in," Joshua said. "I'm sorry. Your name again?" he asked.

"Nicolette. Menderhutt. Did you get my headshot? Judy said she was sending over my headshot. I sure hope you got it. It's my new one. With my dog. He's a cutie-pie."

"Sorry, no," Joshua said. "I only just heard you'd be stopping by. I didn't even realize that Sarah Powers had dropped out."

"Yeah," Alice said. "Sarah. Too bad. Oh, but not for me, of course." She giggled again.

"Do you know what happened? I'd heard she was solid."

"Affair," Alice said, her voice dropping low. "So they told me. But I also heard that, well, that she caught something called an STD. That means sexually transmitted disease."

"I know what it means," Joshua said. "But I thought she was married. Happily, even."

Sandy giggled. I got the impression that Alice was just making stuff up as she went along.

"I'm just telling you what I heard. And what sort of person would lie about something like that?" Alice asked. "So where do you want to practice?"

"Practice?" Joshua asked. "Oh, you want to run lines?"

"I figured we could practice, I don't know, maybe the romantic scenes. I haven't done many romantic scenes. They make me nervous so I like to practice them a bunch beforehand. You know, to get warmed up."

"You mean, our lines, right?" Joshua said.

"Yeah, *and* our lines. But everything," Alice said. "This is my big break. I've got to do my best and I know I get nervous if I have to improvise. I work a lot better when I know what to expect. I've never been good with surprises. Jack-in-the-boxes still totally freak me out!"

There was a pause, and when Joshua finally spoke, his words were slow and steady. "Maybe I should call Lars. I'd like to hear exactly what happened with Sarah Powers."

"I also want to go over our characters—you know, to see if what we're imagining for their motivations match up," Alice said quickly. "I hope I didn't come on too strong. I'm just so thrilled to be working with you, and I bet you've done a lot of great thinking about your character." This seemed to do the trick.

"Yeah," Joshua said. "So what are your thoughts about Elizabeth?"

Alice paused for a moment. Sandy and I crept a little closer to the doorway, to make sure we could hear.

"Gosh, *my* thoughts? That's so nice of you to ask. Well, I see her as sort of…oh, what's that word? What's the word I'm looking for?"

"Conflicted?" Joshua guessed.

"No, that's not it."

"Strong? Passionate?"

"Actually, sort of lusty," Alice finally said. "I want to play her all lusty."

Sandy rolled her eyes at me.

"She's the minister's daughter," Joshua pointed out.

"And like you said, passionate. Sure, she's passionate. About lots of things, and definitely about Josiah Whitcomb."

I couldn't believe that Alice was actually saying that stuff. I loved her for it—but found myself a little scared of her, too.

"I'm planning to come at Josiah differently," Joshua was saying. "You know, he's got all that conflict built up, after his father dies. I imagine there would be a lot of tension between them."

"Oh, okay," Alice said. She sounded bored.

"I don't think lusty goes with that."

"But why do you want to make him so conflicted?" Alice asked. "There's a war. His side wins. He's the pretty boy."

"He's not just the pretty boy!" Joshua snapped. "There's more to him than that."

"But why else would they cast *you?*"

The sting of Alice's words hung in the air, like the silence after a thunderclap, when the dishes are still vibrating. I was pretty sure that our prank had stopped being funny.

Joshua took his acting seriously, I knew that. I'd seen the way he studied the scripts Lars sent. I'd peeked at some of the notes he wrote in the margins, notes about inconsistencies in the characters or the scenes. Notes on how to keep the people and the plots less obvious. And I also knew, from all my fan club work, that most people only wanted him to sit back and smolder. A lot of the interviews I kept on file traced a common theme—Joshua complaining that he wasn't taken seriously because of his looks and because he'd come up through soap operas. Alice's dart hit the bull's-eye. She *had* done her homework.

I turned to Sandy, and in a panic, pushed her into the living room. She entered with a stumble. "Hey!" she said, too brightly.

Neither Joshua nor Alice spoke.

"We're making…I mean, we're getting ready to make…" She paused. I wondered what we were supposedly going to make. "Margaritas!" Sandy finally said. "Either of y'all want one?"

"Thanks, no," Joshua said. I was relieved that he'd finally spoken.

"Oh, not me. Thanks. I'm fine," Alice said.

"Okay!" Sandy spun around and hustled back into the kitchen.

"Margaritas?" I whispered at her. She shrugged and we returned to our hidden spot near the kitchen door.

"Nicolette, it's been interesting, but I don't think I'm up for much character analysis," we heard Joshua say. "Besides, we've still got at least a month before the production gets rolling."

"Okay. Then what do you want to do in the meantime?" Alice asked.

"What do you mean?"

"I came *all* the way out here. And we'll be working *so* intimately." Alice's voice got breathy. "Don't you want to test how compatible we are?" she asked.

In the kitchen mirror's reflection, I watched her take a step closer.

"Maybe find out what the physical will feel like?" she asked. She put her hands on his chest. He flinched a little.

"I think it's going to feel good. Sure you don't want to practice? Or maybe it's true what I read about you—that you have trouble with your follow-through."

Joshua didn't have time to answer. The phone rang. Sandy skittered across the kitchen and tried to pretend that we'd been baking. I grabbed for the phone. It was Judy's assistant, saying that Judy was about to get on the line. That's the way they make phone calls in Hollywood. I'd always found it weird and a little lazy that people didn't make their own phone calls. But for once, I was glad for the few seconds of warning.

"Who is it?" Joshua called out.

When pulled tight, the kitchen phone cord was barely long enough to reach into the living room. I did just that, pushing Sandy into the room before me.

"It's Judy!" I said, brightly like it was good news. "Your publicist."

"Hey, Judy," I said to her, when she got on the phone. "How are you?"

Joshua hurried over and held out his hand to take the call.

"Judy, hold on a minute," I said, but I made sure to drop the phone before Joshua could take it, and the cord contracted, dragging the headset back into the kitchen.

"Damn it," he muttered, and went after it, and in that same second, Alice grabbed her purse and headed for the door. By the time he was saying hello, Alice had opened the door and skipped out, blowing a kiss to Sandy and mouthing, see you later. I could hear Joshua in the kitchen.

"Nicolette," he was saying. "What do you mean? Your office called. I'm serious… That's what Leanne said. Someone from your office called, and…then if you didn't, who the hell is she? Hold on."

Joshua came back into the living room and looked back and forth between me and Sandy.

"Where's Nicolette?" he asked.

"She left," Sandy said.

"She what?"

"She left," I said. "She said she had an appointment. Sorry, I figured you knew that. You guys weren't done?"

"She left?" Joshua said. "Go catch her!"

"Me?" I asked him. "What should I say? I mean, she's *your* co-star."

"But Joshua can't go past the driveway," Sandy said.

"Oh, right. Do you want me to try to catch up to her?" I tried to sound helpful but stupid at the same time.

"Or I could go," Sandy offered. Sandy and I had practiced getting in the way like this for years, mostly on our brothers.

"Do you *want* to go?" I asked Sandy.

"I will, if you want me to," Sandy said.

Joshua had run to the door and was trying to see beyond the driveway. He looked like he might explode. "Forget it. It's probably too late," he said. "What the fuck?" he muttered, then returned to the phone.

We could hear him in the kitchen, his voice rising and falling, first angry, then confused, then exasperated, then resigned. I hoped he wouldn't notice the lack of cupcake supplies.

"So I understand that someone called, saying they were from my office?" Judy said, maybe ten minutes later, after Joshua handed me back the phone.

"Yeah," I said. But I felt guilty. I hadn't thought it through enough beforehand to realize that I might be forced to lie to Judy.

"Man or woman?" Judy asked.

"Woman," I said, making it up as I went along.

"And this woman, she said that someone was replacing Sarah in the film? Who was it? Did you recognize the voice?"

I told her I didn't.

"Was it the same woman who came over to your house?" Judy asked. "Was it the same voice?"

"It could have been, I'm not sure. I wasn't really paying attention." Another lie. I felt low. "Who do you think she was?" I asked.

Judy sighed. "Probably just some psycho fan. It's not the first time this sort of thing has happened. Not quite like this, but it *has* happened. Joshua's a little freaked, I think. I don't think he realized how safe he felt over there with you. But whatever. No harm done. He's a little skeeved. I guess she touched him and said some things. If this happens again—if someone calls and you don't recognize the voice, ask for me, okay?"

I promised that I would. I hung up the phone. Sandy had gone home—or rather, she'd said that she was going to do more baking, though of course there had never been any baking, and she was headed off to meet Alice. I went out to the porch and gathered the magazines that Alice had left there for me. Back inside, Joshua was flipping through papers in the living room.

I wished I didn't feel so guilty. Part of me knew that there wasn't *that* much to feel guilty about. It wasn't like Alice was a real stalker or would ever hurt him. And he *had* been nasty. But all the same, he'd felt safe in our house, and I'd poked holes in that.

"You need anything?" I asked him.

He was reading a script. "I could use one of those margaritas," he said.

"Oh, right. Turns out we didn't have any tequila," I told him. "Whoops." I felt like I was getting better at lying. Or acting.

"Whatever," he said.

"Let me know if you ever want help running lines or something," I said. "I know I'm not a professional. But if it would help."

"Oh, that's okay," he said. "I mean, not being a professional. Thanks. I might take you up on that." He looked up and smiled at me. "Sorry if I snapped at you—about not running out to get that psycho chick. I know you didn't realize what was going on."

I nodded, but I could feel my cheeks get hot. "Yeah, weird, huh? Makes that drunk girl on the lawn look pretty good, doesn't it?" I asked.

He laughed, then gave a shiver.

That night's AA meeting was one of the open ones, and Grant Pearson suggested I sit in. I figured it would be more interesting than sitting in the car or the school hallway for the duration, so I said okay. It was held in the gym and pretty crowded—much more so than the first meeting I'd brought Joshua to. Grant said that open meetings always attracted a larger group, but I wondered if that was the entire reason for the increase.

Poor Joshua—I think he was still freaked out from Nicolette's visit. He kept looking around the room, and he gave a start whenever anyone made a quick move. I was planning to sit in the back, but he said no, why didn't I sit beside him. Part of me was flattered that he asked, like I was important, or a friend. But more likely, in that room of strangers, he wanted as much of a buffer as possible.

I recognized some of the people—the head of the cheese department at the Winn-Dixie, a clerk I often saw in the halls of the municipal building, the car mechanic who changed our oil and gave us a twelve-point service check over at the SpeedLube.

It was interesting to hear people tell their stories. One guy stood up ("My name's Bob," he said, and then everyone said "Hi, Bob!") to announce that he'd just reached five years of being sober. People clapped. Another guy said that it was coming up on the anniversary of his mother's death, and he was getting worried about "the stress of it all." A woman said that she was there because she didn't like the people at the meeting over in Harper's Ferry. Joshua didn't say anything, except to mutter "This guy again" when some old codger took to the podium. The man said that his name was Homer ("Hi, Homer!" the rest of us said, like a responsive reading in church) and that he'd been sober going on twenty years, and that the meetings kept him from going out of his gourd. People applauded when he was finished.

The man named Homer was walking back to his seat when he looked over at Joshua and frowned. That would have been okay, but then he stopped where he was—in the middle of the right-hand aisle—and pointed. Joshua looked like he wanted to disappear.

"I recognize you," the man named Homer said.

This seemed to give everyone in the room permission to stare. I'd noticed a few glances and whispers when we first walked in, but now it felt like everyone was looking around.

Grant Pearson hurried over and took Homer by the elbow. "You know that these meetings are strictly anonymous," he said.

Homer shook Mr. Pearson off. "How do I know you?" Homer pressed. "You come in the store?"

"Nope," Joshua said.

"You buy that old shitbox car from me?"

"What car?" Joshua asked.

"Homer," Mr. Pearson said.

"You just said we was supposed to keep anonymous and then you go using my name," Homer complained.

"You introduced yourself," Grant Pearson said. "Please let this young man be. If he wants to introduce himself, he can do so in his own time."

After the meeting ended, Joshua went to use the bathroom, and Grant Pearson walked over to me while I waited.

"I wanted to ask you, Leanne," he said. "I get the impression that Joshua is kind of going through the motions here. I'm not sure he's committed to the process." He watched me as though waiting for a response.

"That wasn't a question," I said. "Are you asking if I agree with you?"

He laughed a little. "I guess that's it."

"I do," I told him. "He doesn't want to be here—not just here, but in Pinecob, in West Virginia."

Mr. Pearson nodded.

"But it looks like he's been good for your meeting," I said, toward all the people still milling. Some of them met my eyes, then looked away. I realized I was being stared at nearly as much as Joshua. I didn't like it. I wondered whether any of these people had asked Max about me, about what was going on in our house. "I mean, getting people here."

"I suppose so," Mr. Pearson said.

I saw Joshua come out of the bathroom and start looking around. "Listen, I've got to run," I said. "I'm supposed to have him back to the house by nine-thirty."

"See you at the next open meeting?" Grant Pearson asked.

"Sure, okay," I said. I started walking away.

"Leanne," he said.

I stopped and looked back at him.

"You know, you can talk, too. If you ever wanted to."

"I know," I said.

"It might be—"

But I cut him off. I told him I'd think about it, and I left.

Chapter 10

Shutting Up Sandy

My mother wasn't the only person I knew to suffer a mean season in Pinecob. Sandy hit one of her own not long after returning from the beach. When she first got back and told me about her and Alice, it was all gentle, like she was worried that I'd be upset or judge her wrong or something. And hell, I can see her point, but I knew that her leanings weren't anything that should come between us, not after so many years being practically sisters.

A few weeks later, after she'd been harassed about it a few times and read up on where she now perched in the social scheme of things, she got a little mad. Sandy would say she was just more in touch with it all, with the anger *and* the love. Maybe that was true, but her ornery side was the most visible.

Sandy's mean season was wide-open that Saturday when we met at The Buccaneer, one of Pinecob's two bars. I always considered "Buccaneer" a silly name for a bar in a land-locked state like West Virginia, but it sat dead center on the only commercial strip in town. With a good location, I guess the Buck's owner could have named that place anything and still pulled a crowd. Most everyone went there. Well, except Sandy and me, we hardly ever went there. But I was tired of Momma being the only person who got to go out on weekends, so I up and said that I was going. Besides, she wasn't home to stop me, and Joshua had been with us a little over a month by then, so I figured he'd do fine watching Beau Ray.

We sat at a booth near the jukebox, and ordered beers from Loreen Dunbar, the girl Howard Malkin cheated on me with. She'd been a waitress there for a couple of years, which is one of the reasons Sandy and I didn't frequent the place. Not that I held a huge grudge, but a little one, sure.

"So Leanne," Loreen said, after we'd ordered. "Any good stories?"

That was a second reason I hadn't been hanging out at the Buccaneer. I hated all the asking, hated hearing myself tell the same story over and over. Maybe if I had good stories, I'd have felt different. Sandy's news was more buzzworthy, knowing Pinecob, but it wasn't common knowledge at that point.

"Nah," I said. "I don't actually see him all that much."

"How come?" Loreen asked, but I got lucky and she was summoned by another customer. "I'll be back with your beers," she said.

"Guess who I see?" Sandy asked, and then she waved.

It being Pinecob, Sandy might have seen anyone from our growing up. It might have been Howard Malkin, the cheat himself, or Barton Albert or Paulie Pizzoni or Lionel Hutchinson or really anyone. But I turned around and saw Max Campbell walking over, which was better than all of them by a long shot. And somehow worse, too.

"Hey Sandy, hey Leanne," he said. "I like your hair, Leanne. It's different, right?"

I nodded. I'd brought a picture from one of Alice's magazines to the salon the day before. All week, I'd been leafing through her loaner periodicals, but a haircut was all the change I'd managed.

"It looks good," Max said.

"Who are you here with?" Sandy asked.

"My cousins Lisa and Laura are up from Roanoke. They wanted me to show them a good time," Max said.

"So you took them to the Buccaneer? Remind me not to call you when I want a hot date," Sandy said.

"Hey, they're not complaining." Max pointed to two blond women playing doubles pool with a couple guys I didn't know.

"It doesn't look like," Sandy agreed.

"What about you? And don't try to sell me on Leanne being your Saturday-night squeeze," he said.

"Hey!" I said, pretending to be insulted.

Max looked at Sandy, it seemed to me, the way a lot of guys looked at Sandy, like she was a pleasant surprise, like looking at gold.

"None of your business," Sandy said. "But I am seeing someone new. Someone fabulous."

"Someone fabulous?" Max asked. He sat down beside her. "Won't Scooter be crushed. That might do the old boy in."

Loreen brought us our beers, and I took a big sip of mine so maybe I'd be less tongue-tied. Loreen gave Max a big smile.

"Scooter will get over it," Sandy said.

"You're heartless, Wilson. Always have been. Anyone I know?" Max asked.

"You know anyone in Hagerstown?"

Max shook his head.

"Then, no," Sandy said.

"So tell me about him," Max said, and in a space of a blink, Sandy looked ready to spit fire.

"Typical," she snapped. "I said it's none of your business, and I'm serious!"

"Sandy," I said, trying to point out that she'd been way snappier than need be.

"Sorry," Max said. "I didn't realize you had nerves enough to strike."

"Go bother Leanne about her love life," Sandy said. "Leave mine be."

"Sandy!" I said again, this time wanting to shut her up for a different reason.

Max turned to me. "I see Leanne every Sunday," he said. "There's nothing to pick on her about. And even if there was, I promised I wouldn't gossip about her." He winked, like the two of us had a secret. I thought about him standing there, in the doorway of my house and wondered if we did. "But you, Wilson, you've near as hell disappeared off the map."

"How do you know Leanne doesn't have a love life to pick on? You don't know everything about her. Yeah, you see her, but you don't really see her. You hardly know *anything*," Sandy said.

I tried to kick her under the table, but I missed and jammed my toe against the booth-back. Max looked over and sort of frowned. I smiled at him, hoping to seem nonchalant.

"I noticed her hair," Max said. "Leanne holds her cards so close, I can't get anything out of her," he said. "You, I can make all sorts of conjectures about."

"But Leanne's the one with the hunk in her house, isn't she?" Sandy asked. "Right across the hall. Isn't it strange how little she talks about that?"

"We all know there's nothing there," I said, quick as can be.

Sandy shrugged. "So you say," she said. "But if you're so available, why aren't you out and about?"

"Look at me. I'm out," I said, really wishing that the subject would die. But Sandy still wasn't done.

"What about asking out that guy from your office? Otto? Or that guy you think is cute at the SpeedLube? Or Lionel. You could always go back to Lionel. You could even ask Max here out to another play."

"What?" Max asked.

"What?" I asked, only I knew exactly what she was referring to, and I hated when she did this, handing her pissy moods to me like dripping socks. Plus, when Sandy was feeling mean, she'd barrel over the same looks that she'd catch on subtler days.

"You remember…when Leanne asked you to see *South Pacific?*" Sandy asked Max.

"What are you talking about?" Max asked, looking between me and Sandy, like this might be a private joke he didn't get.

I thought it would be better if I told the story, so I cut Sandy off before she could say more. "It's nothing," I said. "It was years ago. There's no reason you should remember. My mother's cousin, Nora, down in Charleston, is a drama teacher and her school put on *South Pacific,* and it won a competition, so it played in a bunch of the county seats, including Charles Town… None of this rings a bell?"

Max shook his head. "When was this?" he asked.

"I don't know—maybe three years back?" I went on. "It was a Sunday, and I was at the Winn-Dixie, and you were there, and I asked what you were doing later that week, on that Friday, when they were going to put on the play. I asked if you wanted to go see it—with me."

"That sounds vaguely familiar," Max said. "What did I say?"

"You told me you were scheduled to work that Friday, but you'd see if you could get off, and you'd call to let me know."

"But," Sandy said, forcing a transition. I braced myself for what had to come next, like when you see a pothole too late to swerve off.

"I didn't call?" Max guessed.

"What happened was...that was the week you met Charlene," I said. "At least, that's what I found out later."

"Oh, fuck," Max said. "I think I do remember that. God, I'm sorry."

"Whatever. No big deal now, you know. Bad timing, is all."

"No, Leanne, I am sorry. That was kind of a crazy time for me. I probably dropped a lot of balls right around then."

"That's putting it mildly," Sandy said.

I knew that she just wanted to be mad at him for having assumed she was dating a guy, even though he'd have to have been a psychic to guess about Alice. I mean, Sandy had practically been engaged to Barton Albert just a few years prior.

"It's fine. I know it's not every week a guy meets his soul mate," I said.

"That's not the word I'd use for Charlene," Max said.

"Better that than, I mean, if you weren't going to call, better it's on account of meeting your future wife. Better than you forgetting, or it just being some other girl. But you know, no big deal." I felt like I was about to cry although I didn't know the reason. It was nearly three years before that this had happened—or not happened—between me and Max, but it suddenly felt like last week. I turned to Sandy for help, and she seemed to see me for the first time.

"Got you over that little crush anyhow," Sandy said. "Right quick, too."

"I guess," I said. "Yeah."

"I feel like such a jerk. I'm really sorry," Max said.

"Like I said, no big deal," I told him. "I can't think why it came up."

I frowned at Sandy, then grabbed my beer and downed it as quick as I could. I put the glass back on the table with a thunk. Sandy and Max looked at the glass, then at me. "Man, that was good," I said.

Max looked into his own beer, still half-full. "Can I get you another?" he asked. It seemed obvious that he was trying to be extra nice for the slight, three years gone.

"Would you mind?" I said. As soon as he got up from the table, I turned to Sandy. "How could you say that? Why did you bring that up?" I asked her.

She blinked at me. "What?"

"About the time in the Winn-Dixie," I said. "About *South Pacific*."

"That was *years* ago. It's funny."

"It's embarrassing."

"But you can't still… It didn't seem to bother you much back then."

"I would think that you, of all people in my entire life, could tell when I'm faking something," I said to her.

Sandy's eyes got wide. "Oh," she said. "It was worse than that?" Whatever anger she'd been carrying evaporated. "Oh damn, Leanne. I'm sorry. You should have told me."

"You were all happy with Barton back then, remember? I didn't want…" I felt myself start to choke up again, and willed it away. "It took me a long time," I said. "You know, first to ask, and then to get over asking."

"So your crush?" She looked at me and I shrugged. "Still?" she asked.

"I can't help it," I told her. "Even knowing about Charlene and him all holding on. Nothing's ever going to happen."

"I never would have said it if I'd known. Please believe me," she said.

"I figured it was obvious," I said.

"The crush? No. Not at all. You're cool around him. Except for that part just now when you almost started to cry."

"It's been a rough week," I told her.

"I don't think he noticed," Sandy said.

"So was it a good play? Did you go?" Max asked.

He put a new beer down and sat beside me in the booth. I moved over to give him room and could feel liquid jostling around in my stomach. It usually took me about an hour to finish a beer, so I didn't even know where to begin with the second one.

"What?"

"*South Pacific.* Your mom's cousin's school. Did you go?"

"Yeah, it was. I did. You know, I'm gonna wash that man right out of my hair," I said, singing it like they do in the musical. "How are your own cousins doing?"

Max turned toward the pool table. "We're going to head home after this game. We've got hours of home movies my mother wants us all to watch. Mostly of my mom and their mom when they were little. We figured we'd come here first and get a couple drinks down, to make the viewing more interesting." Max looked at me. "But I'm just having this one," he said. "I'm driving."

I shrugged.

Chapter 11

The Guys Again

Round about the time Sandy and I were talking to Max, Lionel was calling my house. Me not being there, he talked to Joshua, and by the time I was back from the Buccaneer, the two of them had hatched a plan for another Sunday night movie at our house, and there was nothing I could do about it. Scooter had family obligations, but otherwise, it was going to be the same audience as for *Die Hard,* plus Max's two cousins from Roanoke were invited, since they'd still be in town.

God, I was feeling low all day that Sunday. I had no energy for anything, especially the thought of company. I didn't even have energy for grocery shopping, and when Momma offered to go with Beau Ray, I took her up on it so fast, she asked if I was sick.

I wasn't sick, I was sapped. Maybe it was the summertime heat kicking in, or maybe it was Momma and the way she'd started talking about her and Judge Weintraub as a "we." I swear, I didn't begrudge my mother one minute of happiness, but it still made me aware that I was nowhere near to being a "we."

Or maybe it was Sandy's "we." Since she hadn't told anyone but me about Alice, I was hearing an awful lot on the subject. After Max left the Buck with his cousins, I kept on hearing about her. How great she was, how funny she was, how stylish she was, how everything she was. Sure I wanted to be happy for Sandy, and I *was* happy for Sandy, but I had others moods mixed in, too.

I didn't want to be part of a "we" just so I could use the pronoun more. I could have gone back to Lionel—I was pretty sure of that—if my only goal had been to use the word. But the more I thought about Lionel and me, the more it felt like being in a pool and treading water, refreshing for a spell, but tiresome after a time, and you're always in the same place.

Even Joshua, who didn't seem apt at noticing anything, asked what was up. He was just out of the shower, and I was headed into my room to get ready before everyone showed up.

"What's wrong with you?" Joshua asked.

I told him nothing, I mean, that nothing was wrong.

"You drink too much last night? Are you hungover?"

"No," I said.

"Well, someone's cranky today." He was standing in the doorway of Vince's bedroom with a towel wrapped around his waist. Just a towel and the gray ankle sensor, still beaded with water. He'd gotten quite tan in the previous weeks and was keeping in shape with Tommy's old weight set. His chest seemed like something from a sculpture or a perfume ad. Part of me wanted to reach out and touch it, to see what it felt like, although I'd touched plenty of chests before then. Funny, but his chest being so perfect made it hard to look at it. To see something like that, so close, and to know that it might as well be a mirage, not for you and not ever to be yours—that's no pleasure. Maybe that was my problem with Max.

I don't think Joshua was standing there half-naked because he considered himself a symbol of all I couldn't have. Not right then, at least. He was just standing there. He was a guy out of the shower, after all. The way they tell you, when you've got an interview or a speech to give, to think of everyone in their underwear. He was like that. Real. Human.

"I don't feel like having company, is all," I managed to say.

He shrugged. "You don't have to watch."

For a moment, I thought maybe I *had* been staring, that he'd noticed I was having a hard time looking away from him. But he went into his room, and I realized that he must have meant the movie. I didn't have to watch the movie.

In my room, behind the door, I pulled off my shirt and my shorts and stood in front of my closet in my underwear. It felt good in the summertime heat to be out of the day's sweaty clothes, but there was nothing hanging up or folded that struck me as the right thing to change into. I didn't know what I wanted to wear, because what I wore seemed more than ever like an extension of who or where I wanted to be. If I didn't have the answers to those questions, how could I ever expect to find an outfit to match? I had looked through some of the magazines Alice had brought—the same ones where I'd found my new haircut—and there were so many ideas in there. But none of my clothes looked like the magazine clothes. Everything in my closet seemed too bright and too sunny and too obvious.

I'd read in one of the magazines where a designer said, "when in doubt, wear black." And I'd always heard that people in New York dressed in black all the time. I figured why not—at least my clothing would match my mood. So I wore a plain black T-shirt and black pants and pulled my hair back into a ponytail.

But come to find out the "wear black" rule doesn't work for Pinecob, West Virginia. I should have known that "when in doubt, wear boots," or maybe "wear jeans," is the rule there, and I knew I'd broken it when I opened the door for Lionel and Paulie, and Lionel said, "Whoa, where's the funeral?" and Paulie asked if I'd gone "goth," as he handed me a six-pack. Still I figured, what did they know, and I was halfway to forgetting their comments when Max showed up with Laura and Lisa, his cousins.

Laura and Lisa were both dressed in cute little summery skirts and matching tops, and their blond hair was all bouncy and shiny, as if they'd taken turns blow-drying each other. One had blue eyeshadow and one had lavender, but besides that, they looked an awful lot alike. They were sunny and nice and totally killed whatever good spirits I had left in me.

"Hey, Leanne," Max said. "You feeling okay?"

"Why?" I asked him.

"Your mom did the shopping today, and I don't know, you look a little pale."

"I'm fine," I told him. "I'll get Joshua and we can start." I noticed Laura elbow Lisa, who giggled a little. I hoped they wouldn't fawn over Joshua. I thought that might make me physically ill.

"He's upstairs then?" Max asked.

"I think so."

"Across the hall," Max said.

"Yeah, why?"

But Max just shrugged.

"Who wants a beer?" Lionel asked.

I raised my hand, but it seemed that he couldn't see past Max's cousin Lisa. Blue eyeshadow.

Joshua came bounding down the stairs. "I miss anything?"

he asked. Then he looked at me and did a doubletake. "Don't you look Left Bank tonight," he said.

"What's that?" Scooter asked.

"Leanne's gone chic on us," Joshua said.

Scooter looked over at me. "Since when's a black T-shirt chic?" he asked.

Max interrupted to introduce Joshua to the Roanoke cousins, and Joshua did his charming act and asked all about Virginia and talked about *Musket Fire* and the character of Josiah Whitcomb and how the story was a mix of *Taming of the Shrew* and *Gone with the Wind,* which I'd heard about a hundred times by then. I felt about as chic as our old rug.

I hated being with myself in that sort of mood, much less a crowd of other people living it up. So I excused myself and headed back to Beau Ray's room. The room had been his private domain nearly twelve years by then (he'd laid claim to it as soon as Tommy moved out). But he'd promised, when he first took it over, that as long as his door was open, I was allowed inside. That open-door policy had remained a constant, except during a couple of knockdown drag-outs, and since Beau Ray's room was as far off as you could get from the din of the house and still be inside, I'd sought shelter in there a number of times. There and in his bathroom across the hall.

"Are you lonely?" It was Beau Ray. He sat on his bed, smiling at me. "Are you sad, Leanne?"

"No," I told him. There was so much I never explained to Beau Ray, mostly because he tended to lose his ability to concentrate about thirty seconds into a conversation. Maybe because I felt that, on a lot of levels, his challenges loomed larger than anything I ever faced, even if he didn't realize it. It was habit, by then, to give him the smaller version of everything. The abridged edition. "I'm a little tired," I told him.

"You're wearing a lot of the same color," he said.

I nodded. "Is that bad?" I asked him.

"It's not bad," he said. "I wear all one color some days."

I wasn't sure that was the argument I wanted to hear.

"It's crowded in our house tonight," he said. "More girls."

"That's true."

"I'm going to bring my pillow to lie on."

"That's more comfortable than the floor," I told him.

He laughed. "You can't lie on the floor," Beau Ray said.

"Well, you can—" I started to say.

"For a whole movie?" he asked.

I told him that he was probably right. "You're going to like this movie."

"You're going to like it."

"Maybe," I said. "I might go out instead."

Beau Ray frowned. "Go where?"

"Maybe just to get some milk. Just out. You stay and watch the movie. It's a good movie. James Bond. And Joshua will be here."

"Joshua lives here," Beau Ray said.

"For a little while longer at least," I agreed.

"Be back soon," he said, and it sounded like a decision.

"Leanne? Beau Ray?" It was Lionel from the living room.

Even if I wasn't going to watch, I'd have to walk by them to get out of the house. Whether I left out the front door or the back, I'd have to pass through the living room, and the guys and the matching blondes. I wished I could just stay in Beau Ray's room, but I got the impression that nowhere in the house would let me breathe the way I wanted, not that night. I'd be able to hear the movie from every room.

"Coming!" I called out. I handed Beau Ray his pillow and we left his room.

They were waiting for us, Joshua in Dad's old easy chair, and the girls on the long couch, with Max between them. Lionel and Paulie sat on the short couch, and looked up when we came in.

"You guys ready?" Lionel asked.

"Leanne has to go get milk," Beau Ray said.

"Now?" It was Max. "Why?"

"Why don't you start the movie?" I said. "Really. I forgot something. Earlier. I thought I'd go out for it now."

"Now?" Max asked again.

"You going to a rave?" Paulie asked.

Lionel swatted him. "You don't even know what a rave is," he said.

"I've never been to a rave," Lisa said. "Are they fun?"

"Jesus, let her go if she wants to go," Joshua said.

"I won't be long," I said.

Lionel shrugged and started the film. Beau Ray set his pillow against the side of the long couch and sat down. I grabbed my keys and walked out.

There are some decisions that, when you're making them, you're pretty sure you could go either way. If anyone had piped up to say that they wanted me to stay, I'd probably have stayed. And since no one did, I left. But once I was outside, I knew that leaving was what I'd wanted. The way you feel your deepest desire when the coin is in the air. Even though you've already called heads, and even though you've said you couldn't care less, suddenly, the coin is flipping around and you find yourself hoping for tails.

I drove into the center of Pinecob first, trying to think what to buy, so as to have had a good excuse for leaving in the first place. I thought about getting Beau Ray some ice cream. A prescription would have worked, except it was Sunday night and the pharmacy was closed. Indeed, a lot of Pinecob was closed up and turned off, so I headed toward the Potomac and drove alongside that slow river a while, until I crossed a big bridge announcing the borderline of Virginia. I'd driven there a couple of times in the week following Joshua's arrest, but I wasn't too familiar with the state, and past Harper's Ferry, it was all foreign to me. But I kept on driving and listening to the radio, and singing along, loud as can be because it was dark and who was going to see me crooning like a fool? I kept going, sort of east some of the time, sort of south if I felt the urge. I passed schools and shopping malls and truck stops and fields, most of them dark. I passed a church all lit up, the parking lot overflowing onto the shoulder of the road. Finally, I pulled over at a strip mall to stretch my legs. I looked around. The stores there were the same as we had in Charles Town, but the land around was a lot flatter.

I looked at the gas gauge—I still had half a tank, more than enough to get me farther away, or if I turned around then, to get me home. I sat on the hood of the car, the engine warm and clicking beneath me, and looked into the dark ahead. I wondered whether, on the night he left, Vince's mood had been the same as mine right then. I didn't know if his leaving had been a spontaneous decision, if maybe he had been planning on going out for a soda or a drive, but with each mile told himself, just one mile more, until Pine-cob was long gone behind him. That's how I kept going whenever I went jogging. Just one step more. Just one tree more. Just one block more.

Or maybe he knew, from the moment he left, that he wasn't coming back. I wondered if he'd floored the accelerator on the way out of town. Whether he'd said goodbye to anyone. Why hadn't he said goodbye to anyone?

I found myself remembering an autumn day, back when I was six and Vince was eight. Vince's class had gone on a field trip to Cedar Creek Battlefield Park. Momma had signed on as a parent-chaperone and had dragged me along for educational purposes, she said. After the tour was over, when the rest of the kids were eating their lunches, Vince found a stick and started playing like it was a sword, jabbing and swinging. I remember thinking that it was the best stick ever and that I wanted to play with it, too. I was reaching for it just as Vince wheeled around, and the stick poked me hard in the cheek. I started crying and Momma yelled at Vince something fierce and took the best stick ever and broke it in half.

Vince didn't move a hair while Momma was hollering. It was like he was frozen. But as soon as Momma turned to tend to my face, he took off running, across the big field where the Civil War battle had raged, and on into the trees. The battlefield was surrounded by woods and bounded on one side by the Shenandoah River. Beyond the boundaries of the park stood a forest and beyond that, the start of the Blue Ridge Mountains.

No one could find Vince. The teacher was looking and the park ranger, and I remember sitting in our car and listening to some of the kids from Vince's class calling his name. In a panic, Momma telephoned my father, who drove over to the park straightaway. She was in tears by the time he arrived.

"He'll be back," Dad told Momma. Dad said that Vince was like a dog that needed time alone to lick his wounds. "You wait here," he told Momma. "Leanne and I will find him."

My father held my hand and we walked a path through the woods that sloped toward the Shenandoah River. At a fork, he turned to me and asked which way I thought Vince would have gone. I remember being scared to answer such an important question. I thought hard, then pointed at the river. I knew I wanted to see the river.

When we hit the water's edge, we followed the river downstream and in a ways came upon a man then about my grandfather's age. He sat on a folding stool, with a tackle box and a fishing pole. When he saw us, he nodded and motioned down the bank, maybe twenty feet farther on. Vince was sitting there quietly, fishing.

When Dad called out his name, Vince gave a start, like he was waking up. He reeled in his fishing line, stood up, and walked over.

"I'm sorry for hurting your face," Vince told me. "I didn't mean to."

Dad put his hand on Vince's shoulder. "Your momma's worried over you," he said. "We'd best get along back."

Vince nodded and gave his fishing pole back to the old man.

"I been watching him," the man told my father.

I thought about that man on and off as I was growing up. I used to wonder what he'd thought, seeing Vince emerge onto the bank in tears, like some runaway prince. I wished I could ask him. Whenever I asked Vince to tell the story, he claimed he couldn't remember much, other than his hook, baited with American cheese, sinking into the green river water.

There, in the roadway dark of Somewhere, Virginia, I thought about the old man. Nearly twenty years had passed so I figured that he probably had, too. And now my dad was dead and Vince was gone again. This time, we hadn't found him. He hadn't been found or hadn't let himself be found. Or maybe the worst, he couldn't be.

Somewhere in Virginia, I looked out at the road, both ends disappearing into the dark on either side of the strip mall. Somewhere else in the state, my brother Tommy was going about his life. Somewhere, back behind me, Beau Ray and the others were watching James Bond. I wondered who was having a better time, those who left or those who remained. My parents had lived out their whole lives in West Virginia, and that wasn't so unusual. A lot of folks lived all their years within a few miles of where they grew up. I figured it was people like Joshua who skewed the results—because looking at Pinecob, it seemed like most everyone had always been there and would always be there. I just had to figure out whether I'd be one of them. And if I wasn't, then when and to where?

I didn't even know where I was, just then, and that didn't seem a fortuitous way to start the decision-making process.

So I found a map in the glove compartment and located the town where I'd pulled over. It was a lot farther into Virginia than I'd expected. Maybe it was just that my mind had been elsewhere, but part of me wanted to take it as a sign. I'd traveled that far, singing along with the radio and watching fields pass. I might go even farther if I had a plan.

I wondered whether the same realization had hit Vince. A strip mall, a map. Maybe he'd pulled over to figure out where he was and seen how far *he'd* gone. I thought about California, where people so often went to reinvent themselves. Who said I couldn't do the same thing? What would happen if I just didn't go back? But then I thought about Beau Ray and the movie I was missing in our living room, and I knew I couldn't, not like that at least.

After a while, I turned the car around and headed back toward Pinecob. It took longer than I thought it would. There was construction along the route the map said was the shortest. And also I stopped to get Beau Ray some ice cream. By the time I got back, the house was dark. Everyone had gone.

Chapter 12

Day 36: the Fourth of July

Our backyard in Pinecob looked like this: you'd come out of the house through a sliding door in the back of the dining room, onto a deck Tommy had built years before. Nothing big, but it held a couple of chairs and one of those plastic all-weather tables. Then two steps down, you'd be in the backyard, with grass that Beau Ray kept mowed. Our backyard was much bigger than our front. It ran the length of the house and was maybe twenty-five, thirty feet across. At the far side stood a cluster of pine and oak trees that had felt to me like a deep, dark forest when I was little. Once I was older, it seemed more like a glen, protected and shady but tame, so that I stopped expecting to run across Bambi or Thumper in there.

A narrow ditch paralleled the far side of the trees, and after that rolled the big expanse of Brown's Field. Brown's Field was always called that, though officially its name was "the West Ridge field" and it was county land, facts I learned through my job at the clerk's office. At the far edge of the field sat the Pinecob Elks Lodge and VFW building.

All the time I'd lived there, people rarely hung out in Brown's Field. Teenagers would mess around in there on and off after dark (at least, I did, when I was one), and on Memorial Day and Veterans' Day, the men from the VFW would host a big spaghetti dinner and bingo raffle, and pull tables out to the field's edge. The only other time it regularly saw traffic was on the Fourth of July. The way the field sloped made it a good place to watch the fireworks that were annually set off over at the elementary school.

Beau Ray loved fireworks, and we'd spent many July fourths over at Brown's, a blanket spread out on the gangly grass. That's what I'd planned to do that year, too, though I'd figured on using lounge chairs instead of the usual blankets, since that Fourth of July was set to be soggy. It had rained the whole day before, and the sun had only broken through around three on the afternoon of the Fourth. Momma had gone to Elkins to visit Susan and the kids, so I was expected to stick close to home.

"Leanne, I expect you to keep the house from burning down" was how Momma said goodbye. You might think that we kept a fire stoked twenty-four hours by the frequency of that admonition. But far as I knew, our family hadn't ever suffered a fire, and there was no great Pinecob burn to warrant her worry either. Paulie's family once lost an outbuilding to fire, but that was because his father had been burning trash in a barrel, gone inside for a cold one and got distracted by a playoff football game on the television (another reason Momma had for disliking television). Paulie's father hadn't even known the building was on fire until a neighbor came knocking. Paulie's mother was in charge of all trash burning after that—but they lived on a farm outside of town, so I kind of figured things ran different over there. We took our trash to the dump.

On the morning of the Fourth, Momma packed up early for the trip to Elkins, saying she'd be back the next afternoon. She didn't mention it to me, but I knew she was picking up Judge Weintraub on her way out of town. I'd overheard her say so when she was on the phone with Susan. It bugged me that she hadn't said anything to me. She didn't even give me the chance to be gracious and adult about it.

I haven't taken a poll or anything, but I wouldn't be surprised to find other youngest kids who've had a hard time proving themselves grown-up to their family. To my mind, I should have had an easier time of it, considering all the mothering I was expected to do with Beau Ray. But there were certain things that Momma only talked to Susan about, because Susan was older and had had kids young, like Momma had, and because she had a husband. I figured such things seemed to Momma like proof of being fully human.

Anyhow, around five, Momma was long gone to Elkins and I was about to put a load of laundry in the washer when the doorbell rang. Beau Ray answered it and in walked Lionel and Scooter. They were carrying a cooler and paper bags full of steaks and hot dogs and buns.

"Hey, Leanne," Lionel said. "Happy Fourth."

"What're you doing here?" I asked him.

"We're barbecuing, right? Five o'clock," he said.

"I love bar-cue!" Beau Ray said. He looked thrilled.

"We are?" I asked. That was one more thing I hadn't heard about, but I told Lionel to make himself comfortable—he already knew where everything was kept. I said I'd be right back.

Joshua was down in the basement. As I was walking down the stairs, I heard the doorbell ring again.

"Joshua," I said to him.

He was looking at something on the computer. Without turning from the screen, he held up one hand in a gesture that said hush up and wait.

"Joshua," I said again.

"Just a sec," he said, and I waited while he finished whatever he was reading. "Okay. Yeah? What is it?"

"You tell me," I said. "Did you invite people over?"

"Huh?" He turned around to face me. He looked particularly sour.

"Did you invite people—Lionel, Scooter, I don't know who all—over? To barbecue today?"

"Oh, right," he said. "Yeah, last week." He started to turn back to the computer, but I wouldn't let him.

"Were you going to tell me?" I asked him.

He glanced over at me and rolled his eyes. "I didn't think it was a big deal," he said. He sighed. "Are you making it a big deal?"

"Are you going to go upstairs?"

"Of course," he said. But he tried to turn back to the computer again. "I'll be up in a little while," he said.

I swear, I thought I hadn't heard him right. "You're kidding, right?" I asked him. I mean, say you go out to eat and you order the steak and the person you're with orders the chicken. Both of the meals arrive, and you taste your steak and don't like it. Do you make the other person eat your steak simply because you ordered wrong? I felt like Joshua had just grabbed my day and started in on it. I'd had in mind a mellow Fourth of July, with lounge chairs in Brown's Field, watching fireflies and fireworks blink all together. I stood there, trying to figure out what had just happened and whether I suddenly had to be all social. Swear to God, Joshua could make me feel like the least mellow person alive.

"What's the big deal?" Joshua asked me.

"For one, you didn't ask. And for two, they're *your* guests. And they're here."

He stood up so quickly that his chair bumped the back of his legs and fell over. He didn't move to pick it up. I could tell he was pissed but so was I.

"Fine," he said as he brushed past me and headed up the stairs.

"Wait, so now *I'm* the bitch?" I yelled after him, but he didn't answer. I took that for a yes.

I stood there in the basement, looking at the upended chair, on its back like a dead thing. I listened to the sound of feet and conversation above me and wondered what was the point. I'd felt the same way the first night Joshua had been there, when I'd wondered how I would ever survive the summer. Now we were more than a third of the way through, and I was still trying to figure it out. In the most recent couple of weeks, there'd been a few times when I'd felt like we'd struck a truce. And then something like what had just happened would happen, and I would wonder how a stranger could make me feel so out of place in my own home. I felt like I was flying below the radar, going unnoticed in my own life. I was almost embarrassed that I'd ever imagined Joshua and me becoming friends.

I leaned up against the Ping-Pong table and stared at the wall calendar that hadn't yet been changed from June. The computer was still on.

"Hey, sunshine. You waiting for me to kick your ass in Ping-Pong?"

I turned around and saw Max smiling. "No," I said.

He frowned. "Uh-oh. Serious mood," he said. He went over to Joshua's chair, looked at it a moment, then righted it and tucked it back beneath the desk. "What's up?" he asked.

"Nothing. I'm fine. So how was the movie last Sunday?"

"Oh, right," Max said. "You never came back."

I felt my face redden when he said that. I guess I'd been hoping that he'd wondered about it all week. But it seemed like he'd forgotten I hadn't been there until I reminded him. I felt about as appealing as a spotty mushroom.

"Where'd you go anyhow?" Max asked.

"Just errands. Was the movie good?"

He nodded. "For James Bond, it was okay. Laura and Lisa were thrilled to meet Josh," he said. "I have a feeling they might find a reason to visit me again real soon."

He twirled a Ping-Pong paddle, then found a dusty ball on the floor and hit it over to me. I caught it in one hand. Such a relief when a guy you like tosses a ball or a Frisbee or something of that sort and you manage to catch it without some huge lunge or bobble. Especially when the rest of your moves aren't that graceful.

"You're not mad at me, are you?" Max asked.

I didn't know what he was talking about. "You?" I asked him. "No. Why?"

"First you cut out for the movie, and then I only heard about this barbecue from Lionel."

"You knew about it before I did," I told him. I tossed the Ping-Pong ball back and he lobbed it into the ceiling. "Maybe Joshua wanted to surprise me."

"Gotcha." He put the paddle down. "Let's go up. Paulie brought beer and a kiddie pool, and Scooter has a whole mess of bottle rockets," he said. "It'll be fun. We'll make it fun."

Apparently, Joshua had told Lionel to invite whomever. Apparently, he'd said that he wanted to meet a lot of new people. By five-thirty, there were maybe thirty folks in the backyard, grilling food, dunking their feet in Paulie's pool and drinking beer and whatever else they'd carried in. An hour later, there was near to twice that many, and a steady stream of randoms were finding their way through the trees from Brown's Field. In a bigger town, that might have become a problem, but this was Pinecob.

Of course, it turned out that I knew or least recognized most of them—acquaintances from high school I saw around town, friends of Lionel's I hadn't seen since we'd stopped dating, friends of friends of friends. And it had turned into one of those perfect early evenings of summer, almost but not quite too hot, so moods stayed up and people kept cool by spraying each other with a hose that someone had dragged out to fill the kiddie pool. Plus Lionel, bless his heart, had put a sign in the driveway, telling people to walk around to the backyard. And he'd locked the front door, which kept most people out of the house.

"Don't think I don't remember your momma," he said. "Anything happens and you can blame me. She likes me."

Scooter took charge of the grill, and I was impressed to see that there was a whole setup of coleslaw and potato salad and ketchup and mustard and relish and paper plates and plastic forks.

"You really didn't know about this?" Max asked. "Maybe Joshua *did* organize it to surprise you. I heard he's footing the bill for it."

I wasn't convinced. "Maybe," I said.

"Looks like he's having fun anyhow," Max said.

Joshua was standing with three women, who cocked their heads and played with their hair as he held forth about something. A fourth approached and handed him a drink. He took a gulp and said something that made the girls giggle. No doubt, he could have recited state capitals and they'd have been cooing.

"He's not supposed to be drinking. Alcohol, I mean," I said to Max.

"Maybe it's soda."

"Whatever. His party, his life," I said.

Who came up to me not ten minutes later but Loreen Dunbar. Loreen: Buccaneer waitress, Potomac Springs Senior High graduate, and before then, skank who went down on Howard Malkin while he and I were dating. Sure, it was years back, but since we hadn't been close beforehand and hadn't spoken much after, that betrayal remained the most obvious thing Loreen and I had in common.

Loreen came bopping up to me with Paulie on her tail. It looked to me like he was trying to score, but her posture said that he wouldn't, not that night, not unless something changed her mind. I found myself marginally more impressed with her because of that.

"Paulie, give me a minute with Leanne, will you?" Loreen said, and he shrunk off. "Leanne. Great party," she said.

"Thanks." I asked if the Buccaneer was closed for the Fourth and Loreen nodded.

"I don't think I've been over here since third grade," she said. "Remember your party?"

I nodded. She'd never have been to our house if Momma hadn't invited everyone in my class over for my eighth birthday.

"It hasn't changed much," Loreen said. "That deck wasn't there."

"Tommy built it," I told her, just to say something.

Loreen shifted around a bit, like her skirt was biting at her waistline. She looked at her watch, then back to me. "You still hate me?" she asked, all of a sudden.

I felt myself freeze and get hot at the same time. She didn't look mad, just curious. I took a quick internal inventory.

"No," I said, slowly, like I was listening to myself as the answer came out, trying to figure out if it was correct. "That wouldn't make much sense."

"Oh," Loreen said.

"But I don't like what you did, even if it was a while back."

"No," she said. "It's not something I brag to anyone about. I'm sorry it happened."

I nodded. Part of me started to feel bad for having referred to her as a skank all those years. I told myself that maybe I wouldn't have done that if she'd said all this sooner.

"It was a long time ago," I said. "I don't even know where Howard is. So it seems silly to keep on fighting over him."

"Last I heard, he was living in Martinsburg," Loreen said. I think I shrugged.

"But besides, look at you now, living with a movie star."

"Only literally," I said. "He's more a houseguest. Or house-arrest guest, you could say."

"Man, if Joshua Reed was living in my apartment, I'd be all over him, night and day."

I smiled at her and wished I had a beer. I thought maybe skank had been accurate after all.

"Max Campbell is sure looking good. I been thinking about asking him out, myself," Loreen went on. "We talk whenever he comes into the Buck."

"Oh, yeah?" I said. "What would you ask him to do?"

Loreen looked at me funny. "I don't know. The usual, I guess."

I wondered what her usual was. "I thought he was still hung up on Charlene," I said. "I always hear that."

Loreen frowned. "You think?" she asked. "I guess, maybe. But I see him out. Not so often as Lionel or Paulie, but out."

"You see him with girls out?" I asked.

Loreen shrugged. "But you know how they say that the best cure for a girl is another girl," Loreen said.

"Who says that?" I asked.

"It's just a saying," she said.

I figured I was pretty much done talking to Loreen for the night, so I told her that I needed a beer, and she nodded and let me walk away. On the way to the beer cooler, I looked around for Max, but I didn't see him anywhere.

"So you having a good time?" Lionel asked. He'd come up behind me and put his hands on my shoulders. "Josh mentioned you were kind of tense," he said, kneading his fingers around.

"I'm not tense," I said. But I think getting defensive like that kind of proved it.

"Hey, if it's about the party," Lionel said. "I didn't realize you didn't know. Sorry about that. It wasn't meant to be a surprise."

He kept massaging my shoulders. I remembered as he did how Lionel was one of those too-hard massagers. There was too much kneading and pinching, so that I always ended feeling more wound up than before he began.

"You guys really brought the works, didn't you? Down to my favorite mustard."

"That was me," Lionel said, and I took the opportunity to turn all the way around, so I could face him, but also so he would have to let go of my shoulders.

"Hey, thanks, Lionel," I said. "Nice of you to remember."

"Anything for you, little lady," he said. He said it with a drawl, like he was John Wayne or someone. I winced. Lionel always used that twang when he was giving a compliment or gearing up to be sweet. It was like he had to put on an act if he was going to be gentle. Like, the real Lionel, the manly Lionel, would never be caught dead saying "you matter to me." Instead, some twangy alter-ego was sent in to do the job. I didn't like it when we were dating, and I wasn't in the place for him to be sweet again. I liked Lionel and all, but I'd done enough treading water. That much I knew.

"Leanne and Lionel," Beau Ray said. He was walking by, and somehow he managed to sing that out and stuff a hotdog into his mouth at the same time.

"Aw, Beau Ray, can't a girl talk to an old flame without it meaning anything?" I asked. But it gave me an excuse to slip out of my one-on-one with Lionel. Beau Ray was fighting a summer cold that had socked him with an ear infection, so I told Lionel that I had to go get my brother's medicine. Lionel said he'd catch up with me later.

Scooter cornered me next, but all he wanted to know was where was Sandy. Scooter'd had a thing for Sandy going on four years at that point, but the barbecue was the first time I'd talked to him alone since finding out that Sandy wasn't ever likely to return his affections. Maybe I'd always known that Scooter was out of luck, but Alice was real confirmation.

"So Sandy's not coming? I sure as heck wish you'd known about this party," Scooter said. "Reckon you'd have invited her. I guess I should have called her personal."

"I think she made plans a few weeks ago," I told him. "She probably couldn't have come anyhow."

"She ain't been around much this summer," he said. "You still see her a lot?"

"On and off. You know, she's working in emergency now. I think she needs a lot more down time."

"She seeing anyone, do you know?" Scooter asked. "Oh, hey Josh," he said.

I looked up to see Joshua smiling unsteadily at the both of us.

"Is who seeing anyone? Leanne?" he asked.

"Have you met Leanne's friend Sandy?" Scooter asked.

"Have I ever," Joshua said. "Too bad she's playing on the other team," he said. "Or—wait—is she on my team? We're on the same team. I think that's right." He swayed a little bit.

"What's that?" Scooter asked. "What team is that?"

"Joshua's just kidding around," I said. "You know, he met Sandy early on, and they talked all about baseball." I gave Joshua my best shut-up stare. He didn't so much shut up as wander off, which worked just as well. I smiled at Scooter.

"She likes baseball?" Scooter said. "Maybe I should invite her to a game."

I watched him wander back to the grill to add another round of sausages. I'd always liked the fact that Scooter would talk about how much he liked Sandy. I might talk to Sandy about how much I liked Max, but it scared me to death to think about saying anything like that to his face. But

I knew that if Sandy had been at the party, Scooter would have been telling her the same thing he told me. He put himself out there. I was sorry that he wasn't going to get what he wanted, but then, I figured, who did? What percentage?

The heat and light of the day were both fading, and it was getting on time for the fireworks. I sat down on a corner of the deck, my legs swinging off.

"Mind if I sit?" Max asked, then dropped beside me before I could answer. He took a sip of his beer and looked out toward the trees and Brown's Field. "Lots of people out tonight," he said.

"You having a good time?" I asked him. "Everyone being nice to you?"

"Sure. Why wouldn't they be?"

I shrugged.

"I've seen a lot of people I hadn't in a while. Loreen's sure in fine form," he said.

"What do you mean?" I asked him. "Why would you say that?"

Max looked like he wasn't sure what he should say next. "You two buddies now?" he asked.

"No," I said. "I talked to her for a little while. That's all."

"Huh. I never thought the two of you were tight. She probably had too much to drink, that's all," he said. "It's nothing. Forget it. You like the Fourth?" he asked.

I told him that I liked the general lack of build-up, how it's just one day. The fifth and everything's gone back to normal.

"That's not a very celebratory attitude," Max said. "It's our country's birthday, after all."

"I got Beau Ray's birthday at the month's end. That's enough."

From where Max and I sat, I knew we'd only see the fireworks now and again, the brightest ones that shone through the leaves, or those that shot so high they cleared the tops of the trees. I didn't want to move though. I liked sitting next to him.

I looked down the length of our yard at all the people milling around, talking, laughing, drinking, and I suddenly hit up against a wave of melancholy, smack dead on. I couldn't remember the last time I'd laughed really hard, so hard that you go silent and your stomach muscles feel like they're going to give. I turned to Max.

"Am I a bitch?" I asked him.

"What?" he said. He laughed a little, then looked at me harder. "Why are you asking *me* that?"

"You've known me forever. Do you think I take things too seriously? Am I a downer? Am I uptight?"

"Is this about the barbecue?" Max asked.

"You know, I was fine before all this happened. Wasn't I?"

"Sure you were," Max said. "You've always been."

"Sure I was. I was fine. I was doing my job. I was going to school. I was happy. Or at least fine."

Max nodded.

"And now I've got this movie star in my house that everyone's crazy about and I'm the bad guy all the time. Or a loser. Or a hillbilly."

"You're not the bad guy," Max said. "I'm sure there's a lot that you see that other people don't see."

"There is," I told him. "You have no idea."

Max smiled. "You're not a bitch, or a loser, or a hillbilly," he said. "Maybe you're just tired."

I was very aware of the way our feet and ankles bumped, as both of us swung our legs off the deck. He kept looking at me, and I thought that I noticed him lean in a little bit, so I leaned in a little bit. Most of me was trying to remain all calm, but inside my head, there was this circus of voices saying something like "Oh my God! You're practically kissing Max Campbell!"

But then there was a shriek from someone in the crowd. I thought that the fireworks must have started, but they hadn't, not yet. Max suddenly turned around, so I pulled back. I could see people pointing to our roof, to someone who was up on it.

There's not much to say about the roof of our house on Prospect Street, except that it was slanted, not steep, but not shallow either. I'd been up there only once, when I was a kid and my dad was fixing a leak. I remember holding nails in my hand, and handing them to him one by one each time he asked. I remember him telling me to be very careful because the tiles could get slippery, and there wasn't much to grab if you fell.

"Joshua Reed's on the roof!" someone said.

I stood up. "Hey!" I called out to no one in particular. I left the deck and walked over to where the figure was standing on our roof. "Hey!" I called up to him.

It was Joshua all right. He looked down at me and bobbled a bit.

"Hey, Leanne, favorite fan," he called down. "Come on up. View's great up here."

"How did you get up there?" I asked, then saw a ladder leaning against the side of the house.

"Come on up," he said again.

He lifted his cup in a toast to all of us standing below him, two stories down, but his footing must have slipped. He stumbled backward suddenly, catching himself with one arm, but not before letting go of his drink. A sticky-sweet mix of soda and whiskey poured down. I couldn't duck in time, and got sprayed by it. An ice cube beamed me in the head.

"Whoa!" he said. "My bad. Can someone bring me another Jack and Coke?"

"Why don't you come down?" I said. "It's pretty slick up there." I tried to wipe his drink out of my hair.

"View's better," he said. "I got good balance. Who wants to join me up here? Lionel? Where's Scooter?" He looked around at the crowd below him.

"You'll get the same view from Brown's Field," I told a couple standing beside me. "I'd rather people not go up there."

It didn't look like Joshua was getting any takers when I headed inside to blot his Jack and Coke from my clothing. In the kitchen were two of the girls I'd seen Joshua talking to earlier on. I wondered if anyone else was wandering through our house.

"Hi," I said. "I'm Leanne. I don't think we've met."

"Christy," one of them said to me. "That's Marsha."

"Nice to meet you," I said. "Can I help you find something?"

"Oh, no. We're just looking around." Christy was staring into our refrigerator. Marsha had a cabinet open.

"Yeah, I live here," I said. "Can I help you find something?"

Christy shut the refrigerator door. "Oh, I'm sorry!" she said. "How rude."

I shrugged. I was glad to see that Joshua's drink wasn't leaving a stain on my black T-shirt.

"You live with Josh Reed?" Marsha asked. "She lives with Josh Reed," she said to Christy.

"I heard," Christy said.

"We're sort of trying to keep the party outside," I said. "No offense. It's just, you know, my mother, all these people…"

"Oh, sure," Christy said.

"Of course," Marsha said.

I studied them for a moment. They looked like nice girls—a few years younger than I was in years. Maybe more in other ways. Who knows? Maybe less.

"What's it like living with him?" one of them asked.

"I'm so jealous!" the other squealed.

"You want to see his room?" I asked them. Maybe I offered because they were a lot nicer to me than Joshua was. Or else maybe I just wanted them to look at me with even half the interest they'd shown to him.

It was nice to be able to offer something like that, something that people wanted. To have people think you're cool, without having to convince them first. All evening, I'd felt it. People I hadn't seen in ages kept coming up to me, talking to me with a light in their eyes I hadn't sparked before. It was seductive. I had to keep reminding myself to pay attention. I had to keep reminding myself about the drunk girl on our lawn. My celebrity was borrowed. It had an expiration date.

"Follow me," I told Christy and Marsha, heading toward the stairs.

"This is so cool!" I heard one of them whisper.

Joshua's door was open, and we walked right in. One of the girls stopped at his bed and buried her face in his pillow.

"I'm smelling Josh Reed!" she said.

Joshua's window was open, and I could have sworn that it had been closed just ten minutes earlier. Maybe he hadn't used the ladder after all, I thought. I stuck my head out the window to see if he was still out there. He was, but now he wasn't alone, and I felt a surge of adrenaline sour my stomach. There was Beau Ray, making his way across the roof.

"Hey, man. That's it," Joshua was saying.

"Beau Ray!" I called out. "Stop!"

Beau Ray stopped where he was and turned his head slowly toward me.

"Hey Beau Ray, that's not cool," I said. "Come on back inside."

"The fires," Beau Ray said to me. "I can see them better."

"I know," I said. "But if you really want to see them, we'll go over to the field. Remember how we always watch them from Brown's Field?" I put a hand on the roof tiles. They were still damp, almost spongy from the rain.

Beau Ray took a step and slid a little. His arms wheeled around for balance, and then he was steady again.

Joshua laughed. "Watch it there, buddy," he said.

"Beau Ray," I said again. "Please."

"Leanne, don't be such a spoilsport," Joshua said. "It's fine. He's fine."

"Butt out!" I snapped at him. "You don't know." People down on the lawn were beginning to stare.

"Just chill out," Joshua said.

Beau Ray inched forward a bit more. His posture was rigid.

"Yo, Bobo, you all right up there?" It was Max, from down below.

"Smax," Beau Ray said. He sounded nervous. "I'm high up. I'm up the roof!"

"Why don't you come down?" Max said. "Here—I've got something to show you."

It was eight-thirty just then. It must have been, because the first of the fireworks went off. There was an audible popping sound, and then a bloom of white and red broke into view. I could hear applause and some oohs from Brown's Field. Beau Ray looked up, raised his hands a little, and promptly lost his footing. He fell backward, skidding on his right hip, down toward the gutter and the edge of the roof.

Far off, it seemed, I could hear gasps below me. "Oh, shit!" I heard someone say. And, "He fell!" But my voice wouldn't make a sound.

This was the fire, the house burning that Momma had trusted me to keep from happening, and yet I was frozen there, watching my brother slide, watching his hands grab for something, anything, only there was nothing to hold. His feet hit the gutter and bounced off, his legs kicking a bit, with nothing but air beneath them.

And then, somehow, he slowed down, slowed to a stop, his legs dangling, but his upper body still pressed to the roof. He had dug his fingernails into the tiles and that had managed to keep him from going over. I could see him shaking as he lay there, but he hadn't gone over.

"Beau Ray!" I screamed to him, finding my voice again. "Hold on, okay? Can you hold on?"

"Whoa," I heard Joshua say. He sat back down on the roof.

"Grab that ladder," I heard Max say. In a moment, the ladder was set beneath Beau Ray's dangling legs.

"Can you feel the top of the ladder, Beau Ray?" Max asked.

Beau Ray shook his head. Now that he'd stopped sliding, he seemed unwilling to make another move.

"I'm going to climb up, okay? I'm going to lead you down," Max said. With the ladder propped against the roof, Max climbed up. He put a hand on Beau Ray's leg.

"No!" Beau Ray yelled.

"Bobo, it's just me," Max said. "Is that okay?"

"I was sliding," Beau Ray said.

"I've got you now. Let's get you down."

I felt like I could finally breathe again. I pulled my head back inside and hustled Christy and Marsha out of the room, into the hall and back downstairs.

"Wanna bet the party's over?" I heard Christy say to Marsha.

Down on the lawn, I found Beau Ray in one of the lounge chairs, picking at his fingernails, now black with gunk and tar. He was rocking back and forth. The fireworks continued to pop and sputter through the trees. A few people came up and patted Beau Ray on the shoulders, saying things like, "You okay, man?" and "Dude, that was a close one." He didn't seem to like the attention.

"It's not like you were ever good with heights," Max said. "Remember when you fell out of our treehouse?"

Beau Ray smiled.

"That was, like, three feet off the ground," Max said.

"Sorry Leanne," Beau Ray said. "I scratched the roof."

"Do you want to watch the rest of the fireworks over in Brown's Field?" I asked him.

Beau Ray shook his head. "From here's good," he said.

I pulled up the other lounge chair and sat beside him, and we watched the fireworks, as best we could through the trees, listening to the oohs and aahs around us.

After the big finale, people started to wander off, and within a half hour, the party was pretty much over. Lionel and Scooter hustled people out, then followed, carrying clinking bags of bottles and plastic cups.

"Did Joshua make it down okay?" I asked Lionel.

He nodded. "I think he ended up watching the fireworks with a couple of those girls," he said.

"Keep the wading pool," Paulie said. He left with his arm around Loreen.

"Say hi to Sandy, when you see her next," Scooter said.

"The kitchen's clean," Max said. I was surprised to hear his voice. I thought he'd wandered off during the fireworks.

"You're still here," I said.

"You want me to go?" he asked. "I figured I'd help clean."

"No, I mean, stay. However long you want."

"Well, the kitchen's clean," he said again. He cocked his head. "Who's upstairs?" he asked.

I listened hard, and heard laughter. "Will you check on Beau Ray?" I asked Max. "I'll be right back."

I walked upstairs, and heard the noise again. I clenched my jaw. People like Max were downstairs cleaning up Joshua's party and there he was, behind his closed door, with some girl laughing. I knocked once and opened the door.

Marsha and Christy were sitting on Joshua's bed. One was in her bra. The other wore one of Vince's football jerseys. They were watching Joshua tell some sort of story. He was standing in his underwear and ankle sensor, making a sweeping hand gesture. When he saw me, he stopped what he was doing, dropped his arms to his sides, and shook his head. I shook my head right back at him. Then I turned to the girls.

"Both of you need to go. Now," I said. "You, take off that jersey. You, find your shirt."

The girls started to grab for their clothes.

"Hi, mom," Joshua said.

"Shut up," I snapped at him. "Max!" I called downstairs. "When the girls come down, will you make sure they get the fuck out of my house?"

"You need any help?" Max hollered.

I said no and turned back to Joshua. I could feel my heart beating fast and mad.

"This isn't working," I said. "I'm going to talk to Judge Weintraub. There's got to be another option."

"What?" Joshua asked.

"This. You, here in this house. You throw a party without asking, get drunk, almost get Beau Ray killed—"

"He's fine," Joshua said.

"That's luck, not because it was okay to do it! You hardly know Beau Ray," I said.

"Oh, please. I've lived with the guy for the past five weeks."

"You don't know the first thing about him! You watch TV with him and teach him card games! You don't know that his night vision isn't good. Or that he gets off balance easily. You haven't been here for a seizure. That was dangerous for him! Way more than for you or me. I can't…I can't have you here anymore. I can't deal with it. I feel like I'm the one being punished."

"You're just pissed because of the party, and that I didn't tell you," Joshua said. "Fine. I spaced. Sue me for that if you want. But people had a good time, and everyone's fine, so what's the problem? You're always dumping on me."

"*I'm* dumping on *you?*" I said. I was trying to keep myself from shrieking. "Forget it. You're drunk."

"So what?"

"So you're not even trying."

"What am I supposed to be trying to do? Be happy here in Pinecob? Be your best friend? That's not the deal."

"You're not supposed to be drinking," I reminded him.

"I was in a bad mood, so I had a drink. Big deal. You know, all I've been is nice to you."

"This is you being nice? You've insulted me since you met me. You treat me like a servant. You're arrogant."

The girls were dressed now, standing in the doorway, silent. I turned to them.

"You know, it's not like he actually likes you. He doesn't give a fuck who you are. You're just a couple more girls who were willing to take your clothes off for him. I bet he doesn't even know your names," I said.

They looked over at him. They had pleading eyes.

"Well?" I asked Joshua.

He didn't say anything.

"What are they?" I pointed to the one who'd had her shirt off. "What's her name?" I asked him.

Joshua looked away.

"Either one? No?" I turned back to the girls. "You'd best be going," I said.

Christy and Marsha slipped down the hallway.

"Really nice," Joshua said to me. "You sent them off feeling good about themselves, didn't you?"

"You had nothing to do with that?" I asked him.

"You didn't have to tell them," he said. "They wouldn't have known."

"No, you'd just wait for them to overhear it someday."

Joshua frowned. "What are you talking about?"

But I shook my head and walked out. "Christy and Marsha," I told him from down the hall.

"Right!" I heard him say. "Damn."

"Are they gone?" I asked Max, when I got back downstairs. He nodded. "What did you say to them?"

"Nothing," I said. "Why?"

"One of them looked like she was crying."

"I just—" I started to say "—nothing. God, he drives me crazy!" I slumped on the couch. "I don't know what I'm doing here."

Max sat down next to me but a second later he stood up again. Beau Ray had wandered in from his bedroom. He was wearing pajamas and complaining that he couldn't sleep.

"I'm hungry," Beau Ray whined.

"There's all sorts of leftovers in the kitchen," Max told him.

Beau Ray wandered off, and I could hear him unwrapping foil packages and peeking under plastic lids. He came out with a mug of coleslaw and a plastic fork, and started to wander back toward his room.

"Make sure that doesn't get knocked over," I said. "Remember last time. The ants?"

Beau Ray turned to me, smiled, and with a mouthful of coleslaw managed to sing, "Leanne and Lionel," before disappearing back into his room.

I turned to Max. "He's been saying that since the night we all saw *Die Hard*. It's getting really annoying."

"I'll bet," Max said.

"It's not like anything is going on, with him, Lionel, not anything." But by the look on Max's face, I wasn't sure if he believed me. "You want anything?" I asked him. "A drink? Snack?"

"No, I'm good," he said.

He puttered around the room, picking up things and putting them down. I watched him from the couch, willing him to sit beside me again. He picked up an old family photograph, one with all of us in it, taken when I was nine or ten. I had buck teeth and really bad hair. He looked at it, looked back at me and smiled. And then he did what I wanted—he came back to the couch and sat down.

"Remember when I looked like that?" I asked him.

"You've improved with age," Max said.

I smiled back at him. "So have you," I said. "If that's possible."

"Is my script down there?" It was Joshua this time, yelling from the top of the stairs. Max stood again. "Oh, never mind. I found it," Joshua yelled.

"Listen," Max said. He glanced at his watch. "I should go. I've got to open the store in the morning. Like you said— July fifth, it's all back to normal."

"You're leaving?" I stood up, too.

"Yeah." He shrugged. "But I was thinking, if you have a free evening, maybe we could see a movie. Or a play even, if there's one around. Maybe next week or something. If you want and have the time. I'd even see a musical."

"Are you kind of asking me out?" I asked him. I wanted to be sure.

"We don't have to," Max said.

"I didn't say no," I told him. "I wouldn't say no."

He smiled. "Listen, I'm beat," he said. "I'm not making any sense. I'm sure I'll talk to you later this week." He leaned in and I thought, "this is it, we're going to kiss," but he gave me a peck on the forehead instead.

After Max left, I wandered around the living room, picking up and putting down the same things he had, trying to slip myself into his frame of mind. When he'd said, "I'm not making any sense," did that mean that the whole asking-me-out part had been nonsensical? Had I misinterpreted it? I wished I could go over it with Sandy, but it was too late then to call her.

I turned off the living room lights, and also a lamp in the kitchen that Beau Ray had left burning, so it couldn't fall over in the night and catch the house on fire. There was still a light on in the basement, so I went downstairs to turn that off, too. A little desk lamp by the computer was lit. I bent over to turn it off and doing so jostled the computer enough to bring the screen back up.

On-screen was a window showing an article from *People* magazine. It must have been what Joshua was reading before the party started. Of course, I sat down to take a look. It's not like it was a private e-mail or anything.

The article was called "All-American Dream Come True," and it was a profile of Elise. It talked about how great Elise's life had been in recent months, how her contract with All-American Cosmetics had been renewed, how she'd left a failing relationship (with Joshua) and started a new one that she was swooning over. Joshua was referred to as her "Bad boy-toy ex." Elise's new man, actor Clayton Crawford, was called a "serious Oscar contender" and "one of the hottest names in Hollywood." The article went on to quote Elise as saying that she'd "always known that Joshua wasn't the one, but he was just so good-looking. With Clayton, I get looks and so much more! I'm happy again!"

I felt bad. I wondered if Joshua ever got good mail. I knew he didn't get many phone calls—maybe because his cell phone didn't work in our house—and most were from Judy or Lars. And he never talked about his family. I realized that if I'd been in his shoes, I probably would have wanted to meet new people, too—even if I'd have gone about it differently.

I turned off the light and the computer, and went back upstairs. This time, it was Joshua who couldn't sleep, but I didn't figure that a mug of coleslaw would do the trick. He was sitting on the long couch, flipping through our five channels, over and over.

"Nothing on?" I asked him.

"Are you kidding?"

The channels continued to cycle by. We got a lot of static channels, too. I hadn't realized just how many empty spaces there were.

"Listen, I saw that article in *People*," I said. "The one about Elise, where she says—"

"I know the one," Joshua said.

"You know, you can't let those get you down. They don't know you."

"I know they don't," he said. He still hadn't looked at me.

"I've got piles of articles saying what a great actor you are—you've seen them."

"I know you do." He just sat there, the channels still cycling by.

"Is it that she's dating Clayton Crawford? He's a good actor, but you're at least that good."

Joshua finally looked over at me. "What are you doing?" he asked me, his voice sharp.

"Cheering you up," I said. "Or trying."

"Don't. I don't need it."

I nodded. "Okay."

"I'm the one who's stuck here."

I didn't say anything.

"It's driving me fucking crazy!" he said. I hoped Beau Ray was asleep. "Why doesn't it drive you crazy? How can you be so complacent? How can you just live here, day after day, just live here? How do you not get totally sick of it?"

"I do," I said. "But at this point—"

"Jesus, who's in charge anyhow? Your mom? That guy Vince who left? Your dad? He's dead."

"In charge of what?" I asked.

"You." Joshua spat that out like it should have been obvious.

"I am," I said, but I could hear that I didn't sound sure.

"Oh, please."

"I *am*."

"You do exactly what people expect you to do. You're like the perfect little Nazi. Plod, plod, plod."

"That's not fair," I said.

"Oh, right. I'm not fair. The rest of this sorry-ass setup is just fine, but *I'm* not fair. Don't you see *anything?* Go to bed."

"It's not that simple," I said. "You don't know."

"I don't *care.*" His jaw was clenched. So was mine.

"You want to tell me what about me bugs the shit out of you? Because let me tell you, I'm not trying to bug you. This is just the way I am."

"Whatever you say," Joshua muttered.

I got up and walked halfway up the stairs, then came back down. "You know—" I started, but he cut me off.

"Go to bed," Joshua said. "Go to bed, work your little job, get yourself a little local boyfriend to marry and never leave this shithole little town."

"You think you know everything. You think your way is the only way that's worth anything. You don't know a thing. Elise was right to dump you. Anyone would be better off without you."

I like to think that he started to say something but couldn't think of a comeback. But I'll never know for sure. I turned back around before he had the chance to speak, and I stomped back up the stairs.

Chapter 13

The Truth of It

Two days later was another open AA session. Grant Pearson had called to remind me, and since he used to be my teacher, I felt some weird obligation to attend. Joshua and I hadn't spoken since our exchange the night of the barbecue, and we didn't speak on the way to the meeting. We didn't speak during the meeting either, though others got up and told plenty of stories. Homer recounted the same tale as before, but if he were still trying to figure how he knew Joshua, he didn't say.

Near the end, Grant Pearson stood at the microphone. He said that all holidays can be a tough time, that they brought up both family memories and family stress. I thought about Fourth of Julys as a kid with my mother and father and Tommy and Susan and Vince and Beau Ray. We were our own little army. "The Gitlin Gang," my dad called us. I remembered him buying a huge submarine sandwich, setting it out on the dining room table, and letting all us kids take a bite at the same time. I remember laughing so hard I sucked lettuce up my nose.

I glanced over at Joshua and saw him roll his eyes and suddenly all my anger was sitting there between us. He thought he knew so much, but he didn't know squat, not about me or my family at least. Not enough to play judge like he'd been playing. Grant Pearson paused for a moment and looked around the room. I felt myself stand. Out of the corner of my eye, I could see Joshua look over at me, but I kept staring ahead. I didn't walk to the microphone, just started talking where I stood.

"My name is Leanne," I said. I didn't wait for the room to say "hi, Leanne," like they always did when people introduced themselves. I just barreled into it. "When I was fourteen, a drunk driver killed my father," I said. I could feel everyone's eyes on me. I kept talking.

"My brother Vince, he'd just gotten his license, so my dad was letting him drive back from a football game Vince had played in over in Charles Town. Vince said that Dad had been telling him how he should…how he should slow down before green lights just a little, you know, in case someone wasn't stopping from the other direction. And he did, Vince did slow down, you know, at that light at Main and Bunting."

I took a breath. I could feel a choke starting in my voice.

"But then he forgot…he forgot to slow a little before that light by the post office." I remembered Vince telling me that. "He said there was a song on that he liked, and he just forgot—you know, God, he was only sixteen. What sixteen-year-old boy remembers anything? But there was this guy—he ran the light and he hit the passenger side of our car, where my dad was sitting."

I heard a woman behind me start to cry, but I kept talking because I knew if I didn't say it all then, I never would.

"We heard later how the guy, he'd been laid off that day. He'd been in a bad mood, so he'd been drinking. And he'd gotten into a fight with one of his friends, and stormed out, and I guess he just didn't stop storming. I don't know if he saw the red light or not. He never braked. He died, too, like a week later. Vince, he didn't see anything coming. I don't know if Dad did or not. Dad died right away. Before they even got him out of the car. Vince had this big bruise and a cut on his head, but that's all. You know, physically."

I felt the whole room looking at me. I saw Grant Pearson looking at me. He nodded, like I should feel free to keep going.

"I know accidents happen. They do. That's why it's a cliché—accidents happen—because it's true. And I'm sure the guy, he didn't mean to. He didn't get in his car thinking that he might kill someone, or himself. But that mood of his— that single bad mood of his, it changed my life. It really messed things up and a lot of my plans. You know, why couldn't he just…deal? I mean, I deal. I deal every day."

I had to wipe my eyes at that point. I thought either I was going to make it through or I'd never make it anywhere. So I had to make it through.

"I came back from a movie with my friend Sandy and there were two police cars in our driveway. And Momma told me my dad was dead. And maybe three months later, Vince was gone, just up and left. I was fourteen. Did I say that already?" I sat back down.

No one said anything for a while. Finally, Grant Pearson cleared his throat, and since he was at the microphone, everyone heard it and turned back to look at him.

"We're a small community," Mr. Pearson said. "I know that some of you already knew Leanne's story. Some of you knew Tom. And Vince."

I winced hearing my brother's name. It was easier to speak about him than to hear him be spoken about, especially when it was put in the past tense.

"And for some of you, that was new, and maybe hard to hear." Someone behind me blew his nose. "But all of you here deserve our thanks, because you are trying, one step at a time, one day at a time, so that you don't become part of a story like that. God bless and good night."

With that, the meeting was over.

Joshua said nothing as we walked to the car. We got in and as soon as he'd closed the door, he turned to me.

"You must hate me," he said.

"You didn't kill anyone," I said. "What you did—it was selfish and careless, but you didn't kill anyone."

"I could have hurt Beau Ray. And I almost killed a cow," he said, then he laughed. "I don't mean it like that." He paused. "I'm really sorry, Leanne."

"It was a long time back," I said.

"No. Not that. Not just that," Joshua said. "I'm sorry I didn't ask before now. Here, I've been living in your house. I should have known. I should have asked."

I glanced over at him. He looked very serious, and it wasn't an expression I had seen before. I put the key in the ignition.

"I should get you back," I said. "It's nine-fifteen." I started the car and pulled out of the parking lot.

"Is that why Vince left?" Joshua asked.

"I think so," I said. "I think it was leave or else he would have taken his own life, and that would have killed Momma for sure. You know, so in a way, maybe it was better, him leaving. That's just a guess though."

"Jesus," Joshua said. "Everyone splits, don't they?"

"In one way or another, yeah. So far."

"But you stay."

"So far. Everyone else beat me to the door. Can I ask you something?" I asked. "Speaking of families."

Joshua nodded. "Here it comes. You want to know about mine," he said. "Like why haven't I called them in the past month, or why they haven't called me?"

I nodded. "Why not?"

"Which?"

"Either," I said.

"They never call me," he said, after a little while thinking. "That's not exactly true. My sister will, every season or so. If she needs something. But I'm sure Lars has taken care of it if she's called in the last few weeks. He usually takes care of it."

"You don't call them?"

"Nah," Joshua said, shaking his head. "I used to, more at least. My parents don't approve of my lifestyle. They've never been too interested in anything I've done. They never wanted to see any of my work. You know, I'd invite them, but there'd always be an excuse."

"They've never seen you act?" I asked.

"No, they've seen me," Joshua said. "They came to see a play that I was in, in Austin. I think a friend of theirs must have told them about it, because I never would have. It was a stretch—I was playing this gay guy, and I had to kiss one of the other actors. It was a great role, a really great play. Actually, that's the play that got me the audition for *The Young and the Restless.* It was this really strong role. I loved it. Anyway, so my parents came to see it." Joshua took a breath. He paused for a few seconds, like he was remembering. "My father walked up to me afterward and punched me. In front of everyone. The whole cast. The director. Just clocked me. Said he'd never been so ashamed having a faggot for a son."

"But didn't you explain—"

"What? Why?"

I didn't know what else to say. I told him that I was sorry.

"Yeah, well," Joshua said. His composure had returned. "It's their life. But I figured that, with this house arrest thing, now probably isn't the time to make overtures, you know? The last thing I want is for my father to show up here and get to say, 'see, I always said you were a fuckup.'"

"He wouldn't say that, would he?"

"I don't see why not," Joshua said.

I pulled the car into the driveway, and we unbuckled our seat belts but neither one of us got out.

Joshua turned to me. "I am sorry, though," he said. "I mean it. I'm glad that you told me about your dad."

"I told everyone."

"That took guts."

"I was pissed at you," I said. "That made it easier."

We sat in the car, neither one of us saying anything. The motion lights had gone on when we pulled up, and a light wind was making the lawn shadows dance.

"I didn't make you steal that limo," I said.

"Borrow," he said. "But I know."

"Do you?" I asked him.

"I do. You didn't. You had nothing to do with it."

"And I didn't make you come stay here. I know I mentioned the spare room and Judge Weintraub—"

"I know. I know. None of this is your fault."

"Because you act like you've been blaming me for it. It feels personal."

He took a deep breath and nodded. "I don't mean—" he said, then stopped.

I waited for him to say more. I knew there must be more.

"You remind me of me, I think it is. And I guess that means Rackett and I so hated Rackett. And this house. The whole small-town thing. It's just so familiar. But that's not your fault."

I nodded.

"So can I stay?" he asked.

I looked over at him and considered it. The motion lights flicked off and left us in darkness. "For now," I said. I could make out a smile in the silhouette of his face.

"Are you still pissed at me?" he asked. "You have every right to be."

"I know," I said. But I wasn't. "Not at the moment anyway."

"Thank God. I've got enough people in the yes column." He paused. "Thanks again for all you've done. And letting me stay. I mean it."

"Fifty-one more days and you're outta here," I said.

Chapter 14

Time Passes

After that, it's funny, but we started getting along better. Like clearing a field of rocks before you start to plant. The difference in the car, the easing in his silhouette, these remained. They were present the next morning, when I came downstairs—later than usual—and found Joshua and Beau Ray making a mess of the kitchen and calling it breakfast.

Joshua had brewed some tar-strong coffee I had to water down to swallow. He'd put Beau Ray in charge of making toast, and it was clear that Joshua didn't know about Beau Ray's fascination with the toaster. By the time I set foot in the kitchen, Beau Ray had toasted up more than half a loaf of Sunbeam. I said that would probably do, what with Momma not home yet from Judge Weintraub's.

Later, after I'd dressed for work, I found them in Beau Ray's room. Joshua was sitting on my brother's bed—which was made, actually made—looking at a family photo album from when we Pinecob Gitlins were all under the same roof.

Joshua looked up when I came in. He had this huge grin on his face. "Leanne, I swear to God, you are physical proof of the beneficial aspects of aging," he said.

He held out the album, pointing at one snapshot in particular. There I was, in our backyard, body like a sausage, no curves at all until you got to the top of my head and started down again. I was eleven. The picture snapped Beau Ray and Max—both fifteen—and me and Sandy, all in the backyard at the end of a water-balloon fight that Sandy and I looked to have borne the brunt of.

"Sandy looks pretty much the same now," Joshua said. "But you—it's like I can hardly see your face in this girl. Look at you, eyeing Max. You guys *have* known each other a long time."

I nodded quickly and turned to Beau Ray, who was digging for something in the back of his closet.

"Beau Ray," I said. "I've got to get ready for work. Have you taken your medicine?"

"He did. I saw him," Joshua said. "I asked him to show me these. I hope that's okay."

I looked back at Joshua right as Beau Ray emerged with a laugh and an armful of old high-school yearbooks.

"That's fine," I told Joshua, then said that I'd see them after work.

Momma had asked me to start getting a list together for Beau Ray's birthday party at the end of July. Of course, there was Susan and the kids and Tommy. And Sandy. And Beau Ray's friends from physical therapy. And Max and the guys.

I wanted to give my brother Tommy the most notice, since sometimes he took construction jobs down at the very bottom of the Shenandoah Valley and would likely need a little more advance word to get off work. But everyone was keen to celebrate Beau Ray's thirtieth birthday.

We had talked to a number of doctors after Beau Ray's

accident. The first of them believed that my brother wouldn't make it through the night. And of course, he did. The second one said he'd probably not walk or speak again. The third one said that he'd most likely die from a seizure before he was thirty. And not only had that not happened, but the incidents of bad seizures had lessened in the passing years. We weren't in the clear by a long shot, but Beau Ray's thirtieth still seemed cause for celebration.

I paged Tommy during my lunch break and a few minutes later, he called me back.

"Anything wrong?" he asked.

I said no.

"You knock over any apple carts lately?" He laughed.

If I'd been closest to Vince, I'd surely been farthest from Tommy, both in age and disposition. "I was calling to remind you that Beau Ray's birthday party is coming up."

"Oh, yeah," Tommy said.

"He's going to be thirty," I said. "Momma wanted to make sure it got on your calendar. Where are you?"

"I'm working a job out by Blacksburg," he said.

"That Virginia?"

"Well, duh, Leanne. Look at a map." That's the exact sort of comment that kept me far off from Tommy. "I'll try to make it, but I can't promise I'll be able to get the time off. Summer's the busy season," he said.

"I know Beau Ray'd love to see you," I told him.

"Well, sure," Tommy said. "I said I'd try to make it."

But to Tommy, it seemed like every season or month or week was too busy. Susan, of course, would come, with her kids. And Joshua would be there. The party would go on with or without Tommy, just like every other day did.

That night, Joshua asked if I might help him run lines for *Musket Fire*. I read the part of Elizabeth, who was the minister's daughter—the shrew character, if you were going to compare *Musket Fire* to *The Taming of the Shrew,* like the California crowd always did. I tried to make her sound passionate and conflicted but not at all lusty. But Joshua couldn't concentrate. He kept correcting his words and revising his accent, and finally gave up and threw the script down.

"You weren't in any of Beau Ray's yearbooks," he said.

I nodded. That was on account of our age and grade differences.

"So can I see yours?" he asked me. I wanted to know why. "To get a better sense of you back then. You know, life history stuff."

"Why?" I asked him again.

"Because I want to," Joshua said.

I cut my eyes at him, like Momma did so often, trying to gauge whether it was truth.

"Plus it's good acting practice. I've got to keep myself working. You heard me—I sucked when we ran lines just now."

I didn't think he'd sucked, but he *had* sounded a little more stilted than I'd expected.

"How is looking through my yearbooks practice?" I asked him.

"Show me and I'll tell you."

So I relented and he followed me upstairs. We sat on Vince's bed and I opened up my senior-year annual.

"Choose someone," Joshua said.

I asked who.

"Just anyone. Someone you knew."

There were only seventy people in my graduating class, so I knew everyone, but Joshua sounded exasperated when I pointed this out. He poked a finger at a picture of a boy named Fletcher McCobb.

"Him," he said. "Tell me about him."

I stared into Fletcher McCobb's smile. I wondered where he was right then.

"Fletcher had an older brother who went out with Susan a few times," I started to say.

"Tell me about Fletcher. Not his brother."

I started again. I told him that the McCobbs had moved to Pinecob when I was in sixth grade, and that Fletcher had had a black eye on his first day of school. I told him how the McCobbs had more money than most families in town, and that Fletcher was always sporting one bruise or another. Even when I was little, I knew that his family was the sort that got shushed over.

I told Joshua how Fletcher used to wear a denim shirt with patches made to look like red handkerchief fabric, and how in high school he'd had a motorcycle and had once dropped it on the asphalt just outside the Wilsons' service station. I told him how Fletcher had joined the army straight out of high school, even though everyone figured he could have made more money working for his father. But Paulie had once done some work on the McCobb's house, painting or some such, and I remembered him saying that Fletcher had been smart to enlist.

"Is that enough? How would that even help?" I asked.

"It does," Joshua said, and he got serious. He started saying how every person has a particular way about them and that his job—being an actor—meant trying to recreate real people or make up new ones, and how it's the particular details that jar a character loose from a script, making them into something that feels like life itself. Joshua told me how listening to stories about a perfect stranger, someone like Fletcher McCobb even, helped him remember all the different ways people grew up, so many-sided it could take your breath away. Sometimes, he said, after listening to someone describe a stranger—a friend or enemy or relative—he'd try to wear that person like a shirt, slipping into their posture or anger or laughter or manner of speaking. That's the part that was practice.

"I didn't know Fletcher too well," I admitted. "I don't re-member the way he spoke. He was kind of shy. Kind of flinchy."

"That's okay," Joshua said, standing up. "I'll show you with Lionel."

"Why?"

"It's easy if I know the people in person." Joshua grabbed a baseball cap from the closet and clamped it down over his hair and slung his thumbs through his belt loops. He inhaled deeply and seemed to inflate a little. In an instant, he'd cap-tured Lionel's way of standing exactly.

"Hey there, little lady," Joshua drawled, taking half a swag-ger forward. "What draws you out of yonder holler?"

"Stop," I said. "That's scary. I mean, it's good. It's perfect."

Joshua looked pleased. He took off the hat and stooped a little. He shuffled a few feet, then turned to me and pointed. "Do I know you?" he asked, all cantankerous now.

"The guy at the AA meeting," I said.

"Homer," Joshua said. Now he stood up straight. He shifted his weight from foot to foot and ran a hand through his hair. It was clear he was nervous—or acting nervous. "So, Leanne," he said.

I shrugged. "I don't know," I said.

He picked up Vince's stapler, then set it down, then looked around the room.

"I still don't know. Someone nervous?"

"Max!" Joshua said, like it should have been obvious.

"But you made him look all fidgety."

"He is," Joshua said.

"No, he's not," I told him. "I don't see that at all."

"Oh, right. Max is perfect," Joshua said, back inside his own voice. He came over to Vince's bed and dropped on his stomach beside me. "So show me your skeletons."

Joshua pointed to everyone in my high school class, and even some of my teachers, and for each one, made me tell a story or admit a crush or grudge or say what had become of the person.

"Him?" Joshua said, pointing at a picture of Butch McAfee, whom I'd admitted was my junior-year prom date.

"It's not his best picture," I explained.

"I hope not." He glanced over at me. "You could do better."

"Butch was nice. He sent me love poems."

"Butch wanted to get into your pants," Joshua said. I kicked him. "What? He was sixteen! That's what sixteen-year-old guys want. Trust me. I was one."

I frowned.

"It doesn't mean that he didn't mean what he wrote. Just that there was a motive."

"They were really bad poems," I admitted.

"Leanne," Joshua said. "You make me want to get a van, Leanne."

"Stop it," I told him, but he only gained steam.

"For you I'm working on my tan, Leanne."

"Go ahead then," I said. "I'm not listening."

"I'm making a romantic plan. I must insist on being your man. You know I am your favorite fan, Leanne." Joshua laughed so hard that tears came to his eyes.

"They weren't *that* bad," I said, soon as I managed to stop laughing, too.

That was Joshua's fortieth day.

The next time I went to work, I found myself watching Mr. Bellevue—as he answered his phone or commiserated with a courthouse secretary about the construction that required a detour onto Fountain Street. I made a list of things I hadn't noticed before. He always straightened his tie before correcting someone. He kept only felt-tip pens in the mug on his desk. When he asked you a question, he'd look at you the whole time you were answering.

I didn't know what such details told me. They surely didn't draw an entire person. Could a stranger see Mr. Bellevue's double-knotted laces and know that he was kind? Could you tell by his slightly shuffled walk that he was lonely? I wondered what Joshua Reed would make of the list. If I did the same for myself, what would that show?

I thought of Momma and how I might describe her. I thought of Tommy. I thought of Vince. I skimmed the list of Mr. Bellevue's details and realized that I couldn't make a like one for Vince. I'd lost the ability to describe him. When he was younger, before the accident, I could have done it by heart—the sound of his laugh, the way he'd toss a ball from one hand to the next. But now I wondered whether I would even recognize him, if I'd even recognize his voice, were he to step up to the counter and apply for a hunting permit.

"I know something you don't," Joshua said. It was Tuesday, that next week. He winked at Beau Ray.

"He knows something you don't," Beau Ray said.

"I doubt that," I told them both. That Tuesday had been the first day of bass fishing season, and I was beat from dealing with license applications all day. "Momma home?"

"They're out back," Joshua said. "You don't want to know what I know?"

"What?" I turned to him. "What do you know?"

"Maybe I won't tell you," he said. "Beau Ray, should I tell her?"

"Tell her," Beau Ray said. He clapped his hands together.

"I should tell her who stopped by?"

"Who stopped by?" I asked.

"So now you *want* to know?" Joshua asked. I saw him wink at Beau Ray.

"Smax," Beau Ray said.

"Max stopped by?" I asked.

"I told you she'd want to know," Joshua said.

"Why did he stop by?" I asked. "Did he say?"

Joshua shrugged. "He asked if you were here, and when I said you weren't, he didn't seem terribly interested in keeping me company."

"I was at the store," Beau Ray said.

"What did he say?"

"Who? Beau Ray?" Joshua asked. "He said he was at the store."

"You know who I mean," I said.

"Oh, Max? What did Max say? Just to tell you he stopped by." Then Joshua put on his best Josiah Whitcomb accent. "Leanne, I do believe you're sweet on that fella," he said.

"I don't know," I said, and I didn't.

For one, Judy'd been right. I'd had a thing for Max pretty much since I was eight and he was twelve, and that's a long time for anyone to fan a flame. Sure, my infatuation had waxed and waned at various times—like junior year when Butch was plying me with his bad poems. Or senior year, when I was positive I'd found my match in Howard Malkin (before I found out about him and Loreen). Or when I thought that Otto, who worked as assistant to the assistant county prosecutor, was almost certainly my Mr. Right. And of course I'd set myself to simmer all the time Max was married to Charlene. Like I said, I'm a pretty realistic person. I never figured I'd come out the winner in heart-to-heart combat with the likes of a former Miss Junior West Virginia.

But maybe I'd been simmering too long. Or, holding to the stovetop metaphor, maybe the pilot light had blinked out, but I'd overlooked it. Maybe what I'd taken for a slow burn was instead a long, covered cool-down. Sometimes I wondered if I liked Max because I'd always liked Max, and it was a habit, like chewing on the end of a pen.

Maybe Max would have been right for me a year earlier. Or even six months before. Maybe it was Joshua being there. In our fight on the Fourth of July, Joshua had said some cutting things about my life being small. Part of it, most of it even, had been hot blood talking. But some of his words had sunk in, more and more as the days passed. Did I really want to hunker down with someone who was never going to leave Pinecob? I'd had an ambitious to-do list before the bad luck settled over our house. If I fell for some guy who was never going to leave Pinecob…at least, that's what I found myself itching about.

Timing really is everything, because of course all this started moving through my mind around the time Max seemed to be emerging from his Charlene fog. Sandy was fit to be tied when I stopped by her house late the same day Max had paid his visit.

"You're impossible!" she said. "You did the exact same thing with Otto!"

"That's totally different," I explained. "I liked Otto from across the hall, and when he started talking to me a lot, that's when I realized he had that smell I couldn't stand. Max doesn't smell anything like Otto. Max smells, well, clean."

Sandy shrugged.

"You remember Brennie?" I asked her.

In high school, when Sandy and I were sophomores, Brennie Critchett was a senior and nearabout the most beautiful, have-it-together girl around. At the time, I thought she barely touched the ground. More than idolized her, I wanted to *be* her. I used to keep track of what she wore, then try to hunt out the same clothes. Of course, they never looked the same on me.

"Remember back when we were seniors, around Christmastime, and I saw her at the Winn-Dixie?" I asked Sandy.

She shrugged.

"She was walking with some other girl, and I snuck up behind and heard them talking about how Brennie had been kicked out of college for grades, because all she ever did was sit around and get stoned."

Sandy slowly nodded, like she was remembering. "Oh right," Sandy said. "So you think that because Max went out with Brennie a few times that if you go out with Max, he's going to sit around and get stoned? Or you are?"

"I forgot that Max went out with her," I said.

That wasn't it, of course. Max had been, for me, a similar sort of pedestal crush, and I'd begun to wonder whether he wasn't best left untested. As soon as the guy on a pedestal starts to return the favor, he grows way too human. He needs things, he whines, and it changes the balance. I knew that Max couldn't *always* smell clean.

"What if it turns out he bores me? What if he's a bad kisser?" I asked Sandy.

"You're not serious!" Sandy said.

"Besides, I don't even know whether he likes me at all. Maybe he's been nice because I'm Beau Ray's little sister, or because I've got Joshua Reed in my house, or because he feels bad for blowing me off three years back."

"Does it matter?"

"Of course it matters."

"He ran into traffic for a dog!" Sandy said. She sounded fed up. "Is this because of Joshua? Did he say something to you? Did he make a move?"

"No," I said. But I did think of Joshua acting out Max, all fidgety. Max had always been the body of confidence to me. Had I been making that part up?

"Did *you* make a move?" Sandy pressed.

"No!" I said. "No one made any moves on anyone." I stood up and paced Sandy's bedroom. "But maybe. I don't know."

"What?" Sandy insisted. "Pull on that thread."

"It's just that, Joshua and I are finally getting along, you know?"

"And you think—"

"Let me do the pulling," I told her. "It's not what you think. He's been really nice, recently. You know, interested in my life and family and asking about my job and helping me choose classes for next semester."

"Classes? Plural?"

I nodded. "Judge Weintraub talked to Momma about it and she agreed. I'm going to go half-time," I said.

"Finally!" Sandy said. "But back to Max."

"So, right, Joshua's been, you know, supportive. And don't get me wrong—he's never said anything down-mouth about Max. But he did say something that got me to thinking about whether I want to stay in Pinecob for that much longer."

"And you think that if you start to date Max…"

"Not that we'd even last a month or anything, but what if I hang back on account of him and miss my chance? It's hard enough to think about leaving when it's just my family."

"Where would you go to? New York?" Sandy asked.

I slumped down beside her on her bed. "I have no idea," I said. I knew that Sandy was taking all this in and would spit back something I could use. She was good at that. She always figured things through.

"Well," she said. "You don't have to decide anything this minute. But there's no way Max Campbell is a bad kisser."

I didn't call Max right away, after he'd stopped by. My talk with Sandy hadn't really helped me decide—except to decide *not* to decide—and that meant avoiding the whole decision-making process, including deciding to call Max. So I didn't. Besides, Judy was due in town the next day, Wednesday, Joshua's halfway mark, so there was cleaning after cleaning to do beforehand. Whenever Judy and Lars were around, Momma's list of "Leanne's Chores" got longer. I think she wanted to make sure that they were catered to but didn't like them well enough to do any hostess work herself.

By the time Lars showed up Thursday morning, the chaos those two brought kept me distracted. They got a car to take them to Virginia and took pictures of the fields and old buildings where some of *Musket Fire* would take place. I wondered if I had passed any of the same spots on my dark Virginia drive. Then they spent hours taking Joshua through the pictures and reviewing script changes and making phone calls and trying to answer their cell phones, which would ring once and then conk out. The only place Judy's cell phone seemed to work was in the trees out past our backyard.

Momma had written out a list of fancy party food to have on hand for their visit, and since Lars said he'd be willing to drive Joshua to AA that night, I figured I'd use the time to shop. I was checking what other, more normal food we might need when Judy appeared in the kitchen and offered to lend a hand and come along. I didn't think anything of it, except that it was company and I liked that Judy was choosing to hang out with me special. So we got in the car and drove to the Winn-Dixie.

I didn't see him in the managers' office, but a guy in there confirmed that Max was working, so he had to be somewhere nearby. The guy in the office stared at Judy while he told me that, like she was something he'd never set eyes on before. It made me look twice at her, and I noticed that, sometime between her asking to come along and us arriving at the Winn-Dixie, she'd put on makeup.

We started shopping in the produce area. I pointed out where Marcy Thompson of *Hollywood Express* had cornered me against the apples, and I grabbed an extra bag of carrots for Beau Ray. We ran into Max in the juice aisle. He stood beside a clerk who'd spilled what looked like a bunch of juice concentrate boxes. The floor was covered with a deep purple glaze, and Max and the clerk were watching it spread. The clerk looked worried, but Max wore the beginnings of a grin.

"Hey, Max," I said.

He looked up and waved. He nodded to the clerk who also looked at us—well, mostly at Judy—before hurrying off.

"Hey, Leanne," Max said, pointing at the stain. "You've come at a special time. We're trying out the industrial mop." Then he broke into a certain smile and as soon as he did, most of what I'd said to Sandy and most every excuse I'd made ran clear out of my head. I should have called him, I thought.

"This is Judy," I said. "Judy, this is Max."

Judy smiled and shook his hand. "Judy Masterson. I remember you from the *Hollywood Express* piece. You saved the apples," she said. She seemed to be watching him very closely.

"They train us in fruit-and-vegetable rescue," Max said. "Not everyone passes the final exam."

Judy laughed. "I'm Joshua's publicist," she told him.

"Seems like a guy like that would generate enough publicity on his own," Max said. "He must run you ragged."

I wondered whether he even knew what a publicist did. Not because Max doesn't have a good mind, but because I hadn't known, when I first wrote to Judy. It's not like there's a big need for them in Pinecob.

"Oh, I make time for new talent. It's always an adventure," she said.

He smiled at her and I was suddenly sorry she'd come along. I wanted to be alone with him, to tell him that I was glad he'd stopped by the house, to say that I wished I had been there.

"Judy's been in town for the last couple of days," is what I said instead. "Joshua said you stopped by—I meant to call, but with Judy and Lars here, there's been a lot to do."

"No sweat," Max said. "I was just passing by." I wondered if he thought I was getting back at him for not calling about *South Pacific,* three years before. I wondered if maybe I'd been doing that, at least a little bit. But I knew if he'd give me a chance, I wouldn't do it again.

"So you're from Pinecob, too?" Judy asked.

"Born and raised," Max said. "Just like Leanne here."

"Judy lives in Los Angeles," I said.

"Malibu," Judy corrected me.

"I hear it's nice out there," Max said. "All that sun. Those palm trees."

"We'll have to get you out for a visit," Judy said. "It's just a simple airplane ride." I looked over at her. Nice as she'd always been, she'd never mentioned getting me out to Los Angeles, or Malibu for that matter.

"Yeah, right," Max said. "Not sure it's the place for me. I doubt I'd fit in out there."

I wondered whether Max's hesitance sprang more from his idea of California or from the flight he imagined taking to get there.

"You never know until you try," Judy said. "I used to say the same thing. Now I wouldn't live anywhere else."

I hated that she was so put-together. I wished I had thought to put on mascara before going to the Winn-Dixie. I watched Judy smile at Max, and I realized that I didn't know what she was after. Something didn't feel right, though. I trusted she wasn't interested in him in the same way I was. Judy and Lars had always struck me as a solid, go-getter couple.

"What happened to your ear?" Judy asked him.

Max raised one hand to his torn-off earlobe.

"He got bit by a dog, isn't that right?" I said. "It wasn't his fault or anything," I added.

"Leanne knows all about my sordid past," Max said to Judy. "Killer poodle."

"Ouch!" Judy said. "But it makes a great story."

"Long list?" Max asked me. "Sardines?"

"Not today," I said. "Fancy olives and cheese mostly. But I could use some inspiration for Beau Ray's birthday party."

"Oh, right. Another July birthday for you to get through. First the nation and now Beau Ray."

"In two weeks," I said. "Can you believe he'll be thirty? You guys are getting old."

"Aw, don't say that," Max said.

"Thirty? Really?" Judy said. "You don't look a day over twenty-five."

"I don't know about that." He laughed. "I could arrange for the bakery to do a cake and bring it by when I come to the party," Max said. "You want me to do that?"

"That'd be great," I said. "If you don't mind."

"I am invited, right?" Max asked.

"I'm sure you are!" Judy said, before I could make a sound.

Judy and Lars left on Friday to return to Los Angeles— or Malibu, I guess, if you want to be a stickler about it. Judy said she'd be back in two weeks time, when preproduction for *Musket Fire* was scheduled to begin and there was publicity to be made and managed. Before leaving, she reminded me that the fan club's summer newsletter still hadn't gone out, and could I get it done before she came back. It wasn't really a question.

I'd been avoiding writing the newsletter, and I knew it. Usually, I sent the summer letter out in late June, but there it was mid-July and I hadn't yet begun. It wasn't a huge task or anything. Mostly cutting and pasting pictures and articles. But I knew that the "Joshua in the news" section would have to include his arrest and punishment, and I wasn't sure how best to frame that.

That Saturday morning after Judy left, Joshua and I were eating breakfast in the dining room. He'd been reading the paper when he looked over at me.

"Nice to have the place to ourselves again," he said.

I was surprised and also flattered. I thought he enjoyed hanging out with Lars and Judy. I thought he would have appreciated visitors, and I said as much.

"Oh, they're fine," he said. "They're just so demanding, you know? It's like everything that isn't L.A. is wrong. It's too hot or too humid or it's so green, as if there's something wrong with that." I just stared at him, I think, because he laughed and said, "I know, I know. Me saying that."

"What are you going to do today?" I asked him. Lars had left a new pile of scripts, and I figured that Joshua would probably lie in the sun and flip through them.

"What are you going to do?" he asked back.

I told him I was fixing to draft his fan club newsletter.

"Can I help?" he asked.

I wasn't sure whether he was serious or not, but figured I might as well find out.

We went down to the basement after breakfast, and I showed him the spring edition as an example.

"You did this?" he asked. "I never saw this."

"Judy okays them, then I send them out."

"This is funny," he said, pointing to a quiz I had written, asking fan club members which outfit Joshua Reed had *not* worn in one of his film roles. The choices were a tartan kilt, a toga, surgical scrubs or a cowboy hat and chaps. A lot of people had guessed the kilt, forgetting that he'd had that cameo role in the Scottish thriller, *Bagpipe Dreams.* The answer was a toga.

"It's part of the job," I said while he read through. I was embarrassed just then that I knew so many of his details, as if for the past seven years, I'd been his official stalker or something. When I'd started running the fan club, Joshua Reed felt almost like a made-up person, like a fairy-tale prince, some sort of dashing composite of the characters he played. The more real he became, the more the fan club seemed like a job. But now he was no longer 3,000 miles away, and keeping tabs on his career and coming up with trivia and being an overall cheerleader with Joshua there in front of me—that didn't seem like something that someone with a full life would spend time on.

"How do we start?" he asked. I pulled out my most recent file of clippings and handed them over.

"Go through this, and separate out whatever pictures you want to include."

The newsletter always had the same basic parts to it. There was the "picture page" where I photocopied pictures of Joshua taken from magazines and newspapers (plus any publicity stills Judy might have sent). There was the "Joshua in the news" section where I listed all the articles I'd found, with little blurb descriptions, so that anyone who'd missed an interview somewhere would know about it. I figured that's what they paid fifteen dollars a year for, and that's what I set to working on. There was also the "trivia corner," with lesser-known information about Joshua (that's where I'd stuck the quiz). And usually there would be a listing of appearances Joshua was scheduled to make (benefits, store openings, movie premieres, press conferences—Judy always sent me the dates and I'd paste them in. That's how come I knew Joshua had never been to West Virginia).

"Now what?" he asked. He handed me the photos he'd chosen.

"I guess there can't really be an appearances list this time," I said.

"I appeared in court," he offered. "Twice."

"I'm not sure Judy would approve that."

"I know I don't have anything on my slate for the next forty days. Unless you count AA."

"Which is supposed to be anonymous," I reminded him, although judging by the newfound popularity of the Tuesday and Thursday meetings, that didn't seem to be the case.

"You could interview me. Or I could write something," Joshua suggested.

"Like what?" I asked.

He shrugged. "What do people ask about?" he asked. "I

could tell some story I don't usually tell. Something exclusive. People love exclusives."

"What about something from Rackett?" I suggested. "You never talk about that."

Joshua frowned.

"Or not," I said. "Maybe you had a pet growing up?"

He didn't respond.

"Or something about you and your sister, when you were little?"

Joshua frowned again. It was obvious I wasn't hitting on anything he wanted to share with his public.

"You know, I've never seen anything on how you picked the name Reed."

"I don't suppose you have," he said finally.

"It doesn't matter. I'm sure I can think of something to fill the space," I said quickly. Something in his mood had gone dark, and I wished I could find the switch to bring him back. "I didn't mean for it to be hard. I can do the newsletter myself."

"My sister's best friend growing up was a girl named Jackie Reed," Joshua said. "I had a huge thing for her."

"Jackie Reed?"

He nodded and smiled softly, like he was remembering her. "I got to kiss her once. Late at night. She was staying over and my sister was asleep."

"And?" I asked. "What then?"

"Nothing. She just let me kiss her. But only once. Said that would have to be it. Even then, she knew she didn't want to get too close to my family. Smart girl. Man, she was something. I could look at her for hours."

"She was your Brennie," I said.

"My what?"

"Everyone's got those people they wish they could keep near and maybe actually *be* at the same time. For whatever reason. Girl or guy."

"And it's called a Brennie? You have people like that?" he asked. He sounded surprised.

"Everyone does."

He looked like he hadn't considered this before.

"I bet to a lot of people, you're that person."

"Now, that's scary," Joshua said.

"So did Jackie Reed stay as great as all that?" I asked. I was thinking about Brennie Critchett. She lived on the far side of Pinecob, out by Paulie's family's farm. After she dropped out of college, she had taken a job as a greeter at the Charles Town Supermart, which only required her to greet people with a smile. She wasn't very good at it.

Joshua smiled, sort of sad. "I don't know. But probably not," he said. "She married some guy I heard slapped her around a little. My sister lost touch with her. But I liked her name, so I took it. It reminds me to remember her."

"We could write up *that* story. Only, not the part about her getting hit."

"Yeah, maybe," he said.

"So I've got a question," I told him.

He had gone back to leafing through the picture file. "What's that?" Joshua asked.

"When you introduce yourself, what do you say?"

He looked over at me. "What do you mean?"

"I notice how sometimes you ask people to call you Josh. I know that Judy calls you J.P.—"

"She's known me a long time," he said. "No one but her and people from home—I mean, Rackett—call me J.P."

"You never asked me to call you Josh, and I was wondering," I said. "I always call you Joshua."

"You can call me whatever you want," he said. "Joshua, Josh, whatever." He looked at me, a little closer. "What?"

"It seems like Josh is what your friends call you, but you never said 'call me Josh,' not to me."

"Leanne," Joshua Reed said. "Maybe I like the sound of it when you say Joshua."

I tried to see through him. I thought he was probably lying, or acting, or whatever you'd call it when you're trying to make someone feel better.

"Call me Josh, if you want. Or Joshua. Or J.P. Or Hey You. Whatever you want. I'll answer to whatever you want."

"Now anything is going to sound weird," I told him.

"You asked," he said, but he smiled.

Maybe timing *is* everything, but that doesn't mean you have to like it. Me, I hated that timing was everything.

That next day, Sunday, I went to the Winn-Dixie fully expecting to see Max, all set to suggest we go see a movie since I didn't know of any musicals that were playing. In the managers' office was the same guy who'd been so taken by Judy during my last visit. I recognized him. He was the assistant cheese manager.

"Max in?" I asked him.

"Where's that lady you were here with a couple days ago?" he asked.

"I don't know."

"She live around here?" he asked.

I said nowhere near. I told him that Judy lived in California.

"California." He said it like it was a place in a dream.

"Malibu," I said.

"Malibu," he repeated, the syllables playing off his tongue.

"So, is Max in?" I asked again.

The assistant cheese manager looked back at me. His eyes were flat again, like I'd interrupted something.

"He's out all week," he said.

I felt like such a dolt. It was like the two halves of my brain had two different places to be. I knew that Max would be gone all week because he was where Beau Ray was, and Beau

Ray was gone all week. Duh. That's why carrots weren't on my list.

Lionel, Scooter, Max, Paulie and Beau Ray were all at Lionel's family's lake cabin. It was a yearly thing the guys did, always midsummer. They'd fish and drink and do God knows what else for a full seven days, coming back all unshaven and bleary. Even Max probably didn't smell clean at the end of those weeks. Normally, I'd have hated that sort of thing, but they never once failed to include Beau Ray, so how resentful could I really be?

The following Tuesday, when I picked up Joshua after his AA meeting at the high school, he was grinning like he'd taken home first-prize, though I was pretty sure Mr. Pearson didn't give out ribbons or trophies.

"What?" I asked him.

"I talked," he said. "Back in there. I stood up and talked."

I told him I thought that was great.

"It *is* great. I don't do much improv, but I thought, screw it, I can do this. Leanne did it. Homer does it. I can do it."

"What did you say?" I asked him.

"You know how it goes. I said my name. I said 'My name's Joshua' and that I figured that most people probably already knew why I was there, but it was because I'd gotten my second DUI. You know, I told my story. Not all of it, but some."

"That's really great, Joshua," I said. I had decided to stick with calling him Joshua.

"I talked a little bit about Rackett and how I was staying with you, and that you and your family had been totally cool to me, and how the summer's been a lot different than I thought it would be."

"Different?"

"In a good way," he assured me. "That I've been reading a lot but also getting a lot of thinking done. You know, Elise told me that she thought I needed to focus on getting myself together. At the time, I figured it was just shrink bullshit. Actually, coming from her, I'm sure it was. But still, it's worked out that way. I'm so much clearer about what I want to do when I get back to L.A., what I'm going to focus on."

He was smiling, but that's when it hit me: Joshua was going to leave. The ninety days would end and he would return to California. Part of my brain must have known it. Of course, I'd known it, but as he spoke, it still came at me like a surprise. Were we all expected to go back to the way we were before? How could we go back?

The next night, Sandy and I went for a beer at the Buccaneer. It was the one night she had off between weeks of fourteen-hours on. Alice was coming from Hagerstown to stay with her the following week, so at least they would be able to see each other, even when Sandy was tired.

Loreen arrived at our booth straightaway. I watched her walk up and wondered if anything had happened between her and Paulie after the Fourth of July party.

"Hey Sandy," she said. And then to me, "So I did it. I asked him out."

I knew immediately she wasn't talking about Paulie. And she was smiling this smile, like she was so proud of herself.

"Oh, yeah? Good for you," I said. But I was only acting casual.

"Who are we talking about?" Sandy asked. Neither of us answered her.

"How'd it go?" I asked Loreen. "What'd he say?"

She shrugged. "I guess he's already dating someone," Loreen said. "You know who?"

"Who's this?" Sandy asked again.

"Max Campbell," Loreen told her.

"I don't know," I said. "First I've heard of that." I looked into my beer, then up at Sandy, who had already started looking sorry for me. She was getting a lot of use out of that particular expression.

"Oh, well," Loreen said. "Can't be too serious if no one knows who it is."

"I'm dating someone and no one knows who," Sandy said. "Maybe Max is seeing someone out of town." I looked over at Sandy like she was no help at all.

"Maybe," Loreen said. "But whoever she is better hold on tight. I heard Charlene's coming back through town next week."

"Charlene?" I asked.

"You know, his ex," Loreen said.

I knew who she was. I felt my face sag.

Sandy turned to Loreen. "What did he say exactly?"

Loreen shrugged again. "I said, you want to go out sometime and he said, oh, that would be cool except he was starting to date someone else just now."

"Starting to," Sandy said, mostly to me.

"Well, good for you," I told Loreen. "For asking, I mean. So I guess you and Paulie aren't going to be a thing?" I hated that we both liked the same guy, again. It felt like Pinecob was closing in.

"Get real. Paulie's just a filler. Hey, *he's* cute," Loreen said, looking at some guy shooting pool. "See you two later."

"If you'd been at the Fourth of July party, you'd know all this," I told Sandy.

"If you'd known about it to begin with and invited me," she said.

"She told me she was thinking of asking him out. I wasn't going to say, no wait, I like him, you can't. It doesn't work that way."

"I wonder who he's dating," Sandy said.

"If Charlene's back in town, it won't matter."

Chapter 15

Second Birthday That Month

"Beau Ray, look who's here!" Momma was in full party mode. The backyard was littered with coolers and Paulie's wading pool and the grill, which sent up puffs of smoke each time Judge Weintraub lifted it to check the hamburgers and hot dogs. Our neighbors had lent us their picnic table, which was covered with sodas and small plates of potato salad that people had set down, then forgotten about.

Beau Ray's friends from physical therapy and "Move Your Body, Move Your Mind" class wandered around with their chaperones—parents or sisters or nursing assistants, mostly. Beau Ray sat at one end of the picnic table, trying to explain a card trick to Joshua. Joshua looked like he was paying close attention. Maybe that was his birthday present to my brother. I figured he might have stayed holed up in Vince's room—sometimes even I got overwhelmed by Beau Ray's crowd.

"Beau Ray," I said. "Did you hear Momma? I think Susan

and the kids just got here." Beau Ray dropped the cards and ran into the house.

"Now how am I going to learn that trick?" Joshua whined. But he was smiling. "Hey," he said to me. "Sit."

"A little more than you bargained for, huh?" There had to be forty people milling around our yard. "Come meet Susan," I said.

My sister Susan was talking to Momma while the two of them unpacked the tubs of coleslaw and Jell-O salad she'd brought. Beau Ray was playing rock-paper-scissors with Kenny and Kathy. Kevin, who was fifteen that year, had mono, Susan was explaining, so Tim was looking after him back home. They both sent their love and prayers.

"You must be Joshua," Susan said, as soon as we walked in the kitchen.

I still hated the way people dropped all they were doing to look at him. I hadn't seen Susan all summer, and still, she said hi to him first.

"I must be," Joshua said. "And you're Susan. Nice to meet another Gitlin. I recognize you from all the pictures. You're even lovelier in person."

Susan blushed. "So how have you been enjoying Pine-cob?" she asked.

"To tell the truth," Joshua said, "I haven't gotten out as much as I'd like."

Susan blushed again. "Oh, of course not. What a stupid question."

"But the house and backyard are great. And I couldn't ask for nicer company than your little sister."

Susan finally looked over at me, her eyebrows gone high up. "Is that right?" she asked, as much to me as to Joshua.

"Leanne's a superb hostess," he said. "I think she ought to explore a career in home incarceration."

"Is that really something people do?" Susan asked, frowning a little.

"No," I said to her, then turned to Joshua. "What do you want?"

He laughed and excused himself. Susan grabbed my arm before I could do the same.

"Are you sleeping with him?" she demanded.

"Nice seeing you, Susan. How have you been?" I said. "And no, I'm not. That's crazy," I told her. "No," I said again, when it looked like she didn't believe me.

"You'd swear on the Bible?"

"On whatever you want."

"Well, he wants to. I can tell you that."

"No, he doesn't. Really. He doesn't."

"Is he queer? I don't want him around the kids if he's queer. Even if he is some sort of moviestar—"

"No!" I said. "Get a drink, Susan. Honestly."

"Watch yourself, Leanne. I know men. That one has his sights on you."

"Go ahead and believe that, then," I told her. I turned around and ran smack into Max. I cringed, hoping he hadn't heard Susan. When I turned, I knocked him in the chest with my hands, and I left them there just a second longer than I needed to. I could feel the arch of his muscles beneath his shirt, and the slight heat of them. I didn't want to pull away.

"Hey," I said.

"I, uh, I brought the cake," Max said. "Let me go get it."

"Oh, great. Momma, Max brought the cake."

In a minute, he'd returned with a big box that he set on the kitchen table. Momma opened it up and fawned over the huge frosted sheet-cake inside.

"Oh, Max, that's real nice," Momma said. "Leanne, go get Max something to drink."

"That's okay, Mrs. Gitlin," Max said. "I'm sure Leanne's busy. I can find the cooler myself." I watched him walk away.

"He's looking good, isn't he?" I heard Susan say to Momma.

Joshua came back in the kitchen just then, and pulled me out by the arm.

"What?" I asked him.

"This way." He steered me to the front door and then out onto the porch. He pointed to the end of our driveway. "Who's that?" Joshua asked.

So it was true, I thought. She was back in town. "That's Charlene," I told him. "Someone must have told her we were having a party."

Charlene was talking to our neighbor from across the street, I couldn't hear about what. But she looked up and over toward our porch. I saw her excuse herself, and she started walking up the driveway. She gave us a pageant wave.

I'll admit that Charlene was pretty, in a tight blond way, though I always expected to see a sash and tiara when I looked at her. She was the type of woman that guys describe as having a "body that won't quit" although I have never really understood what that means. At least with Max, she hadn't shown much endurance. Or maybe she'd just needed a rest before coming back for round two.

"Is that you, Leanne?" Charlene called out. "I haven't seen you in ages. Don't you look wonderful!"

"Thanks," I said, as she came close. "I heard you'd be in town."

"I saw you on that thing with *Hollywood Express,*" Charlene said to me. "Funny, with the apples." Then she turned to Joshua. "And you're Joshua Reed, aren't you?" She stepped onto the porch.

Joshua held out his hand, then took hers and kissed it. I wanted to gag. I felt way too tall and gangly, standing there.

"Charlene," she said.

"Charlene," Joshua said. "That's a lovely name. I've got to remember that."

"Charlene used to live around here," I told Joshua. "But

then she left." I smiled at her. She smiled at me. I doubt either one of us actually meant it.

"But now I'm back," Charlene said. She was a lot better at being perky than I was.

"Lucky me," Joshua said.

"If you play your cards right," Charlene said.

"Did you and Max come together?" I asked her.

She turned to me with big round eyes. "Max? Is he around? I should say hi."

"You know Max?" Joshua asked.

I think Charlene was waiting to hear whether I would say anything about her having been married to Max, and having left him. But I wasn't going to do that. Charlene hadn't ever done anything mean to me, not directly. She was inconvenient, and sure, I was sorry that she'd shown up when she did. But if her showing up meant that she and Max would get back together, I figured that nothing was meant to happen between us anyhow.

Charlene turned back to Joshua. "Will you excuse me for a moment?"

I watched Joshua watch Charlene leave. I felt sure she'd be back.

Judy showed up with a gift box in one hand and a man who wasn't Lars. She introduced him to me as Sasha. She said that he was a casting director, come to finish work on *Musket Fire*. Sasha had an accent I couldn't place and wore sunglasses, even when he was inside. He was more pretty than handsome, and he stuck close to Judy. The three of us, Judy, Sasha and I, walked out to the backyard, and as soon as Sasha stepped outside, he stopped, took a deep breath and scanned the entire party.

Judy pointed across the yard. "That's the one I was telling you about," she said to Sasha. She spoke in a low voice, like maybe I wasn't supposed to hear.

"Talking to our dear Mr. Reed?" Sasha asked. He peered over his sunglass frames. "I see what you mean."

"That's Max," I told them.

"And Max is?" Sasha asked.

"He's a friend," I said. "He's a family friend. And a manager over at the Winn-Dixie."

Judy laughed. "I just love that name," she said. "That's what the grocery store is called," she explained to Sasha.

Sasha excused himself, and I watched him go kiss Joshua on both cheeks and then get introduced to Max. I watched Sasha and Max shake hands.

"Sasha is famous for having the eye," Judy said.

"What do you mean?" I asked her.

"No one's better at finding people," she said. "Hey, great job on the newsletter by the way. I've been trying to get J.P. to talk more about Texas for ages. And that story about Jackie Reed? Excellent. That shit sells." She headed off toward Joshua and Max. I followed.

"Hey, Judy," Joshua said, kissing her cheek. "Good seeing you again, as always. It's been a quiet two weeks with you gone. How's the city of angels?"

"Relatively sane with you locked up here," Judy said. "So, boring. We need you back there. I ran into Elise last week. She sends her love."

"Yeah, right," Joshua said.

"You know what I mean. That shirt's a great color on you."

"Leanne gave it to me," Joshua said.

I had found the shirt Joshua was wearing at a garage sale. I'd meant it to be for Beau Ray, but Joshua had commandeered it, soon as I'd returned, and seeing as how he offered to give me the two dollars I'd paid, I relented. It was just an olive green button-down, but it did make his eyes look like evergreen almonds.

"Leanne takes good care of me," Joshua was saying.

Judy turned to me. "I hope not too good," she said.

"No, of course not," I told her, quick as can be. "Where did Sasha and Max get to?"

I caught sight of them at the edge of our yard. Sasha had taken Max by the elbow and seemed to be saying something in confidence. Then he let go and made big, sweeping motions with his hands. Max nodded, then shook his head. Sasha took him by the elbow again. I suddenly noticed Joshua watching me.

"They seem to be hitting it off," he said. "I know people who'd kill for that much face time with Sasha. Lucky guy."

"Who?" I asked.

Judy and Joshua said it together, "Max!" like I should have known.

I tried to ignore Sasha and Max and focus on Judy and Joshua catching up, on Judy complaining about the humidity and what it did to her hair. I caught Judge Weintraub's eye, over by the grill, and he waved at me and offered whatever he was grilling. I shook my head.

Charlene wandered over with a smile that looked custom-made for Joshua. "I'm back," she said to him.

"No lie. Hey, Judy, I want you to meet Charlene. This is Judy, my publicist."

"What a pleasure it is to meet you," Charlene said.

Judy shook her hand and said, "Likewise."

"I'm thirsty," Charlene said. Joshua immediately offered to get her a drink and like that, they were off. And then Sasha was back, talking to Judy, but I didn't see Max anywhere.

"Well?" Judy asked him. I noticed that she was keeping an eye on Charlene and Joshua.

"You are right, Miss Judy. He does have something," Sasha said. "And I adore the West Virginia angle and that crazy earlobe. We will see how he tests, but I have a few ideas."

"I can already tell you, he's great on screen," Judy said. "I saw him."

"You're going to test Max?" I asked. "Where? Where do you test someone?"

They turned to me like I'd asked what color the sky was.

"In Los Angeles," Judy said. "Or New York."

"Max in Los Angeles? You'll never get him there." I laughed.

"But he already agreed," Sasha said. I couldn't see his eyes behind his sunglasses. "I did not even have to twist his arm."

"I'd better see whether my mother needs help in the kitchen," I said. But it was just an excuse to get away. I felt like a bandage had just been ripped clean off of me. My whole body stung. I wandered instead to Beau Ray's room and smiled to see how much he'd straightened it for the party, though the closet door was closed and behind it might well have lurked a pile of chaos six feet tall.

Then I walked into his bathroom, closed the door, and sat on the edge of the tub. I noticed that Beau Ray had not yet opened the miniature bottle of conditioner and the miniature soap I'd given to him, from the resort in Harper's Ferry, so long ago. I also noticed a small spot of something on the counter, and before I'd thought much about it, I'd found a sponge under Beau Ray's sink and started to wipe it off. The spill stuck a bit—it might have been jam, or syrup from an old soda can—so I pulled some scouring powder from beneath the sink, and sprinkled the sticky spot. And then, I kept going. I wiped down the sink, and then the toilet seat, and then the edge of the tub. And of course you can't leave scouring powder around, so I had to rinse it off, too. I was drying the sink when I heard a knock at the door. That brought me back—I was supposed to be at Beau Ray's party, not cleaning his bathroom.

"Just a second," I said. I shoved the sponge and scrubbing powder back under the sink. I straightened the shower curtain and opened the door, then I stepped aside for Max. "All yours," I said, as perky as I could manage.

"Thanks," he said, but he paused at the doorway. He sniffed the air. "Were you just cleaning?" he asked. "It smells like Comet."

"Something spilled," I said. He shook his head like I was crazy.

I tried to imagine him on television, maybe in scrubs like Joshua had worn on *General Hospital*. Or in a cowboy getup. It didn't fit.

"So that guy Sasha says you've got something," I said. "I hear he wants to test you."

"Isn't that the weirdest? The guy walks right up to me and says he wants to get me out to California. I tell you, if Josh hadn't been there, I would have figured he was just hitting on me."

"So that's great, I guess," I said. "It seemed like you were getting sort of bored of life at the Winn-Dixie."

"You really think it's great? I never thought for a second about that kind of life," Max said. "Not before Josh got here, at least."

"It looks like you need to start thinking," I told him.

Max looked at me, and kept looking at me.

"Judy says that Sasha has the eye, whatever that means. I can't even see his eyes behind those sunglasses he has on. Actually, I think it was Judy's eye you caught." I felt like I was babbling.

"You didn't answer my question," Max said.

"What question?"

"Leanne!" It was Momma. She'd rounded the corner and was standing with her hands on her hips. "I've been calling for you. Sally Ann's casserole dish just broke all over the dining room table. There's macaroni and cheese everywhere."

"Jesus!" I just blurted it out, before I could edit myself. "Can't you see I'm trying to have a life? Is no one else at this entire party qualified to clean up Sally Ann's mac and cheese?"

Momma blinked but said nothing.

I turned back to Max, but whatever the moment had been, it was gone.

"I need to use the rest room, anyhow," Max muttered. "We'll catch up later." He stepped inside and closed the door. I hoped it didn't smell too strongly of scouring powder.

"Fine, I'm coming," I told my mother.

I helped Sally Ann clean off the dining table and reconfigure her macaroni and cheese into two smaller dishes, but by the time I returned to Beau Ray's hallway, Max was gone. Joshua now stood outside the closed bathroom door.

"Charlene's in there," he said. "I'm just waiting." Then he gave me his "concerned" look, which I was never sure was real or put-on. "What's up? Something's up."

I looked away. I didn't want to tell him about Max and how it felt like I was about to lose him. All that made me wish that Joshua had never come to town—then Judy wouldn't have come to Pinecob and met Max and introduced him to Sasha. And I would never have started to think so much about leaving Pinecob, and maybe I wouldn't have ignored Max like I had done, and maybe we could have made a small little life together, somewhere on the outskirts of Charles Town. But now it was too late. Now Max was going to Los Angeles or was dating someone else or would return to Charlene in a heartbeat, or a mix of all three.

"It's nothing," I said.

I poked my head into the kitchen, but it was empty.

I walked back outside. Beau Ray and his friends were playing a game of wiffle ball, and Beau Ray said that I had to play, because the teams weren't even and his team needed someone at second base. Judy had been roped into playing for the batting team and was also on second.

"Where's Sasha?" I asked while we waited for the next hit. I hadn't seen him since I'd fled inside.

"He went back to the hotel to meet Lars," she explained. "I think this party was a little much for him. Too much authentic atmosphere."

"Did he bring Max with him?" I asked.

Judy frowned and looked around. "I don't think so. He was using my cell phone, last I knew. Or trying to. He wanted to call his parents to tell them what Sasha said. Pretty exciting, don't you think? Max is totally Sasha's type. I knew it the moment I saw him. Professionally speaking, of course. And Sasha is heading up casting for the next Bond film and thinks he sees a part for Max in it, if the tests go well. Things happen really fast around Sasha. Oh, a hit!" Judy ran off to third, and then home.

"Leanne!" Beau Ray called. "Outfield. Big batter." He waved me back.

I nodded and headed toward the outfield, which in our yard was close to the beginning of the trees that separated our house from Brown's Field. One of Beau Ray's friends from therapy was at bat. I didn't know him, but he *was* big, and when he swung, the crack of the wiffle ball sounded almost like a hit in a real baseball game. It was an automatic home run—the ball whizzed past me and into the trees. I heard whoops from the batting team, and headed back to try to recover the ball.

I picked my way onto the path that had been there since I could remember. I'd always been surprised by how quickly the trees would envelop you, making it seem later in the day than it was, everything a few shades cooler and greener. I looked around for the ball.

"Leanne."

It was Max, standing a few feet away, with Judy's cell phone to his ear. He was holding the wiffle ball out to me in his other hand.

"I've got to go," Max said.

I nodded before I realized that he was talking to the person on the phone.

"I'll call you later. I love you, too." He clicked off.

I took the ball from him. "Well, I," I started. I was going to say that I had to get back to the game, but we both heard the crack of another wiffle bat, and a cheer go up, so it was clear that they weren't waiting on me.

"Figured I ought to tell my parents," Max said. "I'm sorry we got interrupted back there."

"Yeah, well, can't say no to Momma."

"You were answering my question. What do you think of this L.A. thing? Me going out there, I mean?"

"Was I?" I asked. I didn't want to answer that question. I wasn't sure I could. "So, Charlene," I said instead. "It must be nice to see her," I said. "She looks good."

"That's never been Charlene's problem," Max said. "Sticking around was the problem."

"She came back," I said. "There must be a reason for that."

Max seemed to think on something a while. "You know, we're divorced," he finally said. "Not separated. We're divorced."

"But you were married. You made those vows. There's gotta be part of you that…" I paused. I didn't know what to say. "That's glad to see her?" I guessed. "That thinks maybe this time…"

Max shook his head, then he shrugged. "I don't know exactly what I think," he said.

I nodded, trying to look as cool as I could. I flipped back my hair.

"I don't know where my head is just now," Max said. "I'm actually thinking of getting on a plane. Never thought I'd hear myself say *that*."

"So, you're going to Los Angeles?" I asked him.

He looked at his shoes. "Hard to believe," he said. "I guess so. Wouldn't you?"

"I guess so," I said.

"Listen, Leanne. I've actually got to leave now, the party.

That Sasha guy wants to meet with me later today, and I need to figure out who's going to sub for me at work."

"That's cool," I said. "Whatever. I'm sure Beau Ray will understand."

"That's not what I mean," Max said. "I…you're…all this. We've known each other for a long time, haven't we? But, I don't know, I feel like I've been trying, for the past couple of months, or wanting…but I can't tell where you are. It's like, whenever I think, maybe, but then we'll get interrupted, or you'll kind of fade off. I'm not explaining myself well. But do you know, sort of, what I'm talking about?" He dug the toe of his boot into the dirt.

"Maybe," I said, but then I took a step back. I had to remember the facts. "But Loreen said that you said you were starting to date someone. I don't want to get in the middle of anything." I watched a wonderful smile break over him.

"Who do you think I meant?" Max asked. "I don't want to date Loreen." Then the smile faded. "Only now, this whole L.A. thing…and part of me is thinking, great, go and don't look back. I mean, a life like Josh's? Not that anything would actually come of it, but the opportunity—that won't happen twice. And Sasha made it sound pretty cool. But there's this other side of me wondering, why now? Because I thought things were finally going to start, only they haven't, have they?"

I looked down at my feet and took a deep breath. "I had the hugest crush on you all through high school," I told him. "You know, when I was in high school—well, also when you were in high school and I was younger."

"No, you didn't. You did?" He sounded like he really hadn't known. I wondered whether he'd ever be as good an actor as Joshua Reed. I wondered how much of Joshua's style of life Max would want to make his own.

"And after," I said.

"Sandy was pretty clear that you got over it."

"That's part of her job as my best friend. Why do you think I do the grocery shopping on Sundays? I know you work Sundays," I said. "You really think the Gitlins have got some tradition of buying food only on Sunday?"

"I thought maybe you had a thing for the assistant cheese manager," Max said. "So that crush…" He took a step forward. I could see the stubble on his upper lip. "Do you still?"

I shrugged. "With all this happening, maybe it's not such a good idea anymore."

"Why not? Why can't it be a good idea?" he asked, but didn't wait for me to answer.

And with that, I found myself with a wiffle ball in my hand kissing Max Campbell. And of course Sandy was right. No way he was a bad kisser. Not at all. He held my chin in his palm, then held the back of my head and moved me closer still. I had wanted to kiss Max for half my life, maybe, and it was happening, under the trees behind my backyard. I felt like I could kiss him forever, never need to eat, never need to sleep.

Everything I'd ever liked about Max came back in focus. The way he looked, the way he smelled, the way he had those times of utter inarticulation, it all came clear. This was the reason my heart had held tight, even as the years went by, even as he grew up and I did. Even as I got to know who he really was, as the person beyond the name in my spiral notebook.

We stood there, and I dropped the wiffle ball onto the dirt and kept on kissing him. In the distance, there were voices and laughter and the sound of the bat and applause and the smell of charcoal smoke and hot dogs. But close-up, it was all Max, only Max, in every sense.

He wrapped his arms around my back and I leaned in so that my body rode right up against his body—and then Judy's cell phone rang. We pulled apart and Max looked at the phone in his hand, now lit up and buzzing like a thing alive. He handed it to me like he was scared it might bite.

"Damn. I actually do have to go," he said, between rings. "Give this back to Judy, will you?" I nodded. "We'll talk soon," he said. "I'll call you later. But we're good?"

"We're good."

He kissed me once again, more lightly, then disappeared out across Brown's Field. I picked up the wiffle ball and walked back to the party.

Beau Ray's cake was brought out, thirty candles all ablaze. Charlene stood beside Joshua, tucked right up against his armpit, him resting his hand on her waist, as we sang. Sandy snuck up behind me.

"Where've you been? I was looking for you and guess what? Take a look at who Joshua is standing next to," she whispered.

"I kissed Max," I whispered back, and Sandy let out a high-pitched yelp.

"When?" she asked.

"Keep singing," I said. We finished *Happy Birthday dear Beau Ray, Happy Birthday to you,* and everyone clapped when Beau Ray blew out the candles on the Winn-Dixie sheet cake, smiling like there'd never been a better day. I thought maybe he was right.

"Uncle Beau's happy," my nephew Kenny said, pointing to him. He was eleven, at turns full of sass or sweetness.

"He *is* happy," I agreed. "It's his birthday. Cake, presents and wiffle ball. You can't beat that."

Kenny nodded. "I hope it's chocolate," he said, looking at the cake.

Sandy pulled me away. "Well?" she said. "You don't just kiss Max and shrug it off!" she said. "You kissed Max—oh my God, I feel like my kid just won the swim meet."

"It's not that big a deal," I said.

"So when, where, for how long and who started it?" Sandy asked. "Was it before or after Charlene showed up?

And by the way, what the hell is she doing here? You didn't invite her, did you?"

Sandy and I took slices of chocolate cake out to the front porch.

"It was after Charlene showed up," I said, once we were arranged on the stoop, paper plates balanced on our knees. "Apparently she knows one of the nursing assistants. But I think maybe she's here for Joshua."

"That makes sense," Sandy said, nodding. "He can hide, but he can't run."

"It didn't look to me like he was trying to do either. And Judy does not look pleased."

I told Sandy how it happened with Max. I admitted that it *was* a big deal, that it was quite possibly the best kiss ever. I also told her about Sasha, and Los Angeles, and the Bond movie, and testing.

"Wait, so he's going? Just like that?"

"I don't know. I guess so. I think so. Not moving there, not yet at least. But if things work out…"

"Wow. Bummer. Cool for him. But bummer for you."

"Tell me about it."

"So it looks like young Mr. Campbell might be interested in the world beyond the Winn-Dixie after all," Sandy said.

Charlene and Joshua walked out onto the porch then, and Sandy shut up.

"Hi, Sandy. You're looking well. Have you met Charlene?" Joshua asked. He looked up at the sky. "God, it's a beautiful day."

Sandy and I smiled up at him. Charlene took Joshua's hand and whispered something into his ear.

"We're going inside," he told us.

"She's bad news," Sandy said, after they were gone. "But don't be surprised if you wake to bad news tomorrow morning."

"Nope," I said.

Chapter 16

More Bad News

Around nine the next morning, around the time Momma, Susan, me and the kids were sitting down to breakfast, Judy showed up. She had left Beau Ray's party on the early side in order to get back to Harper's Ferry, to the same resort where I'd first met her and Joshua and Lars. Apparently, Judy had gotten wind of a new script development, and she wanted to make sure that Joshua knew about it. I told her that Joshua wasn't awake yet. I didn't tell her that I was almost certain he wasn't alone up there.

The night before, as I'd headed into my bedroom, I'd heard a giggle I knew could only be Charlene. There were low murmurs and another laugh and then a sigh. I had closed my door so that I wouldn't hear them, then sat on my bed and wished Max were there.

"J.P.," Judy called, and marched up to his room. "J.P.," she said again, knocking once and opening the door. I heard her gasp. "Sorry," she said, and shut the door. She turned to me. "So you *aren't* sleeping with him."

"Did you really think I was?" I asked.

"I don't know," Judy said. "I never know what to believe. So give me the rundown on this Charlene chick."

"She just came back to Pinecob," I said, dropping my voice. We headed back downstairs.

"This is just what I need," Judy said. "A groupie girlfriend. And he's got no other distractions. I knew I should have done something about that yesterday. I could tell. She's just his type."

"That's Max's ex-wife," I told Judy. "I thought Max was why she came back to Pinecob, but maybe not."

Judy nodded. "That's Max's ex? The one you said he still had a thing for?"

"I think he *used* to," I said.

"What did he have to say about this?" she asked, motioning back toward Joshua's door. I told her that I didn't think Max knew. I reminded her how he'd left the party before she did.

"Huh," Judy said. "Is there coffee?"

I brewed a new pot, then ran through it pouring for Judy, Susan, Momma, myself and Judge Weintraub, who had come down from Momma's room by then. Beau Ray was still in bed and as a late birthday present, Momma was letting him sleep in.

Beau Ray had spent the evening before going again and again through each present he'd received, describing it and listing who had given it to him and who that person was to him.

"This is my new deck of cards Alex gave me. Alex and I go to therapy at the Y. Then this," he'd said, holding up a sweater, "is a sweater from Momma. Momma is Momma and that's that."

The only present he'd treated any different was a new football. I hadn't seen him open it, so I didn't know where it had come from. And Beau Ray refused to say.

"This is my new football. It's just special."

When most everyone had gone home, I went into Beau Ray's room, where all his presents were laid across his poorly made bed in neat rows. Beau Ray sat on the floor with his senior-year annual open before him. Beau Ray had played varsity football that year, and the yearbook was open to the team portrait.

"Hey, buddy," I said. I crouched beside him and pointed to his face in the crowd of uniformed young men. "Who's that handsome guy?"

"Me," Beau Ray said. "And that's Lionel, and that's Paulie, and that's Vince." He pointed to each one of them in turn. His fingertip lingered under Vince's face, which was slightly blurred, as if he'd been moving when the shutter opened.

I looked away from the picture. I'd been thirteen that same year, and as happy-go-lucky as a girl can be at that age, what with all the body changes often going on. Later that same year, Beau Ray would fall and never fully recover. The next year, my dad would die and Vince would leave. But when the shutter had clicked, none of that had been visible. They'd just been boys on a football team, dressed for the next game.

"Hey, who gave you the football?" I asked Beau Ray. But he turned away from me. "Did Tommy send it to you? Or Joshua?"

Beau Ray looked up at me and smiled broadly.

"I like Josh. He lives here. He said I can come to his movie's place."

"To the set? That's nice of him," I'd said.

Back at breakfast, Judy sipped her coffee and waited for Joshua to emerge from upstairs. Judge Weintraub told her that Sasha had asked whether he might be available to work as an extra in *Musket Fire*.

"Apparently, I have a remarkable presence that has gone unappreciated before now," he said, clearly amused.

Momma laughed. "Unappreciated?"

"Maybe not by everyone," he said. He smiled at her.

"Where's Sasha anyway?" I asked Judy. I wanted to ask him about Sandy and me being extras, too.

"Didn't I tell you? He took Max to New York first thing this morning."

"Max is in New York?" I tried to sound calm but my heart felt like it was getting ahead of itself. "Already? I thought everything, the testing, was in L.A."

"Sasha had to go to Manhattan for a photo session with a few actors he's considering, so he invited Max to go along. It's a great opportunity. Perfect timing. They took a car this morning. Should be there in not too long," she said, looking at her watch.

"When will they be back?" Susan asked.

Judy shrugged. "A few days maybe. If the photo session goes well, and between you and me, I'm sure it will, Sasha can justify getting him to L.A., so Max can take some real meetings. And if those go well, Lars might even be willing to represent him," Judy said. "What? Aren't you happy for him?"

"Sure I am. I guess," I said. "It just all happened so fast."

"I told you—things happen fast around Sasha. Listen, honey, I know you've got something special for Max. But this can only help things, don't you see? If anything great happens to him, it all traces back to you."

"I guess." But I'd quick lost my appetite for breakfast. I hadn't told anyone but Sandy that I'd kissed Max, so there I was looking like a lovesick puppy in front of my whole family.

"Who's Max?" Kenny asked me.

"A friend of your Uncle Beau's," I told him.

Joshua and Charlene finally came downstairs.

"Sorry about that, J.P.," Judy said. "Hello again, Charlene."

"No biggie. No lock," Joshua said. "These pancakes look awesome."

Charlene nuzzled something into Joshua's ear.

"No, not as awesome as you," Joshua whispered back.

I caught Momma frowning at the two of them, but she held her tongue.

"Who's she?" Kenny asked, pointing at Charlene.

"She's Josh's friend," Susan said. "You remember Josh from yesterday, don't you?"

"He's the big star," Kenny said. "He's in trouble so he's living with Gramma now." Joshua laughed.

"Aren't kids great?" Susan said. Then she turned to Kenny. "Only we don't talk about people being in trouble in front of other people, remember?"

"She's got yellow hair," Kenny said, pointing at Charlene again.

"And it's rude to point," Susan said.

When breakfast was over, Joshua stood up, stretched and said that he could use a shower. The rest of us, save Beau Ray who was finally awake by then, had done our washing and dressing beforehand.

It was Sunday, and with Susan around, that meant church. Susan and her husband, Tim, were both active in their congregation, and were always reminding us to attend services every Sunday at the minimum. Momma went on and off, mostly for social reasons but I wasn't sure she'd set foot inside a church since she'd begun seeing Judge Weintraub.

Still, with Susan visiting, Momma had decided that we should all attend church together. Even Judge Weintraub was going. All of us save Joshua, who couldn't leave the house, of course.

"We'll pray for you," Susan told him.

"Every little bit helps," he said.

When Joshua mentioned getting into the shower, Charlene stood and reached for her purse.

"Oh, please. Stay a while longer," Judy asked her.

Joshua agreed. "Yeah, stay. I won't be long," he said, and so Charlene perched like a bug on the long couch in the living room. Joshua smiled at her and headed upstairs.

"So you and J.P.," Judy said. "That was fast."

Charlene nodded. "We get along," she said.

Charlene sounded so wide-eyed that I wondered whether *she* might have a future in acting. I noticed Judy look at her watch, then glance in my direction. Then I heard her suggest to Charlene that the two of them take a sit out on the front porch. It was clear that I wasn't invited, that it was private, girl-to-girl stuff, so I announced to no one in particular that I'd best get started on the dishes. Of course, as soon at they headed outside, I opened the kitchen window. I mean, it was my house.

"Leanne tells me you used to be married to Max," I heard Judy say.

"For a little bit," Charlene said. "Not anymore."

"That's too bad," Judy said. "I tell you, if I weren't happily married," Judy went on. "That boy is poised to go places."

"Max Campbell?" Charlene said. "He's been at the Winn-Dixie since he was in high school."

"Didn't you hear?" Judy asked. "Oh, right, you weren't around yesterday when Sasha saw him. Sasha does casting and the agency he works for sent him out to find the next big thing. He thinks he found it in Max. Between you and me, that boy has got star potential the likes of which I rarely see. More than any of my current clients. Don't get me wrong, I love J.P. He's been with me forever. But this Campbell guy? It's like looking at the next Cary Grant. I'd bet my career on it."

"Max? Really?" Charlene said. "But Joshua… And this movie in Virginia. About the guns?"

"*Musket Fire.* Right," Judy said. Suddenly, she sounded distracted. "God, I need to tell him about that."

"How do you mean?" Charlene asked. "Tell him what?"

"I haven't had the heart, with him locked up here. But it turns out, they've found someone else for Josiah. The producers just didn't think J.P. had enough, well, as I was saying, star potential."

"No! Really?" Charlene said. "Can they do that?"

"He knew it might be coming, but I think he's in denial. I think he's having trouble accepting that he's on a downhill slide. That's why I'm so glad he met you. It's nice that he's found someone to cushion the blow."

There was a long pause.

"I don't know," Charlene said finally. "I'm not sure how long I'll be in town. I've actually been considering a trip west myself. I've always thought about moving to California."

"Really?"

"I don't know if Leanne told you, but I have an entertainment background. Tap dance. I used to be Miss Junior West Virginia."

There was an even longer pause.

"Of course I'd be sorry not to see it work out with J.P.," Judy said. "But if you were already thinking of California, why don't you come to L.A. when Max and I go? I can get you into a few premieres, introduce you to a few people, get a little buzz going."

"You'd do that for me?" Charlene asked.

"I would on one condition," Judy said.

Momma came into the kitchen at that point. "I told Susan you'd ride with her and the kids to church," she said. "Bill's going to drive me and your brother."

I was reluctant to turn away from the window when Judy and Charlene were still talking, but Momma was insistent.

"Leanne, I'm talking to you!"

"Yeah, what?" I said, finally turning.

"What are you doing?" she asked, then Momma walked

to the window and looked out, down the porch. She turned back to me.

"Are you jealous of Charlene?" she asked. "Is that what's going on?"

"It's not Charlene—"

"Because you've got your own gifts, Leanne. Just because Charlene looks like she does don't mean she's a better person."

"I know," I told her.

"I don't think it's right her spending the night when there's kids in the house," Momma said, "but those California types, they live different than us. And Charlene's always had a bit of the California in her, I'd warrant."

"Apparently," I said.

Judy breezed into the kitchen then. "Is there any more coffee?" she asked.

"Don't you think that Charlene's got some California in her way?" Momma asked Judy. "I was telling Leanne."

"Sure, she does," Judy said.

"Where is she?" I asked Judy.

"Who?" Judy asked.

"Charlene."

"Oh, she left."

"To go where?" I asked, but Judy just shrugged and poured herself another cup of coffee.

A moment later, Joshua was down from his shower. "Where's Charlene?" he asked.

"She said she had some errands to do," Judy said. "She said she'd call you later."

Joshua seemed to accept this.

"Lars wanted me to give you this first thing," Judy said, pulling a sheaf of papers from her bag. "It's the newest script. I think you'll be pleased. Josiah gets three pages more face time than before. You are going to be amazing," She squeezed his shoulder.

"Yeah?" he said. "You're the greatest. I'll take a look right now." He wandered off to read the revised screenplay. My mother left to check on Beau Ray's progress getting dressed.

I couldn't stop myself from staring.

"What?" Judy asked me.

"How could you do that?"

Judy opened her hands, palms up, and blinked. "Do what?"

"Push Charlene at Max. You sent her back to Max!" I said. I could only try to keep my voice steady.

"I only suggested that she consider all her options. You should *always* consider your options, Leanne. That's a good lesson for you, too."

"But you wanted her to go to Max." I felt like I might cry. I remembered then what Joshua had said, back on the first night I met him. How Judy got people to do what she wanted.

"No, I wanted her away from Joshua," Judy said. "I have seen what girls like that can do to a career. No one's going to mess with J.P.'s career on my watch."

"But Max?" I said. "Of everyone. You pushed her back at him."

"I'm sorry, Leanne. I guess I forgot about your feelings for him," Judy said.

"You didn't forget," I said. "You decided they weren't important."

"Please. You know that's not true," Judy said.

But I didn't know it. I thought about all the birthday cards she'd sent over the years. Every stray typo she'd found in the newsletters. She'd always been so good at details.

"How could you do that to me?" I asked her.

Judy took a deep breath. "It's not about you," she said. "It's not personal, it's priorities. My priority is J.P. and J.P.'s career. It always has been."

It's a gift, I guess, to catch sight of people as they actually are, and to recognize the moment when it's happening. I knew, looking at her then, that this was the real Judy, not the person I'd so long wanted to be, and not some beast, either. Much as I hated hearing her say it, and likely I hated her as she said it, at least I finally knew. It's a lot harder to fight in the dark.

But this was still fuzzy to me, right when it happened. I didn't have the words to react and so instead, I left. I'd explain it to my family after the fact. They all thought it was about Max and the casting director anyhow.

I told Susan she'd have to pray for me as well as Joshua, and I hightailed it instead to Sandy's place, stalking out the back way, through the itchy high grasses in Brown's Field. Soon after she'd returned from the beach, Sandy had moved from her parents' house into a rental place of her own, a sweet little bungalow on Valley Road over at the west edge of Pinecob, where she didn't have to ask permission for her girlfriend to stay the night.

Sandy was working, but I knew where she kept the spare key, so I let myself in. In exchange for the safe haven, I cleaned her kitchen and bathroom. I knew she didn't have the time or the inclination, and also I'd always found that cleaning when your blood is up can be near to exhilarating. Especially when it's someone else's mess. My own mess, I didn't know how to start on that.

I knew my problem—I felt useless. I couldn't help or hinder Joshua's career, not living in Pinecob the way I did. And Joshua's career was what mattered to Judy. She'd said so. Sure, my years with the fan club gave me some knowledge, but truth be told, Judy could have gotten any number of willing volunteers to take it over at that point.

In an economics course I had taken at the extension campus, my professor talked about something called a "sunk cost." When a business, say, is trying to figure out its next strategic move, it's supposed to ignore the time or money or resources it might have invested in its last move. You start from where you are on that day and move forward. What's past is past, and you're not supposed to let history sway current or future decisions.

But my past felt like roots that bound me to people and places. It wasn't something I could easily extricate myself from, even if I'd been certain I wanted to. My past had made me who I was and advised me whom to trust, if not what to do. That's the way I looked at it. I was sunk into it. Not sunk away.

When I was done cleaning, I dropped onto Sandy's couch and flipped television channels a while. She got the same dull five as we did. No cable on Valley Road.

Later in the afternoon, I called home.

"Where are you?" Joshua asked. "Yesterday a crowd, and today no one."

"Judy's gone?" I wanted to make sure.

"She went back to Harper's Ferry a while ago. Hey, you don't have Charlene's number, do you?"

I told him that I didn't. Her family wasn't from Pinecob— I didn't even know what town they called home—and I didn't know where she might be staying.

"Are you coming back soon?" Joshua asked.

"Why? You lonely?" I said.

"Well, yeah," he said. And though I'd meant it to be a joke, his answer dug at my heart a little. I told him I'd head home shortly.

Joshua was out on the deck when I returned, two glasses of lemonade on the table. He handed me one.

"You've got this great, distinctive stomp, Leanne. I knew that had to be you from all the way on the far side of the field," he said.

I sipped the lemonade and took the lounge chair beside him. He said that Momma had called to say that Susan and the kids left straight from church with Beau Ray, who was going with them to Elkins for a few days' visit. Momma and the judge were spending the afternoon out at Antietam, over in Maryland, as Judge Weintraub was something of a Civil War buff. I wondered how the afternoon would unfold for them, seeing as how Momma's family was originally from Tennessee and still called it the Battle of Sharpsburg, not Antietam as they do in the north. But long and short of it, Sunday afternoon was just me and Joshua and the hot almost-August sun and a pitcher of lemonade.

Joshua wanted to talk about Charlene.

"You were there when she left. Did it sound like she was coming back?"

I said I didn't know. I said that Judy was the only one who might say for sure. "Did you ask her about it?" I asked.

Joshua shook his head. "I could tell what Judy thought of Charlene. But I thought for sure she'd be back. Hell, I was surprised she wasn't waiting when I got out of the shower."

"I don't know what to tell you," I said.

It was true. I didn't know how much to say about what I'd overheard. It seemed a precarious thing—if Joshua knew that Charlene was leaning toward Max, he might say good riddance. If he heard me speak ill of Judy, he might think I was making it up, jealous of any number of things. Luckily, at the core, Joshua was more interested in himself than he was in Charlene.

"Want to know what the hardest part is?" he asked me.

"Do I?"

"When people expect me to *be* these characters. People actually expect me to be Colin Ashcroft or Nate Cummings. I didn't even invent those characters. I just said some writer's dialogue. I didn't even *like* Colin Ashcroft."

"You didn't like Colin Ashcroft?" I asked. "How could you not like Colin Ashcroft? He was perfect!"

"Please. He was a pussy," Joshua said. He counted on his fingers as he spoke. "He was smart, sure. But he was way too nice to all the old ladies. He always offered to work extra shifts—even when he'd been in surgery for, like, seventy-two hours. And he never got the girl."

"He got the girl," I said. "He had that thing with Miranda. And then he dated Chastity."

"Yeah, but remember, he wanted Fern. But he never had the guts to go get her. I kept yelling at the writers. You know, let him ask her out."

"But her father ran the committee that wanted to take away his fellowship," I reminded him. I'd always found Colin's shyness around Fern endearing.

"So what? He was a prodigy, for God's sake! He should have asked for what he wanted. You've got to say what you want. But I can't tell you how many times I've been on a date with some girl and I'll say something like that and she'll get a look on her face like it's a personal affront. Like I've been misleading her. On our first date!"

I nodded. The problem in a town the size of Pinecob was the opposite. Everyone knew everyone else almost too well. There weren't enough surprises. And there was too much talk.

Max had said that I held things close, and maybe it was true. But that was a learned habit. Like Joshua with his acting, I'd practiced long and hard not to give much away. As the youngest Gitlin, I'd grown up hearing about my brothers and sister second- and third-hand. Good and bad, but gossip all the same, and that's how you got a label. And in a town the size of Pinecob, labels are hard to pull off. My brother Tommy was the wild one who could be trusted to pick fights. Susan was the cheerleader whose first pregnancy kicked her off the squad. After his fall, Beau Ray was "that poor Gitlin boy."

"Or sometimes," Joshua went on. "They only want to be with the movie star," he said.

"That's not you?"

Joshua smiled at me, then looked out toward the stand of dead oaks at the far side of our house.

"You know what I like about you?" he asked.

I shook my head.

"That you've got only you. There's just Leanne. You ask for Leanne, and you get Leanne."

"I don't follow," I told him. But I figured as labels went, "just Leanne" was okay.

"I hate Rackett, and, you know, that I wish I weren't from that shithole. But that doesn't change the fact that, deep down and way back, I *am* from Rackett. I sprung from that shithole."

"Okay," I said. I wasn't sure where he was going.

"Most of the time, the celebrity gig is fine. There are a ton of perks. But part of me...you know, nobody knows you like the people who were there when your past was your present day. For me, that's knowing some drama geek named Josh Polichuk."

"So bring back the drama geek," I said. "You can't fairly expect people to know him if you refuse to talk about him."

"*You* know him," he said.

"From one geek to another."

"Yeah, I guess," he agreed, which wasn't exactly what I wanted him to say.

"I feel I've got to tell you something," I said. "I think maybe Judy sent Charlene away."

Joshua stood up then and walked to the edge of the deck, his back to me. I couldn't guess his expression and what he meant by standing there, looking like he might dive into the green spread of the backyard. Then he turned back around, his face in a sort of sad smile.

"I don't know why I didn't see that," he said. "Guess I've been around your family too long. No secrets and all. Thanks for telling me."

I shrugged.

He got a little more mad then. "But that's not fair! I'm stuck here!" He paused. "Max doesn't have Charlene's number, does he?"

"Max is gone, remember?"

That night, the phone rang, and I could gather from the way Bill Weintraub smiled as he handed me the headset that it was a call I'd want to take. I shushed everyone out of the kitchen for a little privacy.

"So how's New York?" I asked.

"Hot," Max said. "Crowded. Dirty. Loud. But cool, too. It kind of smells."

"So do you love it?"

"Not yet. It's different. Lots of people wearing black. Sasha says that Los Angeles is the total opposite of New York. But I was thinking that Pinecob was the total opposite of this place, so I don't rightly know what to expect, aside from palm trees. Sasha's already got me booked to meet a bunch of people."

"It must be going well, then. I think Sasha has a crush on you."

"I think you're jealous."

"Not of him." I asked Max if he knew yet when he'd be flying west.

"Wednesday, I think. I can't believe I'm actually going to get on a plane. I hope I can do it."

"Of course you can do it," I told him. "Will you be coming back through Pinecob first?"

"Yeah, and then I'll leave when Judy does. Hey, what do you think of Judy, anyhow? I never really asked you about her. I never figured she'd suddenly come to matter so much."

"She's good at her job," I said. I didn't think it was my place to tell him any different. I didn't want to jeopardize anything. "I don't really know her that well. I mostly know her on the phone, but I think in person, she's different."

"She seems really nice."

"I know," I said. "She met... I think she liked Charlene," I said.

"I don't want to talk about Charlene," Max said. "I told you."

"I know."

"I was thinking how I want to kiss you again," he said.

I blushed into the phone. "You do?"

"But for longer. Just, more."

"Okay."

"Just okay?" he asked.

"More than okay," I said.

"Good. So I'll be back Wednesday some time. I'll call or stop by or something."

I told him that I'd be waiting.

Chapter 17

All I Didn't Know

I hated waiting for Max to return. I wanted to see him again. I wanted to kiss him again. I wanted to get down to the business of him being my boyfriend, to make it an official thing. One kiss was great, but it was still just one kiss, the start but not the thing itself. There are plenty of guys out there I've kissed only once.

Monday night, I was trying to read, to get my mind off of him. And off of Beau Ray and the football he'd brought to Elkins with him, which Joshua still hadn't given me a straight answer about. Sitting on my bed, I could hear Joshua in the bathroom, brushing his teeth. Times like that, things felt intimate. As soon as I heard him, I put my book down and listened. Who'd have thought, even six months before, that I'd be sitting there, listening to Joshua Reed brush his teeth. He'd been with us more than two months at that point, but it still seemed something magical strange at times.

On the flip side, of course Joshua Reed brushed his teeth. He was Joshua Reed, movie star and all, but he was also just a guy practicing good dental hygiene.

I turned back to my book as soon as I heard him twist off the taps, so as not to seem too weird and stalky. He stuck his head in my bedroom doorway.

"I'm going to bed," he said. "I'll see you in the morning."

"Sleep well," I said, and he nodded. I looked at my window and thought about Max again. Then I heard a noise from Joshua's room, a panicked, gasping sort of chirrup.

"Leanne!" I heard him say.

I scrambled out of bed and ran across the hall. He was standing stiff up against the doorjamb, staring at the window. I probably gasped, too, seeing a person there. A face with a beard. A man's face that, for a moment, I thought looked familiar. But it was a second before I could react.

"We're posted no trespassing!" Joshua yelled. He pointed his finger at the bearded man, but me, I reached out my hand. The man looked at it, but when I took a step forward, he seemed to startle and hustled down the ladder he'd been standing on.

"That's right. Get lost!" Joshua said. "Goddamn invasion of privacy. Jesus! I could have been doing anything!"

"Wait!" I said, and turned and ran from the room, down the stairs, and back toward the dining room and the backyard. But the man was down the ladder by the time I reached the sliding doors. He'd disappeared into the trees by the time I got them open.

"Hey!" I yelled. "Hey, don't go!" I couldn't see anyone, and didn't know if he could hear me. "Was that you? Will you come back?" I listened for any sound from the woods, but heard only crickets and wind. "Vince?" I called out.

I sat on the deck steps and stared into the trees until a padding of feet told me Joshua had followed me downstairs. He sat next to me and looked out across the yard.

"You don't think that was Vince?" he asked.

"I did. At first," I said. "But I'm not sure. You've seen pictures of him. What do you think?"

"I don't know. I figured it was some freak fan or something. Did you recognize him? For sure?"

I shook my head. The truth was, I hadn't. Something about the bearded man felt familiar, but he could have been a fan who vaguely resembled Vince. Or a rogue tabloid stringer. Or maybe I'd seen him at one of Joshua's AA meetings. Or in the Winn-Dixie.

"Has Vince ever done that before? Shown up at the house?"

I shook my head. "No. I don't know. No one's been in his room for ages."

"Have you heard from him recently?"

"Not for years."

"We should ask Judy if she's gotten any weird fan mail in the past month or so."

"I suppose so."

"If it was Vince, is he unstable? Would he be dangerous?" Joshua asked.

"I don't know," I said. "It probably wasn't him."

"I wonder if he had anything to do with that creepy Nicolette chick who showed up here," Joshua said.

"I doubt it," I told him. That was the one thing I was certain of.

"Why is our ladder up against Vince's room?" Momma asked at breakfast. I could see Joshua watching me.

"I was cleaning that window," I told her. "I forgot to put it away."

"Do it today, would you?" Momma said. "It could fall. Someone could get hurt."

I told her I would.

Later, at work, Mr. Bellevue mentioned that a man had stopped by and asked for me.

"What man?"

"Some guy. About your age, maybe. He didn't leave his name."

I asked what the guy had looked like. "Did he have a beard?"

"Nah. No beard. But your color hair. Sort of wiry." That might describe Vince, as well as about a million other people. Mr. Bellevue motioned with one of his felt-tip pens. "Maybe you're getting your own fan club."

I smiled at him. In the light of morning, the bearded man seemed most likely another fan with boundary issues, even if he had looked a little like my missing brother.

Of course, I wanted to believe it had been Vince. I wanted him to come back. I wanted all of my family to come back. Joshua was right, everyone had left Pinecob. Even Beau Ray did—his fall had taken a huge part of him away from us. Everyone had left but me and Momma, and she wasn't even around too often in those days. It got me to thinking. Maybe the door was still open, if I could figure out where I wanted to go once I walked out of it.

At home that evening, I thought, I have to ask. I couldn't just leave it to wondering.

"When was the last time you heard from Vince?" I asked.

Momma was piecing squares for a new quilt, sitting in the living room beside Judge Weintraub. She looked up at me, then over at the judge, like she was trying to tell me not to ask such a thing in front of him.

"He's practically family," I said. I rocked back and forth in Dad's old easy chair.

"Why, thank you, Leanne," the judge said. But he stood all the same. "I think I left something in the bedroom," he said and climbed the stairs. Momma turned back to her quilting.

"Well?" I asked her.

"Why?"

"What do you mean why?" I asked. "Have you heard from him recently? Have you seen him?"

"Leanne, now you listen to me. You got to get over thinking Vince is coming back," Momma said. "You got to let him go."

I asked Momma how she could sound so certain, like she wasn't just guessing. Momma put aside her squares.

"Heavens when was it...? Maybe seven years ago now, September, we got a phone call here at the house. From the police. You were at school."

"The police? You never told me this," I said.

"I'm telling you now. I meant to for years, and then...I guess it became something you didn't need to know. Leanne, I know how you were about him."

"You were the same way," I reminded her.

"That's how come I knew."

"What did they say? The phone call?" I tried to think back seven years. I'd been seventeen, maybe eighteen. Around September, I'd been starting my applications for college.

Momma looked like she had to gather her strength. "The policeman who called, he said they'd found a body in some building that was getting torn down, somewhere in Kansas. They didn't have much to go on for ID, because he'd been dead some time, but they found a ring on the body. You remember Vince's class ring?"

I felt a chill pass through me, like something dead had flown through the room. I wondered if it was Vince, or maybe my father, trying to act the shield.

"It was his? I mean, did they know for sure it was his?" Momma nodded.

"But did they know for sure it was Vince?"

Momma shrugged. "They didn't—they don't—know that it *wasn't*. And Vince loved that ring of his."

"But you don't know. It could have been someone else," I said.

"Leanne," Momma said, strong enough that I had to look at her. "I can't do this. It was hard enough back then. I had to make a choice."

I thought back to that September. It was the beginning of the period Momma referred to as her unraveleds, the beginning of those long, mean seasons of time. I wished she had told me about the phone call. I'd been so frustrated—quietly, but still frustrated as heck—by her weakness back then, a weakness that sucked every bit of light from our house. But here she'd been trying to keep me strong, trying to keep at least one of us strong.

"I know your daddy never liked secrets," Momma said. "But I didn't know what else to do. I was afraid you'd do something crazy. Maybe run off to Kansas. They said he'd been shot through the head. Fast, at least. I tell myself that."

Part of me nearly broke in two right then, but another part of me now clung to the man in the window. Why couldn't it have been Vince?

"But what if it wasn't him? Maybe Vince had sold that ring, did you think about that? Or maybe it got stolen. Maybe he's still alive," I said.

"I hoped. But the police said it was a good match, age and hair color. I don't know, Leanne. Him being alive, that would be a gift from above, but God's been down on us Gitlins for a while now, don't you think?" Momma asked. "I couldn't hold on to that. I can't. I still can't." Momma reached over and patted my hand. "I should have told you sooner."

"You should have," I said.

Momma looked far off. "You want to protect your children," she said. "Even when they're not children no longer, you still think you can, maybe, make things not hurt so bad."

"I know," I said.

"I couldn't protect my youngest boy," Momma said. "That

near to killed me, I'll tell you. And there you were, my baby. How could I talk about this thing? But Bill says I got to remember how old you are, even if I still see a six-year-old when I look at you."

"You still see a six-year-old?"

"Crying your eyes out when your tadpoles died, of course I do. You feel things real strong, Leanne, even if you pretend you don't. You're my girl that way."

I just nodded.

"You know, I really appreciate how you've been getting on with Bill. Especially with what your sister says."

"Susan doesn't like him?" I asked.

"He's not a churchgoer. Well, to her church," Momma said. "She keeps calling it a character flaw. Like she's so perfect."

"Susan doesn't live here," I said.

Momma smiled. "You going to be okay?" she asked.

I shrugged. I honestly didn't know.

Chapter 18

To Those Who Wait

I put in a call to Max's parents on Wednesday when I got home from work, and I left word that I'd be around our house all evening. I couldn't wait to see him, but of course, I'd have to. I didn't know when he was supposed to arrive back from New York.

Wednesday had been one of those unseasonably cool days, but bright, almost like the beginning of fall, and we'd kept the curtains open and shades wrenched up to burn the place full of light without heat. I'd been home from work a while, had eaten dinner and watched a little television, and the sun was finally sinking. I considered drawing the curtains again, but didn't make a move to.

Whoever the man in the window had been, he hadn't returned. I restored the ladder in our shed and tried to forget everything new—my brief hope and the thought of Vince dead in Kansas. I just didn't have the energy.

A little past eight, Momma left to pick up Beau Ray from the bus from Elkins. Joshua and I were sitting on the long couch, watching television. I asked him if he'd rather read a script, but he said he was bored with scripts. I asked him if he'd prefer a book, but he said he was bored with books, too.

"But I was thinking, Leanne," he said.

"Yeah? What? Cards?"

"I was thinking that I'd like to try kissing you," Joshua Reed said.

Had I heard him right? But I knew I'd heard him right. And part of me started smiling all over, even as I tried my best to hold it in.

"What?" I asked.

So he said it again, only slower, like a grammar lesson on the parts of speech. "I'd. Like. To kiss. You."

I looked at him as hard as I could. I tried to see him as though I hadn't seen him a thousand times before. "I can't tell if you're acting," I said.

"Oh, come on. I'm not that good an actor," he said. He looked at me. Oh, how he had gorgeous eyes.

"Yeah, you are," I told him.

He smiled. "Now I want to kiss you even more," he said.

"Why?" I asked. I wanted to hear him explain it.

"I don't know why," he said. "I'm an experiential guy. I just want to. I like you. You've got such sweet brown eyes."

"You're bored," I said.

"Maybe," he agreed.

"And a little lonely," I said.

He nodded. "Could be."

"And first your supermodel girlfriend went and dumped you," I pointed out. "And then I ruined your chances with Christy and Marsha—"

"Who?" he asked.

"Exactly." I waited for him to remember.

"Oh. Them. Yeah, you did," he said.

"And now Charlene's off and left you in the dust," I said.

"Leanne, are you trying to flatter me?"

"I'm only saying that when you met me, you thought I was a hick. You called me a fucking hick." I froze. I hadn't planned to say it, but my voice had rushed ahead of my mind. "I heard you," I said, more quietly.

Joshua nodded. He looked down at the couch and his hands.

"And ditzy," I added.

"No," he said, cutting me off. "I only expected you to be ditzy. I told you I thought you were smart. And I'm sorry about the rest. Really. I was an ass."

I wasn't ready to let go yet. "But you're stuck in my house, and you want something to do and Sandy won't touch you so why not Leanne, right? Plus, you'd be getting back at Judy for sending Charlene away." I felt myself getting pissed at him, for all those reasons, and even for his pretty green eyes.

"You're the one who'd be getting back at Judy," he said, and I was a little embarrassed. He was right on that score. Part of me did want to kiss Joshua for that reason alone. "But I can see your point. A lot of that is probably right. I like the way Sandy looks, sure. But I like who you *are*. And how you look. It's different. I know you. But I don't see us traipsing off together—you know, in part because I can't leave your house, but also—for all sorts of reasons. I'm not a good traipser, I guess. I don't want to fuck with you, Leanne. You've been good to me. I don't want to ruin that."

"Then don't," I said.

He nodded. I nodded, too.

"I guess that settles it," I said. I got up off the couch and stretched my legs. Part of me knew that this had been my chance. There was a high road, and I had taken it and as much as I knew it was right, I also knew that I was sorely tempted. Besides, it was just one kiss, and Max still hadn't called. And right doesn't always feel right, in the middle of any single moment. Even an internal compass needs calibration now and again.

"But—" Joshua said. He looked up at me.

"But what?" I asked him.

He took hold of my hand. "I still want to. Sorry." He smiled. "Oh, come on. Don't you want to, at least a little bit? Just once? Just for kicks?"

"Maybe. Part of me might," I admitted. "Only I don't think I want to be any closer to your life. I don't think I really like your life."

"I don't like a lot of it either," he said. "And I don't mean the part about being stuck in Pinecob. Maybe if I'd grown up around here, I'd be more like you. I'd be content."

"Content or resigned?" I asked. "Or complacent?"

"Don't say that. You don't mean that, do you?" He actually sounded worried.

"Of course not," I said, but it rang false to me. I wasn't the actor that he was. I wasn't content with what I had. Not anymore at least.

He nodded. I thought I heard a car door and turned toward the window. But it was light inside and dark out and I couldn't see a thing. It could have been Momma. It could have been a neighbor or a television van. It could have been some mad fan or Vince or a stranger or no one at all.

"You hear that?" I asked. "I think someone's outside."

"Nothing," he said. "My heart, maybe. Don't change the subject."

"I'm not. I thought I heard something. Maybe Momma's back."

"Come on. Just one kiss? I won't be able to sleep." He was still holding my hand, and I let him pull me beside him on the couch. "You can pretend it's acting if you want. Pretend you're on a stage. Or I'm Colin Ashcroft and you're Miranda."

"Why would I do that?"

"You liked Colin Ashcroft, didn't you?"

"Of course. But that was years ago. And you're not Colin Ashcroft," I said. "I mean, you know what I mean."

He kept looking at me. "One. Kiss," he said. He put a finger on my lips and traced around them. I'll admit it felt good.

"You don't get turned down much, do you?" I asked.

He shook his head.

"I don't know," I said. "This is weird."

He smiled and stared at my mouth.

"I'm too self-conscious," I said.

He didn't say anything, but put a hand on the back of my neck and moved me closer.

"This is crazy," I said. I realized that I was the only one talking, and thought I'd better shut up before I said something really stupid or bit him by mistake. I looked at him in the eyes, then looked at his lips, then swallowed.

"Shh," he said, and he kissed me.

Joshua Reed kissed me. Joshua Reed, movie star. I barely remembered to close my eyes. It was sweet and light and lasted for just a few seconds. Then he pulled away and smiled at me again.

"Nice," he said. "Thanks. Now I know."

He got up, went into the kitchen, and brought me a mug of ice cream. We sat on the couch and watched the end of *Cool Hand Luke.* That was it.

Max hadn't called by the time Momma got home with Beau Ray. And he didn't call after that, either. Or on Thursday, even though he had said he would before heading to L.A. There was no sign of him around the house, and no messages on the answering machine. I figured Joshua might know if Max had left or not, but I didn't want to ask him.

The upside is the kiss. The downside comes afterward, when you realize you can't launch into the same conversations as before. After a kiss, you can find yourself in that deserted place—where even if it's not leading to anything, you and the other person have both admitted something that tugs at the friendship, pulling it out of shape. Either you plunge forward and start to date and through that, keep talking, or you sneak backward and pretend like it never happened. But backward takes a little time, and while you're waiting, it feels weird to ask questions like, "Do you know where Max is?"

What I'm trying to say is that, having kissed Joshua—or been kissed by Joshua—I suddenly felt naked or obvious on the subject of Max. It's stupid, I know, because it's not as if I thought that one kiss meant that Joshua Reed and I were an item. The opposite, maybe. I knew we weren't.

Still, one kiss from Max and that's exactly what I'd thought. But there was so much more history there. Max had been so long coming. Joshua's kiss was because I could and because he asked. Max's kiss was for everything that had gone before—and that was a lot. And so it stung something sharp to think that Max had not stopped by or at least called. It stung and ached at the same time.

On Thursday midmorning, I made Beau Ray call Max's parents' house, and they said what I had started to suspect, that Max had left for California a few hours before. I listened in on Momma's extension. "He got on a plane with that Judy woman," Mrs. Campbell said. She didn't sound too happy about it.

I told myself that he was probably really busy. I told myself that Judy might be miffed at me and making it hard for him to get to a phone. Or maybe Charlene's appeal had suddenly grown stronger in the midst of all those California strangers. I didn't really know what to tell myself, though. Even Sandy didn't have any good suggestions. Of course I didn't have to decide anything right then. There was nothing *to* decide. I didn't have any choices left.

Max finally called about a week later. I say that like I don't know exactly how long it had been—but of course, I know—it was six days. Six days after he'd left without calling. Ten days after Beau Ray's birthday when he'd kissed me and I'd kissed him back in the trees at the edge of our yard. He called on a Wednesday. Right around ten in the morning.

I was surprised to hear his voice—I was just getting back on kilter, but that's what guys do. They use some sixth guy sense to know exactly when you've almost hauled yourself back to dry land, and then they show up and take you down with them, one more time. I don't mean to say that Max called when he did because he was a typical guy, but it was striking. That Wednesday was the first day I'd gotten out of bed without thinking of him first.

I heard Beau Ray telling a story about physical therapy, but I figured it was Susan or maybe even Tommy, apologizing for missing Beau Ray's birthday. I wandered into the kitchen, and Beau Ray said "yeah, she's here," and handed me the phone. Max sounded so close, it made me well up and my stomach go all fluttery.

"It's you," I said. "Are you still in California?"

"Yup," he said. "You know, they really do have palm trees everywhere."

"Are you still testing?"

"The testing is over. I guess you could say I'm being graded now. A lot of waiting. Maybe I have a couple meetings. But it's still early in the morning here. I haven't talked to Judy yet today."

"You seeing her a lot?" I asked him.

"Some," he said. "She explains things better than Sasha. He just tells me to show up places, but doesn't say why or what I should expect. It's kind of annoying."

"You don't sound like you're suffering," I said. I meant it as a joke.

"Neither do you, Leanne." The words came out of him sharper than I expected. He didn't sound like he was joking.

"Oh, you know," I said, not sure how to respond. He sounded different. "It's all the same stuff out here."

"I'll bet."

"So have you seen Charlene?"

"Sure," he said.

"She still out there?" I asked. I hated hearing my voice get all pleady.

"Yeah. I don't think she'll ever go back. She thinks she was made for California," he said. "Listen, I just called because, well, I said I would and I don't know when I'll be back in Pinecob."

"You don't?" I asked him. "I mean, is that like a week or a month…"

"I don't know. I didn't want to, you know, mislead you."

"What about your job?" I asked him, my words rushing all together.

"I quit."

I felt hollow, hearing him say that. Half his life at the Winn-Dixie and he'd up and quit, no notice. I didn't know what else to say after that, so I told him that I had to be going. I lied and said that a pot on the stove was boiling over. Of course, when I hung up, I sat there. The pot and I, we were both empty.

I started to get over it, him. You do that. You have to. Vince was dead in Kansas and Max was gone to California, so what could I do but get up and go to work like I was supposed to? I registered for the fall semester of extension classes. I invited the guys over for a movie with Joshua. I took Beau Ray to get his hair cut, and got my own trimmed as well. I even brought Beau Ray to the Buccaneer one night, when Lionel and Scooter were there. I was glad that none of them knew about me and Max and the kiss in the trees behind our backyard. It made things easier when his name came up.

Not that Lionel would have noticed. He was all over Max's cousin Lisa, who had visited from Roanoke a few times in the previous weeks, and not to see Joshua it seemed. And Scooter wouldn't have noticed—he had set his sights on Loreen, having heard a rumor that Sandy was seriously involved with someone in Hagerstown. But hanging out with that crowd felt different than it had before. It didn't feel like home any longer, and set me to brooding something awful.

A couple afternoons later, Beau Ray and Joshua were out back, tossing around Beau Ray's football. Beau Ray could still throw high and fierce, but Joshua not so much. Theater geek that he'd been, I don't think Joshua ever played on a football team, and on one of his weaker tosses, I hustled out into the middle of the yard and intercepted the ball.

"Hey, give it," Beau Ray said.

I said I wouldn't until he told me who he'd gotten it from.

"Secret," Beau Ray said. So I held it from him and dodged away when he tried to grab it from me.

Joshua stood back, watching us. "Now, now, kids," he said.

"We don't have secrets. We're not supposed to," I told Beau Ray. "Like locks. Dad said."

"Not with presents," Beau Ray said. "Give it!"

"That's only *before* you give a present. It's not supposed to be a secret after." I turned to Joshua. "Tell me the truth, did you give this to him?"

Joshua shook his head. "I didn't," he said. "Should I have?"

"Give it back, Leanne!"

I could tell that Beau Ray was getting mad. "Why won't you tell me?" I yelled at him, but he'd started to shriek, so I tossed the football back and stomped inside.

Joshua came up to me a while later. "You should go a little easier on him," he said.

I knew it, but it was hard to ease up.

"I asked him about it, after you left."

"Did he tell you?" I asked.

"He told me someone."

"Who?"

"Who do you think?" Joshua asked.

I shook my head. "It's stupid. It'll sound stupid," I said. "It can't be Vince, but I want to say Vince."

"Then say it," Joshua said.

"Maybe it's from Tommy," I said. "That's the kind of thing he would do."

"Or maybe it's not," Joshua said.

Chapter 19

Come Crashing Down

The next time I answered the phone, who was on the other end but Marcy Thompson, hostess of *Hollywood Express*.

"Leanne, we met before," she said. "This ought to be a cinch."

Judy had granted Marcy another exclusive interview with Joshua, to coincide with the first days of the filming of *Musket Fire*. Joshua hadn't been to the set yet and wouldn't start commuting there for another week or so, but *Hollywood Express* still wanted his take on the mood of the project. Apparently, Marcy's first exclusive interview had earned them high ratings.

Marcy said she was calling to confirm that some of her technicians would arrive on Sunday to test out their equipment and signal.

"They'll stay in the driveway, out of your hair," Marcy said. Marcy herself would arrive at eight on Monday morning.

They would interview Joshua out in our backyard, as before. "Hopefully it won't rain. Do you know if it's supposed to rain?" Marcy asked.

I said that I didn't think so, but that a lot could change in four days.

The vans showed up on Sunday around five. There were two of them, and it seemed like they were hardly in our driveway five minutes before Beau Ray was poking around at the equipment and listening through the sound guy's headphones. When Momma finally dragged Beau Ray inside for dinner, he wolfed his food and talked nonstop about putting up the antenna and how the technical team was headed to the movie set right after Marcy's interview ended. One of the technicians, Hank, remembered Beau Ray from earlier in the summer and had invited him along. Beau Ray asked Momma whether he could eat his dessert in the van, with Hank and the other guys. She just smiled and shushed him out.

I could hear the wind coming through when he opened the front door to go back outside. It smelled like a summer thunderstorm was headed for us, the smell of dirt and electricity. I was glad to see Beau Ray beside himself happy. I still felt a little guilty for having bugged him about his birthday football, though I'd dropped the subject by then. I wanted him to believe that Vince had sent it. I wanted one of us to believe he was still out there.

Beau Ray was still outside when I started to get ready for bed. Judge Weintraub was staying over, an occurrence that had become so regular, it seemed strange when he didn't, though Momma asked me to keep it to myself if Susan called. I went up to the bathroom that Momma and I normally shared and gathered my toothbrush and scrub. I was walking toward Joshua's bathroom when he came out of his bedroom, headed in the same direction.

"Go ahead," I said.

"No, you go," Joshua said. "I don't mind."

"I just need to wash my face and brush my teeth," I told him.

"I don't mind sharing," he said.

"There's not very much room," I said.

The bathroom was narrow, so I let him go in first and get his toothbrush and toothpaste started, and then I did the same. We stood on the tiles, brushing away. I watched him out of the corner of my eye and smiled through my toothbrush, because it felt like such a kid thing to be doing, like a slumber party, the two of us crammed in there. I remembered being a kid and jostling around with Beau Ray and Vince, the toothpaste stinging my mouth, and being forced to spit into the toilet, because there was no room at the sink.

Joshua started to nudge me out of the way of the sink, so I nudged him back and then we were both pushing into each other, each trying to own the tiles in front of the basin. He laughed and toothpaste flew which made me laugh. Another shove and my elbow hit the bathroom door, which slammed shut. It didn't hurt, but the bang was loud enough for Momma to call out, "Everything okay up there?" and finally I spit into the sink and yelled back through the door that it was.

I was laughing and leaned against the door, making just enough room for Joshua to spit out his toothpaste. He leaned over to rinse his toothbrush, mashing me farther into the corner, pretending like he didn't know I was there. He put his toothbrush on the counter and wiped his mouth, then he moved a few inches off, so that I was no longer smashed between him and the door.

"Bully," I said to him. He still had a dot of toothpaste at the edge of his mouth.

"Brat," Joshua said.

I reached out to poke him, but suddenly he took hold of

my hand and moved toward me at the same time, pushing me back up against the door and kissing me on the mouth. He moved so quick that I thought the kiss would be hard, but it wasn't. And it wasn't short either. I kissed him back. We were both minty.

He dropped my hand, and then his hands were everywhere and then my hands were everywhere and we were in that full-scale make-out phase that happens the first time, when you're practically trying to inhale the person and you only stop when you need to breathe.

I could hear the howling of the wind outside. I could hear Joshua fumbling for the light switch but hitting the wall, and then the bathroom went dark. We kept kissing and hands moved everywhere and I was thinking, "what am I doing?" and "I don't care" and "yes" all at the same time.

The bathroom was narrow, but long enough to lie down in, if you didn't mind resting your head against the bath-tub, or the cold of the tiles where the bathmat didn't cover them, or the sound of feet bumping up against the wooden door. We were down on the floor, him on top of me, that comforting feeling of a warm body pressed close by grav-ity and mood.

"God, Leanne," Joshua Reed whispered. His voice was low. "I want to. Are you sure?"

By then, my eyes had adjusted. In the strip of yellow light that bounced through the bottom of the door, I could see him, above me. I could feel him, on me, hard against my thigh. There was only cotton between us, which hardly seemed to matter, and my heart was racing. I wasn't sure of anything, except that I was lying down, him on top of me, and it was dark, and I wanted to be there, and I'd always wanted to be there. I reached up and started to take off his shirt, then let him finish until he was bare-chested. My fingertips brushed that beautiful chest of his, feeling the heat of it. He wadded his T-shirt into a ball, then gently lifted my head and placed it under me, like a small, wrinkled pillow.

"Better?" he asked. "Can't have you hitting your head." I put my palms flat against his chest and could feel his heart beating fast, and for that alone, I kissed him again, and we spun off, back into another round of kiss and press and rub. I ran my hands down his thighs, and he shivered and pulled away a little.

"Are you sure?" he asked again. "You know I want to. But you were right. All those things you said. You were right."

"Don't you hate it when I'm right?" I asked him.

He pulled back and looked at me. There was just enough light to see him frown. "No," he said. "I don't. I like it. It gives me something like faith." He kissed my right shoulder, and then my left. "I like how you know why you do what you do."

"You think I know what I'm doing right now?" I asked him. "I have no idea what I'm doing here with you."

He kissed me again and I kissed him back and I felt his hands explore beneath my nightshirt and mine pulled back the elastic band of his shorts. He gave a little shudder.

"Oh, you know what you're doing," he said.

There's a line, and then, there's no line at all. You step across it and it falls away, like an old cobweb, or fog, or even a cotton jersey T-shirt. The boundaries between us were gone, there was just skin on skin.

"Jesus, I want to do this," he whispered. "God, you feel so good."

I felt like I'd won something, after all that time. I felt like I'd won something I'd wanted so long, and suddenly it had been placed in my arms, and still I couldn't quite believe it was happening. I wanted to stay there, in that bathroom, the whole time. I didn't want to drift off for even a moment of it. I wanted to stay sharply aware of where I was and how my body moved and how his body moved.

And so we rocked together, nothing fancy, nothing too hurried or too slow either, the wind howling outside and the bathroom dark and the narrow space along the floor. We rocked and we rocked, trying to keep our feet from bumping against the door in a giveaway rhythm, listening to the click of his ankle sensor as it hit the tiles each now and again.

There was a huge whoop of wind, later, after, as he rested his head on my chest, heartbeat and breath slower now. There was a crack and a crash. I remember him giving a start at the sound, and feeling a brief burn from his day's end beard.

"That sounded close," he said. He lifted himself up a little. "Quite a storm."

It hadn't rattled me at all. I felt a deep calm.

Everything went quiet and darker in an instant. The yellow light beneath the door snapped off, and the air conditioner down the hall stopped humming.

"Electricity's out," I said. Everything seemed cottony and quiet. I felt like I could lie there forever. Even the tiles didn't feel cold anymore.

But a few moments later came a scream. Not a yell or a holler, but a scream that hit me in the spine, and knocked my head hard against the bathtub.

Someone was screaming, "No!"

"Fuck!" Joshua yelled, and he jumped off of me.

"That sounded like Momma," I said, and we bumped into each other as we both tried to stand and dress and turn on the light that didn't work and open the door at the same time. I felt under the sink for a flashlight I knew was there, and we found our clothes in the haunted beam of it. I handed Joshua his shirt, and he pulled it on as he followed me down the stairs.

"What, what, what is it?" I was yelling out as I ran. Through a window, I could see the dance of flashlight beams on the front lawn. I almost hit Judge Weintraub, who was rushing in the door when I got to the bottom of the steps.

"An accident. A tree came down on the power lines. They hit one of the vans. You brother was in it. And another man," the judge said. He sounded panicked in a way I'd never seen. It scared me to my core. "I've got to call." He rushed off into the kitchen.

"Momma?" I yelled, running out the front door. The gravel in the driveway dug into my bare feet. One of the vans was idling, its headlights illuminating our driveway. A dog barked, somewhere across the street.

"Oh Jesus, oh Jesus, oh God," Momma was saying. "Hold on, angel. Just hold on."

Beau Ray was lying in our driveway, unconscious. His eyes were clamped shut, and a thin line of blood trickled out the side of his mouth. There was a singed smell, like an iron had been left on. Two television people stood over the other man, who was curled in a fetal position, like Beau Ray, not moving. One of the television guys talked into a cell phone, nodding, saying yes and no and "I don't know, I didn't see," in a hurried, high-pitched voice.

"What happened?" Joshua asked.

"That tree over there," said the man who wasn't on the phone. He pointed toward the stand of moth-eaten oaks. "Maybe the wind. It just came down. And the wires hit the van. We could see sparks. There was this popping sound. Beau Ray and Hank were…Hank was showing Beau Ray…we pulled them out, but the line might still be live. Don't get too near."

I couldn't have gone near the van if I'd wanted to. I felt frozen into place, Momma at my feet praying, even as the wind whipped circles around us.

"What can we do?" It was Joshua, right behind me. I could feel him there and straightened my shirt. I saw it then, one of the oaks from the craggy, hollow stand of them, now diagonal, held aloft by an electricity pole that pitched at a strange angle, like a broken bone.

The judge came back outside. "An ambulance is on the way. Joshua, I forgot, can you call the fire department?"

Joshua nodded and immediately headed inside.

"Any change?" the judge asked.

I remember thinking, yes, everything. From one moment past to the one I was suddenly stuck in, everything had shifted. I recognized it. I knew the feeling, like you're falling and wish you could rewind time, for a few seconds only, just enough for a chance to catch yourself. It seems like such a simple request, but it's never granted. Time is only forgiving in the long-term.

I don't remember getting to the hospital, although I know that Judge Weintraub must have driven me there. Momma rode in one of the ambulances with Beau Ray, and Joshua couldn't leave the house, of course, so he handed me his cell phone.

"Maybe it'll work at the hospital. Call me when you know anything, okay? Whatever time."

I remember being in the hospital waiting room. I remember calling Susan and waking her up, but not what I said after that. I remember leaving a message on Tommy's pager and wondering where he was at that hour.

I remember thinking that I should call Max, but I hadn't brought his California number with me. Then I saw Sandy run into the waiting room, tears in her eyes, and we hugged for minutes. Sandy, looking pale through her tan, just crying. Not what you'd expect from a nurse in emergency.

Sometimes, I think how strange pregnancy is. One person goes into the hospital and two people come out. But with pregnancy, you know beforehand. You have time to get ready. There's a sense of life in your belly, the kicking and fussing of it. You have time to get it in your head that there's going to be more of you now.

It's not the same at the other end. You go into the hospital beside someone, maybe even holding their hand, and they leave without you. They leave whether you're ready to say goodbye or not. There's the minute that they're with you, and the minute after, when the doctor says it's over now, he's gone. You think, this is a dream. I didn't mean to be here.

It seemed hard to believe but there was nothing to do. In a car accident, at least, you have a broken car. You have to get it fixed or get a new one or stock up on bus schedules. But when someone dies, they're just gone. People tell you to go home, get some sleep, like that can fix anything. You try but you dream of him, alive and doing something so everyday that it must be real. Then you wake and remember, and you would pay anything to crawl outside of your life for even an hour.

Sandy drove me home and offered to come in and make breakfast or wash dishes or do anything, anything at all, even though she must have known better than most people that there was nothing. I told her it was okay, even though it wasn't. I told her I was going to try to sleep even though I didn't think I could. She said that she would come by in the morning. She didn't ask, she just said it, which was a relief.

I think it was around two in the morning when I got back home. The electricity was still off, but the vans were gone, and the newsmen were gone. Joshua had lit all sorts of emergency candles, so the inside of our house cast a romantic glow. I wandered into the kitchen, then into the living room, then took a flashlight and headed toward the back hall. I stood in the doorway of Beau Ray's room. In the flashlight's arc, I could see all of his things, his bed, his lamp, the clothes in his closet, the football he believed that his younger brother had sent.

"Hey," Joshua said, coming up behind me.

I turned around.

"Well?" He opened his hands, waiting for me to speak. He looked so hopeful, standing there. As if he'd only known happy endings. I closed my eyes and felt my lids burn. I must have managed to shake my head, because he pulled me to his chest and let me sob there for I don't know how long.

He brought me back into the living room, and sat me on the couch. I cried so hard I thought I would throw up, and then it subsided, and I lay my head on his lap. He kept stroking my hair, and I must have dozed off because I remember waking and it was barely beginning to get light out and the candles were burnt way down. Joshua was blowing his nose and when I realized I'd been asleep, I sat up and looked over at him.

"I'm so, so sorry," he said. His eyes were red.

"I know," I told him. "I know you are."

"If I hadn't been—" he said.

I put my arms around his shoulders.

"It's because I was here. That stupid interview."

"Don't," I said.

"I keep thinking, I did this." He choked up as though no more words could fit through.

There was a small sound, then, like a soft knock. A tapping. And then again.

"Do you hear that?" I said.

Joshua sat up and listened. The tapping came again.

"Please don't let it be Marcy Thompson," I said.

I pushed myself up off the couch and went to open the front door. Outside, stood a man who'd been knocking, softly, seeing the candles but knowing the time. He stood very straight, very serious. His clean-shaven face was shaded with the beginnings of stubble, the stubble of a grown man, not a sixteen-year-old. His face held all the time that had passed. I stared at him a moment, then stepped aside.

"I'm sorry," I said. "Of course, come in."

Vince walked back inside our house.

"Do you know?" I asked him. "You must know."

He nodded. "Still the same rug, I see," he said, and I knew it was really him. It was the same voice I had found impossible to describe. I recognized it in an instant.

I reached out a hand and touched his shoulder.

"Little Leanne," he said. "I swear I thought of you all the time."

"You couldn't call to tell me that?" I asked. That may not be the best way to say hello to a brother who's been gone for so long. My voice was something between a snap and a whine. But it's only those you appoint to a higher plane who can disappoint. "Even once on a birthday or something?"

"I wasn't sure you'd want to talk to me," Vince said.

"There's not a day gone by I haven't wanted to talk to you."

I introduced him to Joshua.

"Yeah, we met earlier," Joshua said. "You'd already left for the hospital. I didn't think it was my place to tell you, Leanne. I'm sorry."

"You were there?" I asked Vince. "Did you see Momma?"

He nodded. "Bad timing, I guess," Vince said. "Story of my life."

"It's not your fault," I said.

He looked into the kitchen and the dining room, but stayed at the doorways, like he was nervous about exploring any farther. "It doesn't feel real, being back here. I'm sorry I didn't come in the other night, Leanne. I just wanted to see what everything looked like, you know, to have it in mind before I actually came in."

"You shaved," Joshua said, nodding.

"Sorry if I gave you a start," Vince said. "Thought they'd have you in Susan's old room."

"You knew he was here?" I asked.

"I saw that piece on *Hollywood Express*. You and the apples. I thought, look at my little sister all grown. Time to get back. But first I had to tie up some loose ends. And once I got here, it was harder than I expected to get to the door."

"You lost your class ring," I said.

"I had to pawn it."

"Momma thought you were shot in the head in Kansas."

"I didn't mean for anyone to think that. I needed some space. I would have called. Tommy knew I was okay."

"You think Tommy talks to anyone? That's like saying Dad knew."

Vince blanched, and I remembered why he'd left in the first place.

"Beau Ray knew," he said quietly.

I apologized and he shrugged.

"I must have just missed you at the hospital," he said. "Momma asked me to come back here, to see that you were okay. She's still sitting with him."

It was too much just then. I needed to lie down for a while. "I want to talk to you and hear everything," I told Vince. "But I can't right now. And it would kill me if I went to sleep and you were gone when I woke up."

"I'll be here," Vince said.

"You've got to promise her," Joshua told him.

"Yeah," Vince said. "I'll be here. I shouldn't have run the other night. I just—I wasn't ready. I didn't expect to see you. It wasn't you."

Joshua walked me upstairs and in the hallway put his arms around me. "Listen," he said. "Earlier. In the bathroom."

"It's fine," I told him. I was so drained I thought I might fall over if he took his arms away. "Whatever." I wasn't sure what he was going to tell me, and I wasn't sure I even wanted to know.

"All this, right now—this is a horrible time. And I think it's going to be horrible, and I swear if I thought there was any way I could protect you from it, I would. You've got to believe me, I would." He looked hard at me.

"I believe you," I said.

"But in the bathroom, earlier, that was a great time, our great time. I don't want you to feel weird about it. You really do mean something to me. I…" I guess he ran out of words then because he just looked at me, smiling and awful sad both together.

"We'll be okay," I said. "It'll all work out."

"I'm going to be right here, right across the hall. If you need anything, call or come over. Anything."

I nodded.

"Anything," he said again. "I'll leave the door open."

He smiled and gave me a hug and I breathed in his smell and wished he were wrong about not being able to protect me.

I didn't know what time it was, because the electricity was still off, but I heard weeping the moment I woke up. That's likely what woke me, so I couldn't pretend, for even a minute, that it hadn't happened. I put my hand against the top of my head and winced at the bump from the wall of the bathtub, from Momma screaming out. That wasn't a dream either.

I think it was Momma crying, but it could have been Susan, or Sandy, who'd come back by, like she'd promised. Susan had started driving toward Pinecob near three in the morning and had reached our house around seven. My eldest brother Tommy showed up an hour later, so by the time I came downstairs around eight-thirty, there was a crowd of family the likes of which I hadn't seen in years. Momma, Susan, Tommy and Vince, grim and tired, but all around the same table.

Tommy had taken the call when Marcy Thompson rang earlier that morning—seems that Hank had died, too. That's what they were discussing when I showed up downstairs. To Marcy's credit, she hadn't asked Tommy to reschedule her interview with Joshua.

Around ten, the phone started ringing and didn't stop for the rest of the day. It seemed like the whole of Pinecob had heard what happened. Judge Weintraub did most of the answering, only filtering through those he knew we'd want to speak to. One of the calls was for me in particular.

"Leanne," a man's voice said. It was Max.

"Listen, I'm sorry I didn't call you," I said. "I wanted to, I was going to from the hospital, but I left the house so quick and I didn't have your new phone number."

"Don't apologize. Please. God, I only wish I could be there with you."

"So how, who told, did Judy tell you?" I asked him.

"Sandy tracked me through my parents," he said.

"Oh, right. Good. That makes sense."

"How are you doing? No, I'm sorry—that's a stupid question."

"What else do you say, you know? There's nothing to say," I said. I bit my lip to keep it together. "Everyone's being really nice." I told Max that his parents had called and already brought over an apple pie.

"I just. God, you must know—" Max said, but I cut him off.

"I do," I said. "I do know. I'm glad Sandy told you. It would have been really hard for me. But of all people, you should know."

"I feel so helpless, being all the way out here," Max said.

"It's no different here. At least you're doing…well, I don't know what you're doing. But it's different, right? No more Winn-Dixie, right?" I blotted my eyes, then my nose. I was not keeping anything together.

"I'm coming back, of course. For the funeral," Max said.

"You're going to be a pro on planes before long."

"Leanne, don't—"

"Vince came back, did you hear?"

"Vince, your brother?"

"Yeah." I looked over to where he sat, next to Tommy on the couch. A baseball game was on and they were watching it without commentary or cheering.

"Wow. That's great. Isn't it?"

"Yeah, it means he's not dead. Apparently, Tommy knew almost the whole time, but he just assumed the rest of us did, too. We're all kind of meeting him again. Vince, I mean. I guess he went through a bad time for a few years, then joined the army and ended up in Alaska. He seems level enough now. He's got a teaching degree, if you can believe that. Says he's going to try to find something around here."

I didn't know what else to say. Asking about Los Angeles seemed so inappropriate, but it was the only thing I could think of, so I just stayed quiet. Max said he'd see me in a few days.

Joshua stayed up in his room most of that first morning after.

"He's got some balls to still be staying here," Tommy had said at breakfast. He'd sounded spitting mad.

"He can't leave," I reminded him. "He'll get arrested."

"Leanne's right," Judge Weintraub had said.

"Well, he shouldn't be here," Tommy said. "This all happened on account of him being here. And let me tell you I plan to give that sonofabitch some whatfor—"

"Thomas Robert, you'll say nothing like that!" It was Momma, and she was serious. "Your brother Beau Ray adored that boy. And those TV vans. If you'd been here once this summer, you'd have seen how happy he was. Leanne, tell Tommy how happy Beau Ray was."

I nodded. "The guys were teaching him broadcasting."

"Lord knows, I'll feel my anger over this," Momma went on. "But we are *not* blaming Joshua. This was an accident. If I know one thing, I know that."

"God knew what He was doing," Susan said. "He must have had a reason."

"That's bullshit!" Tommy said. "You're telling me there was a reason when he took our father and fucked up Vince?"

"Hey!" Vince said.

"More of a reason than you not telling us Vince was alive!" I yelled at Tommy.

"I didn't know you thought he was dead!" Tommy said. "It's not like we were allowed to talk about him."

"Hey!" Vince said again.

"Stop it!" Momma snapped.

There was a lot of staring around the table. Angry staring, sad staring, uncomfortable staring. Joshua interrupted it by showing up, and as soon as he did, the electricity flicked back on.

"Well, that's something," Judge Weintraub said.

Chapter 20

What I Can Remember

To this day, I don't really know how it all got done. I don't look to know, either. I don't need to open up and inspect that week again, not just to figure out who brought which casserole.

I know that the power company guys righted the pole that had fallen, round about the time our electricity snapped back on. I know that Lionel dropped by to mow the lawn and that he was in tears as he did. I know that Scooter and Paulie restained the back deck and the front porch and oversaw the professional guys who took down every dead tree in the stand of oaks at the far side of the house.

I remember that there were all sorts of flowers and cards. People from town, from my work, from Momma's work and even Tommy's work. Grant Pearson sent a bouquet and Judy and Lars did, and even the folks from *Hollywood Express,* which I thought was quite considerate, seeing as how they had lost someone, too. Someone from "Move Your Body, Move Your Mind" must have phoned all the way to Mexico, because Raoul—Beau Ray's favorite physical therapy assistant who'd left the day Joshua arrived—he sent a big basket of fruit and a card full of funny things that he recalled Beau Ray had once done or said to him. Of course, none of us could read it straight through for at least a month, but I've still got it somewhere.

We buried my brother that Thursday. There had been talk of waiting until Saturday, but most everyone Beau Ray had known still lived around Pinecob—or had arrived by Thursday. Susan's husband, Tim, came up with the kids, and Momma's cousin Nora, the one with the gift for musical theater. So there didn't seem reason to postpone the inevitable.

Time doesn't really matter in those circumstances anyhow. That's one thing you forget and then learn again. Nothing makes a day pass any faster or slower. Waiting to put Beau Ray in the ground wouldn't have kept him more alive. And rushing to get him buried wasn't going to let us slog through our grief any faster. Like a cut you get on the bottom of your foot, the kind that won't keep a bandage on for anything. The body will do what it needs to do in its own time. The mind, too, it turns out.

There was a wake the day of the funeral, but no in-church memorial service. Beau Ray's death put Momma in a mood to have at God, and who could blame her? So Susan got voted down and we held the wake at the funeral home in Charles Town where Beau Ray had been taken after the hospital. It was crowded. Lionel told me afterward that it near to shut down Pinecob, but like I said, I wasn't too much involved in logistics.

The police called it a special dispensation, letting Joshua leave our house to attend. I don't think they'd have fought the request even if Judge Weintraub himself hadn't filled out the forms. I was glad they'd let him out. Joshua had stuck pretty close to me in those first couple of days. Not in a romantic sense—that wouldn't happen again—but it seemed like he was often nearby, like I could reach an arm out and nearly always grab hold of him.

He looked about as terrible as someone that beautiful can look. The only time I remember seeing him smile was on Wednesday, the day before the funeral. I don't know what time it was or what we were doing, but the phone rang and I answered it to a woman's voice.

"Is Joshua there?" she said. "Joshua Reed…or Polichuk."

I asked who was calling.

"I'm…can you tell him that I know him from way back? My name's Jackie. Reed? I knew his family in Rackett." She sounded nervous. "You're not Leanne Gitlin, are you?"

"That's me," I told her.

"You run the fan club," Jackie Reed said.

"I did," I said.

"Someone sent me the newsletter. I read that interview you did with him. About his name?"

"He told me all about you," I told her. I didn't mean to sound standoffish, but I had a hard time working up good cheer those days. All the same, I knew he'd want to talk to her—or if he didn't, that he ought to anyway.

"I can't believe J.P. actually remembered me," she said. "He hardly knew me."

"Some people put down deep impressions," I told her. "I'll get him for you—"

"No, wait!" Jackie Reed said. "I'm sorry. I don't know why I'm so nervous."

I listened to her hem and haw a little.

"Can you maybe tell me a little what to expect?" she asked. "What's he like these days?"

"Joshua?" I said. "He's a good guy." And what's funny is that I meant it.

Joshua and Jackie talked a while, and when he hung up the phone, it was the first time in days he'd looked anywhere near to happy. I was jealous—not of her, but of that emotion.

"So, the famous Jackie Reed," I said. "Of Rackett, Texas."

"I'm going to see her," Joshua said. "She's going to come to the set."

"Do you think she's the same?" I asked him.

He seemed to think on that a while. "I don't," he said, finally. "But I don't think that matters. I think she's still something."

Thursday morning before the wake, I noticed Vince and Joshua sitting together in the backyard. It was one of those all-over, way-too-hot August mornings—the afternoon was sure to be even more oppressive—and they were just sitting here, in chairs with their feet in the wading pool Paulie had given us.

From the back, they looked so much alike. Vince's hair a little lighter, a little redder and a little shorter, but their shoulders were the same breadth across, and the way they sat, each slouched a little, like they were depressed and casual at the same time. I wanted to go out and sit between them. I had my hand on the handle of the sliding glass door even, but something told me to let them be.

I couldn't hear what they were saying. The voices clouded on their way through the glass and humid air. But I could tell that Joshua was talking and Vince was listening, leaning forward a little now and nodding his head. Joshua's hand motioned. Something about the backyard, maybe? Then he hunched forward and dropped his head into his hands. Vince glanced at Joshua, then turned his gaze toward the trees, and said something.

I stepped back from the sliding door when I saw Vince stand and head for the deck. When he came inside, I grabbed for his arm and pulled him near.

"What's going on? Is everything okay?"

"I'm getting us some iced tea," Vince said.

"Is Joshua okay?" I asked him.

"He'll get there."

"He's not still blaming himself?" I asked, and then it was clear to me why Vince might have something to say on that subject.

"Well, if he could leave, he would," Vince said.

"You know what that's like."

Vince nodded. "I do remember it, yes. I ought to get him that tea."

I stepped aside to let Vince get by. I knew I could trust that he'd be back.

The first time I saw Max again was at the wake. He and Judy and Lars walked in, Mr. and Mrs. Campbell right after them, like maybe they'd all shared a car. I watched Max head first to Momma and give her a long hug. I watched him make his way around the room, greeting Lionel and Paulie and Scooter, greeting Susan and Tommy, and seeing Vince again for the first time, saying "Wow, look at you," then shaking his hand. Eventually, Max made it over to me.

"Leanne," he said. He opened his arms and I let myself lean into him. He smelled the same and that's what stung. I figured he'd smell of palm trees and suntan lotion and whatever else California smelled like, but he just smelled like Max, as if whatever was Max at the core would remain such, no matter where he paid rent.

That got me to crying something fierce. I pulled my arms in and pushed at his chest until he released me.

"Are you okay?" he asked, which was a stupid question, because it was my brother's wake, and me, a mess of tears and still mad at him for leaving without a phone call and so, no, of course not. I turned from him and made for the back room, which the funeral director had shown us was a good place for privacy. But Joshua caught me right before I could duck inside.

"Hey," he said. "Here." Joshua handed me a tissue and put his hand on my shoulder. I think he'd learned, in the four days past, that extra words were unnecessary.

I stood there a while, Joshua beside me, hand still on my shoulder. I looked up once and caught Max looking our way, but after that, he was scarce. There were a lot of people, like I said, and I figured he'd gone outside with Lionel and the rest of the guys.

Once I'd pulled myself together, Joshua and I walked back into the wake. We were headed toward Vince and Grant Pearson, who'd been talking for quite a while, when I saw Sandy, Alice at her side. I froze. Joshua saw them, too, and waved at Sandy.

"Who's that standing next to Sandy?" he asked. "Why do I know her?"

Without the wig and heavy eye makeup, Alice looked different. But I was still afraid that Joshua might remember his meeting with Nicolette.

"Just a friend of Sandy's," I said. "Maybe she's at AA?"

Joshua shrugged.

"You know, I think she came by the house for the Fourth of July party."

"Maybe that's it. What's her name?"

"Alice."

Joshua nodded, but frowned. "That doesn't ring a bell. But I swear I've seen her. So is she a friend of Sandy's or more than a friend?"

"She's Sandy's girlfriend."

"Man, there are good-looking lesbians in West Virginia," he said. "It's not fair."

Joshua was headed for the bathroom when someone tapped me on the shoulder.

"Leanne." It was Judy.

I didn't want to turn around and look at her, but knew that the sooner I did, the sooner it would be over. So I turned. "Judy," I said, right back at her.

"I just wanted to say how sorry I am for all that's happened. I wish you'd think about continuing with the fan club."

"I can't," I told her.

She nodded. "And I'm sorry about our misunderstanding over Charlene," she said.

"It wasn't a misunderstanding," I told her.

"Okay, *my* misunderstanding," she said.

"It wasn't a misunderstanding," I told her again. "Like you said, it was priorities. Only I wish you'd told me that from the start."

"Point taken," Judy said. "I'm truly sorry for your family's loss."

"Point taken," I said, before excusing myself.

After the wake, there was the funeral itself, and after the funeral, some folks came back to our house to eat some of the food that the people of Pinecob kept bringing by. Lionel was there a while, and Scooter and Paulie and even Loreen dropped by to pay her respects. But Max stayed away. I didn't even see him leave the funeral.

By dark, just the core of us Gitlins remained, and we were all wretched tired anyhow, so I don't even know how it began. Susan was down in the basement putting the kids to bed, and Momma had already gone upstairs for the night. But I was there. As usual. And suddenly, Tommy and Vince were sniping at each other.

Tommy said something like, "What do you know, you've been God-knows-where for the past ten years. You let our mother go on thinking you were dead."

And Vince said, "Like you couldn't have called and said something? Like you've been around?"

And Tommy said, "At least people knew I was alive."

And Vince said, "You didn't even send Beau Ray a present for his thirtieth birthday."

And Tommy said, "I have a job. I have a life I'm trying to keep together. He knew I cared."

And Vince said, "Yeah, well, he knew I cared, too."

And finally I told them both to shut up, just shut up, because there were kids trying to sleep downstairs and Momma trying to sleep upstairs and it hadn't exactly been an easy day for anyone. They looked up at me.

"Face it—neither of you were here. Neither of you have been around for years now. It doesn't make a lick of difference at this point. It's all sunk. You want to come back, come back. But only tomorrow and every day after that should matter when you think about it."

"I was thinking maybe I'd come and stay a while," Tommy said.

"I was planning on staying here," Vince said.

"It's not like there isn't space," I said. "Maybe one of you can take my room."

I knew I had to talk to Momma about what I'd been thinking, so I caught her in the kitchen the next morning. We were the first two people up in a house crowded with family.

"It sort of feels like it used to," Momma said. "Doesn't it? There's a huge hole, but around the hole, it feels a little bit the same."

I could see that, and at the same time, I was afraid I was about to pull the hole larger still.

"You think Vince coming back is a gift from God?" I asked her. "Like Susan said?"

Momma shook her head. "I think it was time, like he says. I think he had to get past things his own way. He always did. I do miss your pa, but I can't say I'm sorry I wasn't doing the driving. I'd hate to live life thinking I might have been able to stop that damn drunk." Momma turned off the stove and looked hard at me. "You want to tell me something?"

"I don't know," I said, which wasn't exactly true. "Tommy said he was thinking about coming to stay here awhile."

Momma nodded. "He mentioned that. That son of mine could use a little solid ground."

"And Vince," I said. Momma kept on nodding. "That's two more people to take care of—"

"Leanne," Momma said. "You're not a child no more, but I want you to listen to me all the same. You take care of *yourself*. We'll all get through this. All of us."

"It's not like I was looking to go far."

"Why not?" Momma asked. "Bill's poked at me about it over and over this summer and he's right. It hasn't been fair on you, me pressing you to hang back so long. You were always so good with your brother, with Beau." Momma's eyes began to well.

"I can stay," I said, not sure what I wanted anymore.

"For heaven's sake, girl. You've already proved that. Go prove something else."

Chapter 21

Getting Somewhere

People tell me that running a marathon isn't about physical stamina so much as mental. You've got to train your lungs and legs of course, but mostly, you've got to train your mind, because that's what's going to want to stop. Your mind's the thing that's going to want to take a break at every mile. Heck, it might not even want to haul out of bed the day of the race, and somehow you've got to convince it that pushing forward is the thing to do.

I wouldn't know. I don't run marathons. But I know from experience that regular old life can be much the same. And that, too, you've got to keep pushing through.

Beau Ray died and was buried next to my father, and the rest of us were left trying to figure out what to do next. After the wake, Grant Pearson had come by our house and talked some more with Vince and a little with Momma. Turns out that he had been made head football coach at Potomac

Springs Senior High and had asked whether Vince might be interested in being his assistant. Vince said yes and that Saturday, he unpacked his green army duffel in Susan's old room, where he planned to stay for a few months while he got settled. Joshua offered to switch rooms, but Vince said that a different scene out the window was probably a good thing.

That same Saturday was Joshua's first scheduled day on the set of *Musket Fire*. Sunday was his second, and on Sunday, Susan and Tim and the kids all headed back to Elkins, so the house was quiet again, even more than before. It was so quiet that I dragged myself out to the Winn-Dixie—I hadn't been there since before Beau Ray died—just to hear a little noise.

I got my cart, and found myself glancing over at the managers' office where Max once took his breaks. He'd given notice weeks before, but of course I still expected to see him there. And of course, he wasn't there.

I carried a lot of regrets about Max—some my doing, some his, some that seemed the result of life butting in uninvited. I wished we had spoken more during Beau Ray's wake or the funeral or afterward, but Max had kept his distance from me, and I had to figure that he'd done so on purpose. In sunnier times, I might have had the strength to poke and prod him. Or even the strength to walk toward him and hold out my hand. But you lose someone dear and it seems a superhuman feat just to make it into the shower.

I was Momma's daughter, that's for sure. I knew I was giving up Max the same way she'd given up Vince, those long years back. To an outsider, it might look like a harsh thing, like inaction of the worst sort or a purposeful forgetting, but when you're the one choosing to look away, you know it's because your heart is simply trying to make it to tomorrow. Your heart is scared to death, and it would rather not know than take a chance on being destroyed by the whole truth.

So I'd looked away, and as the days passed, it seemed more

and more like a dream, me and Max, like I'd made up the whole thing. I'd heard from Lionel that Max was headed back to Los Angeles that Monday. Lionel said that Sasha had been true to his word and that Max had been offered the part of a scientist in the next Bond film. I had concentrated on looking happy when he told me that.

And there I was, in Max's old Winn-Dixie, pushing a shopping cart, same as ever. Then I turned down the condiment aisle, and he was there, Max Campbell, looking down at a jar of olives with the slightest smile on his face. In the moment before he saw me, I was tempted to spin my cart around and high-tail it out of the store. But I reminded myself that Pinecob was as much my turf as his. I might not be a brave person, I might not run *after,* but I sure as hell didn't run *from*.

So I stood my ground beside the mustard display and in a moment, Max looked up, then turned toward me, then walked the few yards between us, until he was standing up against my cart.

"Leanne," he said. "How are you? How's your prisoner?"

I told him how Joshua had started commuting to the *Musket Fire* set the day before. "A car came to pick him up at something like five this morning."

"You didn't go with?"

"At five in the morning?" I repeated. "Even I'm not that much of a morning person."

Max nodded, then looked away. "Well, anyway," he said. He looked like a tired and fidgety version of the Max Campbell I'd stood beside, under the trees at Beau Ray's party. Frankly, he looked like he wanted to be gone, away from me and the Winn-Dixie and Pinecob altogether—rather like Joshua looked when he had first arrived.

"What?" I asked him, trying to get him to meet my eyes. "Are you okay? Smax?"

"Don't call me that," he snapped. Then, "Sorry. I'm fine. Just busy, that's all."

I looked around, down the aisles. There was no one in sight except a bored cashier chewing gum and picking at her nails. It didn't even look like he was planning on buying the olives, so I figured it had to be me.

"My family really appreciates you coming all the way back for the funeral," I said.

Max just nodded. The muzak in the Winn-Dixie suddenly seemed loud, what with so few words filling the space between us. I thought, this is that point when it's time to give up, when both the heart and the mind turn toward home.

"I guess I ought to be going then," I said.

Max said okay, but didn't move. Since I'd said I was going, I knew it was up to me to turn away, but I didn't want to. I couldn't wait for the next James Bond movie before I saw him again.

"No," I said to him.

"No?" he asked.

"It's not okay. Why are you being like this?" I asked. "I thought…" I started to say but wasn't sure how to finish. Thought what? That a kiss from him meant everything? Was that so far-fetched?

"Why am *I* being like this?" Max asked, then shook his head and said nothing more. He was looking at me with an expression I couldn't read, and I felt my face go hot.

I knew I had to say it, had to stop being scared and just say it. What was the point, otherwise? Where were we ever going to go if I stayed where everyone expected me to stay? Dad had been killed, Vince had left, Beau Ray had died and still my heart went on beating out the days. I had to trust that that fist of muscle in my chest would keep beating, tomorrow and the next day, no matter how Max reacted.

"I thought," I started again. "At Beau Ray's birthday. I thought things—I thought we were different. I thought you said you wanted to be with me. I thought I was the person you wanted to start dating."

"You were," Max said.

I felt a wave of relief even as I noticed how he'd used the past tense. At least I hadn't been making it up. "So what happened? You left and you didn't call. You said you were going to call and you didn't. You've got to tell me."

"I said I'd call or stop by," Max said, his expression still frozen.

"So what happened?" I asked him again.

"You kissed Joshua Reed is what happened," Max said. His expression flashed to reveal something, frustration maybe, or bitterness, but at least it was something alive. He sounded angry, like I should have known this all along. I felt sort of side-swiped.

"How?" I began, but what he'd said was true, so how didn't really matter. Maybe my father had been right about secrets. What good had it done me to hold my cards close? "You're right," I told him. "I did. I kissed Joshua Reed."

"I saw you," Max said. "All that stuff you said about how there's nothing going on and how much you're into me. Then I come by to see you and the two of you are on the couch," he said. "I mean, look at me and look at him. How am I supposed to compete with that? How could anyone?"

"There's nothing to compete with," I said. I thought of Joshua, of the kiss on the couch that Max had seen, and the time in the bathroom that remained only our own. Joshua was beautiful to behold and to hold. But he wasn't Max, and he couldn't become Max, as talented an actor as he was.

"Yeah, right," Max said. He shook his head.

"You left," I pointed out. "You went to California."

"Temporarily," he said. "I came back."

"Not for me," I said.

He closed his eyes. "I would have, if I'd thought—" he said. "Jesus, Leanne, I told you—"

"And then there's Charlene," I said.

"I'm not with Charlene! That's over."

Maybe I could trust him about Charlene, but not about the rest of that California sort of life. I'd seen the way Joshua lived. I'd heard the stories.

"You're going to have girls taking their shirts off on your lawn. You'll be going out with models. I'd just be some girl who never left Pinecob," I told him.

"What are you talking about?" he asked. "I mean, some of that sounds good, but you don't know the part about people being nice for no reason I can figure, people acting like they know me when they don't. Hey," he said, and waited until I met his eyes. "Before this summer, I didn't leave Pinecob *either*. I thought that was something we had in common. I *liked* that we had it in common."

He shoved the olives back onto the shelf and leaned against the row of cans and jars and squeeze bottles. He shook his head, then looked at me again, like he was willing himself not to be angry.

"You want to tell me what the real deal is with you and Josh?"

I studied him hard, wondering whether there was enough of an opening, in time or space or fate or luck, for both of us to slip through.

"There's nothing. There's no deal," I told him.

"Yeah, right," Max said. "At the birthday party, I believed that. And then I saw you—"

"Listen, everything I told you at the party was true. Every word of it and a lot more, besides," I said.

Max frowned, not like he didn't believe me, but rather like he'd heard something he hadn't expected to hear. He looked like he was about to say something, but I wasn't finished. All I'd long held close was biting at my hands to get loose.

"And meanwhile, no one asked me to date him exclusively," I told Max. "Including you. Far as I can tell, I'm not dating anyone. Not you, not Joshua Reed, not Lionel, not any-

one. And did you ever actually ask me? Did you say anything?"

Max looked a little scared then, like he was surprised I
could bark like that. But I didn't care any longer. If he didn't
like what he heard or saw, he could walk away. He'd done it
before.

I rambled on, my voice rising. "I'm so sick of making it
easy for every damn person I know, picking up after everyone and doing the shopping and organizing. How about
someone making it easy for me? How about someone saying, 'Leanne, I don't want you kissing any other guys because
I want you next to me.' Not one guy has ever come up to
me and said that! And I know it, because if someone I liked
ever said that, I'd remember. I'd say, 'damn straight, now we're
getting somewhere!'"

This is when Max took my hand. He took it, even before
I held it out to him. I didn't realize how loud my voice had
gone until I heard Max speak, quiet and calm. He said my
name and he didn't sound fidgety at all.

"Leanne Gitlin," he said, softer than he had in a while.

"What?" I asked him. I thought maybe he was going to
tell me to simmer down or go home. But he didn't.

"I don't want you kissing any other guys." I looked down
at his hand, holding my hand. I looked up at his face, at the
crazy half earlobe and those denim eyes, looking back at me.
"I want you next to me."

"See, now that makes things different," I said. "Now we're
getting somewhere."

Epilogue

Day ninety came right after the week they filmed the love scene between Josiah and Elizabeth, where they're frolicking by the stream, and things get steamy. If you look close, right at the end of the scene, you can catch a glimpse of Joshua's house-arrest sensor, a gray plastic thing that looks out of place in 1863 Virginia. Right before they walk off into the woods. But you have to look close for it, and to know what it is you're looking for.

Joshua wasn't shooting on day ninety—Lars had arranged a free day for him. First a car came to take all his stuff from our house, and then the police arrived to escort him back to the courthouse where Judge Weintraub had to declare that he'd served his sentence and tell him something about probation and something else about his license still being suspended. They took the sensor off, and Joshua just nodded, glancing repeatedly at his ankle like he didn't quite believe it was gone.

"Usually this is where I'd say that I don't want to see you back here," Judge Weintraub said.

I was standing by the door, listening. Mr. Bellevue and I had come over from the county clerk's office to watch it all happen.

"But I hope you'll understand the sentiment if I say that you're welcome back in these parts at any time," the judge said.

"Thank you, sir," Joshua said.

The judge nodded, and then he came out from behind his bench and gave Joshua a hug. It made me want to cry, really, when Judge Weintraub told Joshua that he had family in Jefferson County. And I think I saw Joshua choke up a little, too. Then Lars pointed to me, standing there by the door, and Joshua came over. Mr. Bellevue politely excused himself.

Joshua smiled at me and ran his fingers through my hair. "It's a great cut," he said. "Very Left Bank."

"We have your address, right? If you forgot anything…I can mail it."

"Oh, yeah," he said. "But I'll be down at the shoot for the next month. You should stop by if you change your mind about being an extra. I told the judge to convince you to give it a try. Or you could just hang out in my trailer."

"You'll have enough distractions," I said. "Besides, I've got a lot of stuff to get done in the next couple weeks. I don't want to be a bother."

"You can't bother me anymore. It's only the other way around." He smiled. He was still the most beautiful man I'd seen up close like that. "You know, I brought a lot of crap with me this summer. I know that." He held up his hand because I was starting to interrupt him. "And you just…I don't think it was a fair trade."

It was true and not true. Without Joshua's crap, I doubt that Momma would have met up with Judge Weintraub. And who's to say if Vince would have been spurred to come back, if he hadn't seen me on that *Hollywood Express* exclusive, upending a pyramid of apples? And maybe it did take a nudge, a bump in the guise of Joshua Reed, incarcerated movie star, to get Max to move from the shadows into my life. You can't know things like that.

I think about those twists of fate, the strange run-ins that can alter everything in the blink of an eye, or the shift of a single season. I think about Sandy and Alice, living up in New York, who might never have met if Sandy's brother's boss had given him vacation time. I am certain that if Momma hadn't found her Pat Boone picture, I wouldn't ever have written to Judy for a photo of Joshua Reed. And if I keep tracing back, I know that Momma wouldn't have been sorting through that box if Dad hadn't died. So good does come from bad.

I think about Beau Ray, of course, because bad can come from good, too. It doesn't really matter whether you think there's a reason for the events that hit your life or no reason at all. They still happen.

But on that day in the courthouse, saying goodbye to Joshua, I didn't know the half of what was coming, no more than I had known the day of Beau Ray's football picture. It seems a well-walked path now that Lionel would marry Lisa, that Jackie Reed would come back to Joshua and that I would finally get my law degree. But the only thing clear back then was that the ninety days were over. Joshua had done his time, and things were supposed to fade back to the way they'd been before. But of course, they could not.

They could not, for me at least, because I knew that I was leaving Pinecob. Twenty-five years old, and I was finally leaving. Max and I, together. In two weeks time, he'd be flying back in from California, so I'd have someone to sit next to on the plane ride out. These days, when I look at Max Campbell, I still see that gangly twelve-year-old I met when I was eight. I still see the boy who ran into traffic for a dog. But now I also see a man, nearly thirty and nervous as hell to be flying, sitting beside me all the same.

On sale now

girls' night in

21 of today's hottest
female authors

1 fabulous short-story collection

And all for a good cause.

Featuring *New York Times* bestselling authors

Jennifer Weiner (author of *Good in Bed*),
Sophie Kinsella (author of *Confessions of a Shopaholic*),
Meg Cabot (author of *The Princess Diaries*)

Net proceeds to benefit War Child, a network of organizations
dedicated to helping children affected by war.

Also featuring bestselling authors...

Carole Matthews, Sarah Mlynowski, Isabel Wolff, Lynda Curnyn,
Chris Manby, Alisa Valdes-Rodriguez, Jill A. Davis, Megan McCafferty,
Emily Barr, Jessica Adams, Lisa Jewell, Lauren Henderson,
Stella Duffy, Jenny Colgan, Anna Maxted, Adèle Lang,
Marian Keyes and Louise Bagshawe

www.RedDressInk.com   www.WarChildusa.org

Available wherever trade paperbacks are sold.

™ is a trademark of the publisher.
The War Child logo is the registered trademark of War Child.

RDIGNITRR